"Yes," *Mistystar agreed, baring her teeth* as she confronted Tigerstar. "I thought you were as eager as the rest of us to get rid of that StarClan-cursed impostor. But no—you have chosen your own kin over the good of all the Clans!"

"What else can we expect from ShadowClan mange-pelts?" Lionblaze added.

The two sides surged closer, with claws unsheathed; Tawnypelt slipped to Tigerstar's side, joining him to protect Shadowsight. He could see that they were moments away from springing into an attack.

"Stop!" Shadowsight meant the word to be a commanding yowl, but instead it sounded more like the wail of a frightened kit. But it had the effect he wanted: The enraged cats eased away from one another, and their yowls of accusation sank to near silence as they turned to face him.

"I don't need any ShadowClan blood shed on my account," Shadowsight continued. "I'll go willingly."

WARRIORS

THE BROKEN CODE

THE BROKEN CODE

WARRIORS

THE PLACE OF NO STARS

ERIN HUNTER

HARPER
An Imprint of HarperCollinsPublishers

Library of Congress Cataloging-in-Publication Data
Names: Hunter, Erin, author.
Title: The place of no stars / Erin Hunter.
Description: First edition. | New York, NY : HarperCollins, [2021] | Series: Warriors: the
    broken code ; book 5 | Audience: Ages 8-12. | Audience: Grades 4-6. | Summary: "The impostor
    walking in Bramblestar's pawsteps retreats to the Dark Forest, where the other Clans must
    follow if they hope to restore their connection with their ancestors in StarClan"— Provided
    by publisher.
Identifiers: LCCN 2020056025 | ISBN 978-0-06-282378-6 (pbk.)
Subjects: CYAC: Cats—Fiction. | Fantasy.
Classification: LCC PZ7.H916625 Pl 2021 | DDC [Fic]—dc23
LC record available at https://lccn.loc.gov/2020056025

Typography by Jessie Gang
22 23 24 25 26   PC/BRR   10 9 8 7 6 5 4 3 2 1
❖
First paperback edition, 2022

Special thanks to Cherith Baldry

ALLEGIANCES

THUNDERCLAN

ACTING LEADER   SQUIRRELFLIGHT—dark ginger she-cat with green eyes and one white paw

ACTING DEPUTY   LIONBLAZE—golden tabby tom with amber eyes

MEDICINE CATS   JAYFEATHER—gray tabby tom with blind blue eyes

ALDERHEART—dark ginger tom with amber eyes

WARRIORS   (toms and she-cats without kits)

THORNCLAW—golden-brown tabby tom

WHITEWING—white she-cat with green eyes

BIRCHFALL—light brown tabby tom

MOUSEWHISKER—gray-and-white tom
APPRENTICE, BAYPAW (golden tabby tom)

POPPYFROST—pale tortoiseshell-and-white she-cat

BRISTLEFROST—pale gray she-cat

LILYHEART—small, dark tabby she-cat with white patches and blue eyes
APPRENTICE, FLAMEPAW (black tom)

BUMBLESTRIPE—very pale gray tom with black stripes

CHERRYFALL—ginger she-cat

MOLEWHISKER—brown-and-cream tom

CINDERHEART—gray tabby she-cat
APPRENTICE, FINCHPAW (tortoiseshell she-cat)

BLOSSOMFALL—tortoiseshell-and-white she-cat with petal-shaped white patches

IVYPOOL—silver-and-white tabby she-cat with dark blue eyes

EAGLEWING—ginger she-cat
APPRENTICE, MYRTLEPAW (pale brown she-cat)

DEWNOSE—gray-and-white tom

THRIFTEAR—dark gray she-cat

STORMCLOUD—gray tabby tom

HOLLYTUFT—black she-cat

FERNSONG—yellow tabby tom

HONEYFUR—white she-cat with yellow splotches

SPARKPELT—orange tabby she-cat

SORRELSTRIPE—dark brown she-cat

TWIGBRANCH—gray she-cat with green eyes

FINLEAP—brown tom

SHELLFUR—tortoiseshell tom

PLUMSTONE—black-and-ginger she-cat

LEAFSHADE—tortoiseshell she-cat

QUEENS	(she-cats expecting or nursing kits)

DAISY—cream long-furred cat from the horseplace

SPOTFUR—spotted tabby she-cat

ELDERS	(former warriors and queens, now retired)

GRAYSTRIPE—long-haired gray tom

CLOUDTAIL—long-haired white tom with blue eyes

BRIGHTHEART—white she-cat with ginger patches

BRACKENFUR—golden-brown tabby tom

SHADOWCLAN

<u>LEADER</u>	**TIGERSTAR**—dark brown tabby tom
<u>DEPUTY</u>	**CLOVERFOOT**—gray tabby she-cat
<u>MEDICINE CATS</u>	**PUDDLESHINE**—brown tom with white splotches
	SHADOWSIGHT—gray tabby tom
	MOTHWING—dappled golden she-cat
<u>WARRIORS</u>	**TAWNYPELT**—tortoiseshell she-cat with green eyes
	DOVEWING—pale gray she-cat with green eyes
	HARELIGHT—white tom
	ICEWING—white she-cat with blue eyes
	STONEWING—white tom
	SCORCHFUR—dark gray tom with slashed ears
	FLAXFOOT—brown tabby tom
	SPARROWTAIL—large brown tabby tom
	SNOWBIRD—pure white she-cat with green eyes
	YARROWLEAF—ginger she-cat with yellow eyes
	BERRYHEART—black-and-white she-cat
	GRASSHEART—pale brown tabby she-cat

WHORLPELT—gray-and-white tom

HOPWHISKER—calico she-cat

BLAZEFIRE—white-and-ginger tom

CINNAMONTAIL—brown tabby she-cat with white paws

FLOWERSTEM—silver she-cat

SNAKETOOTH—honey-colored tabby she-cat

SLATEFUR—sleek gray tom

POUNCESTEP—gray tabby she-cat

LIGHTLEAP—brown tabby she-cat

GULLSWOOP—white she-cat

SPIRECLAW—black-and-white tom

HOLLOWSPRING—black tom

SUNBEAM—brown-and-white tabby she-cat

ELDERS   **OAKFUR**—small brown tom

SKYCLAN

LEADER   **LEAFSTAR**—brown-and-cream tabby she-cat with amber eyes

DEPUTY   **HAWKWING**—dark gray tom with yellow eyes

MEDICINE CATS   **FRECKLEWISH**—mottled light brown tabby she-cat with spotted legs

FIDGETFLAKE—black-and-white tom

MEDIATOR   **TREE**—yellow tom with amber eyes

WARRIORS   **SPARROWPELT**—dark brown tabby tom

MACGYVER—black-and-white tom

DEWSPRING—sturdy gray tom

ROOTSPRING—yellow tom

NEEDLECLAW—black-and-white she-cat

PLUMWILLOW—dark gray she-cat

SAGENOSE—pale gray tom

KITESCRATCH—reddish-brown tom

HARRYBROOK—gray tom

CHERRYTAIL—fluffy tortoiseshell and white she-cat

CLOUDMIST—white she-cat with yellow eyes

BLOSSOMHEART—ginger-and-white she-cat

TURTLECRAWL—tortoiseshell she-cat

RABBITLEAP—brown tom
APPRENTICE, WRENPAW (golden tabby she-cat)

REEDCLAW—small pale tabby she-cat

MINTFUR—gray tabby she-cat with blue eyes

NETTLESPLASH—pale brown tom

TINYCLOUD—small white she-cat

PALESKY—black-and-white she-cat

VIOLETSHINE—black-and-white she-cat with yellow eyes

BELLALEAF—pale orange she-cat with green eyes

QUAILFEATHER—white tom with crow-black ears

PIGEONFOOT—gray-and-white she-cat

FRINGEWHISKER—white she-cat with brown splotches

GRAVELNOSE—tan tom

SUNNYPELT—ginger she-cat

QUEENS   NECTARSONG—brown she-cat (mother to Beekit, a white-and-tabby she-kit, and Beetlekit, a tabby tom)

ELDERS   FALLOWFERN—pale brown she-cat who has lost her hearing

WINDCLAN

LEADER   HARESTAR—brown-and-white tom

DEPUTY   CROWFEATHER—dark gray tom

MEDICINE CAT   KESTRELFLIGHT—mottled gray tom with white splotches like kestrel feathers

WARRIORS   NIGHTCLOUD—black she-cat

BRINDLEWING—mottled brown she-cat

APPLESHINE—yellow tabby she-cat

LEAFTAIL—dark tabby tom with amber eyes

WOODSONG—brown she-cat

EMBERFOOT—gray tom with two dark paws

BREEZEPELT—black tom with amber eyes

HEATHERTAIL—light brown tabby she-cat with blue eyes

FEATHERPELT—gray tabby she-cat

CROUCHFOOT—ginger tom
APPRENTICE, SONGPAW (tortoiseshell she-cat)

LARKWING—pale brown tabby she-cat

SEDGEWHISKER—light brown tabby she-cat
APPRENTICE, FLUTTERPAW (brown-and-white tom)

SLIGHTFOOT—black tom with white flash on his chest

OATCLAW—pale brown tabby tom

HOOTWHISKER—dark gray tom
APPRENTICE, WHISTLEPAW (gray tabby she-cat)

FERNSTRIPE—gray tabby she-cat

ELDERS   **WHISKERNOSE**—light brown tom

GORSETAIL—very pale gray-and-white she-cat with blue eyes

RIVERCLAN

LEADER   **MISTYSTAR**—gray she-cat with blue eyes

DEPUTY   **REEDWHISKER**—black tom

MEDICINE CATS   **WILLOWSHINE**—gray tabby she-cat

WARRIORS   **DUSKFUR**—brown tabby she-cat

MINNOWTAIL—dark gray-and-white she-cat
APPRENTICE, SPLASHPAW (brown tabby tom)

MALLOWNOSE—light brown tabby tom

HAVENPELT—black-and-white she-cat

PODLIGHT—gray-and-white tom

SHIMMERPELT—silver she-cat

LIZARDTAIL—light brown tom

APPRENTICE, FOGPAW (gray-and-white she-cat)

SNEEZECLOUD—gray-and-white tom

BRACKENPELT—tortoiseshell she-cat

JAYCLAW—gray tom

OWLNOSE—brown tabby tom

GORSECLAW—white tom with gray ears

NIGHTSKY—dark gray she-cat with blue eyes

BREEZEHEART—brown-and-white she-cat

QUEENS　　**CURLFEATHER**—pale brown she-cat (mother to Frostkit, a she-kit; Mistkit, a she-kit; and Graykit, a tom)

ELDERS　　**MOSSPELT**—tortoiseshell-and-white she-cat

THE BROKEN CODE

WARRIORS

THE PLACE OF
NO STARS

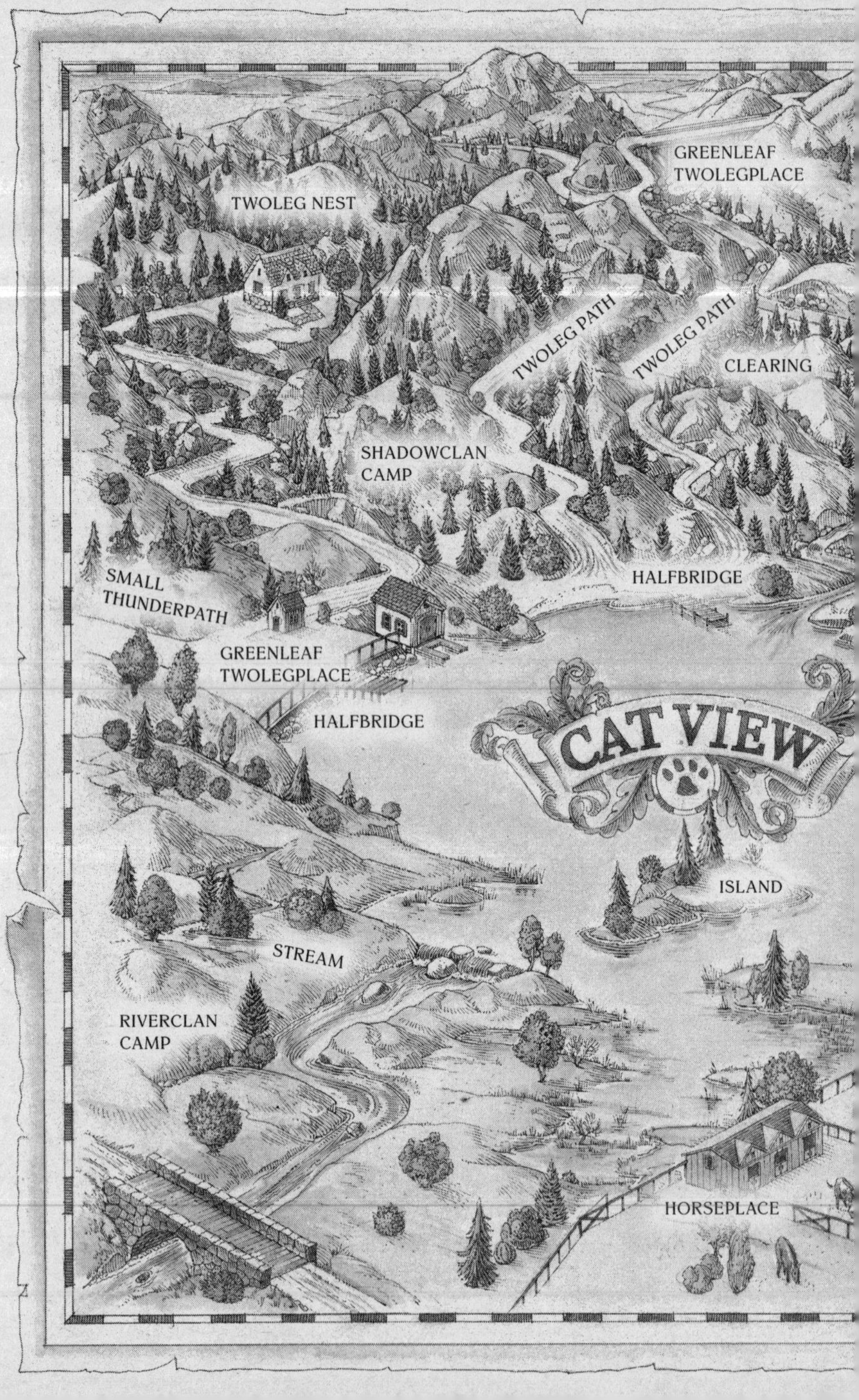

CAT VIEW

GREENLEAF TWOLEGPLACE

TWOLEG NEST

TWOLEG PATH

TWOLEG PATH

CLEARING

SHADOWCLAN CAMP

SMALL THUNDERPATH

HALFBRIDGE

GREENLEAF TWOLEGPLACE

HALFBRIDGE

ISLAND

STREAM

RIVERCLAN CAMP

HORSEPLACE

HAREVIEW
CAMPSITE

SANCTUARY
COTTAGE

SADLER WOODS

LITTLEPINE
ROAD

LITTLEPINE
SAILING
CENTER

TWOLEG VIE

LITTLEPINE
ISLAND

RIVER ALBA

WHITECHURCH ROAD

KNIGHT'S
COPSE

PROLOGUE

❧

Squirrelflight flailed her legs frantically as the water of the Moon-pool surged around her. Ashfur's grip on her scruff was dragging her down, far away from the warmth and light at the surface. The icy water penetrated her pelt; sodden fur hindered her as she tried to struggle. Her chest ached with her need for air, but she dared not open her jaws. She knew that she was growing weaker; with the last of her ebbing strength she tried to lash out at Ashfur, but her claws met nothing except the swirling water.

He's drowning me! she thought, panic gripping her like a massive claw. She'd known that Ashfur was dangerous, even if he wore the pelt of her mate, Bramblestar. But Ashfur had come to the Clans to trick her, and when she'd made clear she didn't believe him, he'd decided to make her suffer. *Would he kill me, though?* Her heart ached at the thought of dying without ever seeing the true Bramblestar again.

Her senses were spiraling into darkness when she felt herself thump down onto a hard surface. She heard a drip and looked down to find water slipping from her pelt to drop onto the dry ground. *It isn't wet here. But where . . . ?* Her head was beginning to clear, but her shoulder, throat and cheek were still in pain from her fight with Ashfur beside the Moonpool. Exhausted, she lay where she had fallen, her chest heaving as she drew in great gulps of air, which felt like thorns tearing deep inside her.

From somewhere above her, a familiar voice meowed, "Welcome to my territory, Squirrelflight."

Staggering to her paws, Squirrelflight shook the remaining water out of her fur and looked around. Standing nearby was the muscular form and dark tabby pelt of her mate and Clan leader, Bramblestar. His amber eyes were gleaming in triumph.

But Squirrelflight knew that this was still Ashfur, the former ThunderClan warrior. He had gone to hunt with StarClan moons ago, but now he had somehow managed to return to the living world by taking over Bramblestar's body. His leadership of ThunderClan had ended in bloodshed and chaos. Renewed guilt and anger flooded through Squirrelflight at the thought that he had done it all "for her."

He was always obsessed with me, she thought. *Even when he was alive. All of this—taking over Bramblestar's body, making himself leader of ThunderClan—he did it all so that he could have me for himself. I should have known . . . oh, I should have known right from the beginning that he wasn't my mate!* But now, when she looked at this cat's covetous gaze, Squirrelflight's guilt hardened into disgust and anger. *Ashfur tricked me,* she reminded herself, *and that's no cat's fault but his own. He tried to murder my adopted kits when we were Clanmates, and even after moons in StarClan, he hasn't changed at all. He's an evil cat!*

The false Bramblestar took a pace toward her. Squirrelflight recoiled, baring her teeth in a threatening snarl. "Stay out of my fur," she warned him. "What is this place? Where have you brought me?"

"Can't you guess?" the impostor asked.

As he finished speaking, Bramblestar's body slumped to the ground. Squirrelflight watched in horror as a faint mist rose from it, gradually solidifying into the form of a different cat: a tom whose pale gray fur was flecked with darker spots, and whose malignant eyes were dark blue. The frosty light of StarClan glimmered at his paws and around his ears.

She had known that the impostor was Ashfur. But it still raked icy claws of terror through her pelt, seeing him as he had been when he was alive.

"It's good that I'm finally able to be myself with you," he purred.

All Squirrelflight wanted was to escape. But how? She spun around, her muscles bunched and ready to flee, but before she could run she got her first good look at her surroundings. Her body froze as she gazed at the trees that stretched away in every direction. They looked sickly, with drooping leaves; and instead of lush undergrowth, the spaces between them were bare, except for the occasional clump of bracken, brown and brittle. She could not see where the pallid light was coming from. When she looked up, the sky was dark, and there were no stars. Terror seemed to freeze every drop of blood in her body as she realized at last where Ashfur had brought her.

"This is the Dark Forest!" she rasped.

Squirrelflight had never visited the Dark Forest in dreams, but she had heard about it from Ivypool and the other cats who had trained there before the Great Battle. She cast a nervous glance around, half expecting to see a crowd of the worst cats who ever lived just waiting to attack her. But the forest was silent, and felt even more desolate than she had imagined: a barren wasteland. Were she and Ashfur truly the only cats there?

The silence was almost creepier than seeing a horde of evil cats. She remembered what StarClan had told her when she'd walked among them after she and Leafpool were gravely injured: The Dark Forest was nearly empty. But it was much stranger to see than to imagine.

"I know you were accepted into StarClan," she told Ashfur. "I saw you there. So what are you doing here? And where are all the others?"

"Life after death is more complicated than that," Ashfur replied, an answer that told her nothing.

Fresh horror thrilled through every hair on Squirrelflight's pelt. "Am I *dead*?" she choked out, wondering whether she had drowned in the Moonpool after all.

Ashfur shook his head. "No. I have brought you here so that we can be together."

The gray tom's eyes were full of adoration. Squirrelflight found that more terrifying than open menace would have been. Slowly, keeping her eyes fixed on him, she began to back away.

But before she had taken more than a couple of paw steps, she stumbled over something soft and yielding, lost her balance, and crumpled to the ground. Her vision swam for a heartbeat; when it cleared, she saw that she had fallen beside a painfully familiar form.

"Bramblestar!" she gasped. Even though she knew it was hopeless, she stretched out a paw and shook her mate by the shoulder. "Wake up . . . please wake up, please!" There was no response to her anguished cry. Squirrelflight drew back. "He's dead," she whispered.

She suspected that Ashfur had stolen one of Bramblestar's nine lives to take over his body when he died. Bramblestar's spirit had been spotted among the living Clans, and later Shadowsight, the young ShadowClan medicine cat, claimed he had released the spirit from where Ashfur had imprisoned it in the Dark Forest. But that was the last time any cat had seen Bramblestar. Now, looking down at his lifeless form, Squirrelflight's whole being ached with the fear that her mate was gone forever.

"A body without a spirit does not last very long," Ashfur told her, his voice unemotional. "Bramblestar has served his purpose."

Squirrelflight wanted to leap at this cruel, arrogant cat with all her claws unsheathed and her teeth bared, ready to sink into his throat. She wanted to let out all her revulsion in a screech of pure hatred. Instead she forced herself to stand still and think.

Everything she had done, every plan she had made since

she realized that an impostor had taken over Bramblestar's body, had been to save her mate and her Clan. Now she faced her most dangerous opponent. Ashfur would do anything to keep her here, or to make her suffer if she refused him. *And we're in the Place of No Stars,* she reminded herself with a shudder—a place of terror and desolation, where Ashfur knew the rules and she didn't. How could all her years as a warrior and ThunderClan's deputy prepare her for this?

But I'm going to figure out what to do, she resolved. *I'm going to get out of here, and back to my Clan—and when I do, I'm going to bring the real Bramblestar with me.* Flexing her claws, she braced herself and summoned every scrap of her courage. *Whatever it takes.*

CHAPTER 1

❧

The moon had slipped down behind the trees at the top of the ThunderClan camp; Bristlefrost guessed that dawn could not be far off. She paced restlessly around the edge of the stone hollow, so tired that every paw step was an effort, yet something inside her wouldn't let her keep still. And she was not alone. No cat was sleeping: Her Clanmates were also padding to and fro, exchanging nervous glances as their tails and whiskers twitched. Bristlefrost could feel their tension like strands of cobweb clinging to their fur, stretching from one cat to another until they enveloped the whole Clan.

Lionblaze and a few others were gone, and none of the remaining cats seemed to know what to do. *Because they're probably killing Ashfur in Bramblestar's body right now,* Bristlefrost mused. *How are we supposed to feel about that?*

Her heart lurched in her chest, as though buckling under the weight of the grief and fear flowing through her. She could not imagine ThunderClan without their wise and brave leader. Squirrelflight would be a most worthy successor, but without the guidance of their spirit ancestors, could she ever truly lead her Clan? Some of Bristlefrost's Clanmates had already left. Were the rest of them doomed to split up and become no better than rogues, without the warrior code to guide them?

How can ThunderClan ever come back from this?

At last she detected the sky beginning to grow pale, so that she could see the outline of the trees above her head. Dawn was breaking. The long and weary night was finally coming to an end.

At the same moment, she spotted movement at the opening of the thorn tunnel. Twigbranch, who was on watch, sprang to her paws, and Bristlefrost, thankful for something to do at last, raced across the camp to her side. She was ready for an invasion, or for the return of Lionblaze and his patrol, but instead it was a single cat who stepped into the clearing.

"Flipclaw!" Bristlefrost's joyful cry echoed around the camp.

Her brother had been one of the cats who had left the Clan for a "wander"—as he and some of the other cats had explained it, a "wander" was the chance to think things over in peace. None of the cats had been sure they would return to the changed Clan, so she had resigned herself to never seeing him again. Yet here he was, looking strong and vigorous, with a surprised expression as he gazed around the camp and saw every cat out of their den. Nuzzling his shoulder, breathing in his familiar scent, Bristlefrost felt a stab of hope that life would not always be dark and full of grief—that there might be a time when ThunderClan would live, and thrive, again.

More welcoming yowls broke out behind Bristlefrost as the

rest of the Clan bounded up to greet Flipclaw. Their sister, Thriftear, and their parents, Ivypool and Fernsong, thrust their way to the front of the crowd, almost overwhelming the young tom as they brushed their pelts against his, twined tails with him, and covered his ears with licks.

"Hey, give me room to breathe!" he exclaimed happily.

"I'm so glad you've come back to us!" Ivypool's purr was full of joy as she pressed herself against the kit she'd thought she might have lost forever. "It's been nearly a moon, so I was worried you wouldn't come home."

Bristlefrost stepped forward and met her littermate's eyes, hoping that he could see how pleased she was. Squirrelflight had told all the cats who'd gone on the "wander" to return to ThunderClan within a moon or they wouldn't be welcomed back. None of the others had returned except Thornclaw, an older cat who'd wandered home within a quarter moon, musing that he wasn't young enough to start over.

"I'm glad to be back," Flipclaw responded. "I faced so many dangers out there, it made me realize that if there has to be danger, I wanted to face it with my Clan by my side. I know now that ThunderClan is the right place for me. But . . . what's happening?" he went on, gazing at the cats swarming around him. "Why are you all up and about so early?"

A chorus of voices began to answer his question, but Flipclaw fixed his attention on Bristlefrost. "Tell me," he meowed.

"It's bad, Flipclaw," Bristlefrost replied. "The leaders have agreed to kill Ashfur, and it's happening now—or maybe it's already happened."

Flipclaw's happy expression faded; his jaws gaped and his eyes stretched wide in a look of shock and devastation. "But that means . . ." His voice died away as if he couldn't bear to speak the words.

"Yes, Bramblestar's body will have to die," Bristlefrost finished for him, her voice steady though her heart was wailing in grief and fear.

For a moment, every cat was silent, until Twigbranch spoke, clearly just trying to break the tension and move on. "Flipclaw, where are the other cats who left camp with you? Thornclaw has returned, but will the others come home?"

Flipclaw shook his head sadly. "We split up, a couple of days after we left camp. Graystripe and I went to the mountains to visit the Tribe of Rushing Water, where Graystripe's son Stormfur lives." His voice grew livelier as he continued. "It was great! I made friends with Stormfur's son, Feather of Flying Hawk, and he taught me how the Tribe cats hunt in the mountains, and then a whole bunch of rocks fell on me and I hurt my leg, but—"

"Wait," his mother Ivypool interrupted. "Did you say that *rocks* fell on you?"

"Yes, but it was okay." Flipclaw waved his tail dismissively. "But then—"

"You hurt your leg?" This time the interruption came from Jayfeather, pushing his way forward until he stood beside Flipclaw. "Which leg?"

"This one." Flipclaw lifted one hind leg, then, remembering that Jayfeather couldn't see what he was doing, gave him a prod with it. "Stoneteller healed my injury. I had to rest it for a few days, but it's fine now."

"It's not fine until *I* say it is," Jayfeather grumbled. "You'd better come to my den and let me check it out."

"Okay." Flipclaw sounded quite cheerful, and Bristlefrost reflected that if his leg had carried him all the way back from the mountains, there couldn't be very much wrong with it. "Anyway," he went on, "living with the Tribe made me realize that I wanted to come home and work to make ThunderClan as strong as it used to be. But Graystripe—"

"Yes, where *is* Graystripe?" some cat asked from the back of the crowd.

"I can't tell you where he is right now," Flipclaw replied, as other cats echoed the question. "All I know is that when he left the Tribe, he said he was going back to the old forest territories."

"What?" Cloudtail exclaimed, his eyes stretching wide and his tail flicking straight up in the air. "But that . . . that's mouse-brained! We left the old forest because Twolegs were tearing it down. There'll be nothing left!"

"There might be something," his mate, Brightheart, murmured. She rubbed her muzzle against Cloudtail's ear. "I'd like to go back and see it again."

"So would I," Birchfall agreed. "I was only a kit when we left, but I can remember our old camp very clearly."

Cloudtail snorted. "Even if it is still there," he meowed, "I can't understand what good Graystripe thought it would do, trekking all that way."

"He wanted to see if he could make contact with StarClan through the Moonstone," Flipclaw explained.

Murmurs of amazement rose from the cats gathered around him.

"Oh, if only he could!" Alderheart exclaimed fervently.

"I think he might," Flipclaw responded, his eyes bright with hope. "Graystripe's a clever cat, and if he thought it was worth making that long journey, then surely there's a good chance it will work."

Every hair on Bristlefrost's pelt prickled with reviving hope. *If Graystripe can get through to StarClan there, then maybe he can bring them back here, too. Maybe everything can get back to normal—at last!* More than that, Bristlefrost couldn't help wondering whether, if StarClan could return, they would be able to send Bramblestar back with a new life. *Maybe our leader will be himself again.*

"But Graystripe *is* going to come back, after he visits the old territory?" Fernsong asked.

Flipclaw nodded. "I think so."

"And what about Flywhisker and Snaptooth?" Cinderheart asked, slipping through a gap in the crowd to stand in front of Flipclaw. Her blue eyes were filled with anxiety. "As Ivypool said, it's been nearly a moon, and we've had no contact. Do you have any news of them?"

Bristlefrost could understand why the gray she-cat was so desperate to hear what had happened to her kits. No cat had seen or scented them since they had left, and most of the Clan—except for Cinderheart and her mate, Lionblaze—had been far too preoccupied with the Clan's troubles to give much thought to them. But Squirrelflight's deadline was approaching, and if they came back after that—if Squirrelflight held to her word—they would be turned away.

"They're okay," Flipclaw reassured Cinderheart. "But you probably won't like what I'm going to tell you."

Cinderheart blinked in confusion. "Why not?"

Flipclaw paused before continuing. "When Graystripe and I left, Snaptooth and Flywhisker were talking about trying out life as kittypets. So when I was on my way home, I detoured around our territory and headed for the Twolegplace, to see if I could find them. And I did—they're both living with a Twoleg now. I stayed—"

Flipclaw broke off as yowls and hisses of shock burst out from the cats around him. Spotfur hung her head, and Bristlefrost's heart ached with sympathy. *She's about to bear the kits of her dead mate, and now she's lost her littermates too.* She tried to give the queen an encouraging look, but Spotfur wouldn't meet her eye.

"Traitors!" Hollytuft growled.

Cinderheart whirled around to confront her daughter, her neck fur beginning to bristle. "How dare you!" she snarled. "Can you tell me that you haven't—that *any* cat hasn't—thought about finding some way of escaping from this awful mess that we're in? If you do, I won't believe you!"

Bristlefrost noticed Twigbranch and Finleap exchanging troubled glances. *They were Snaptooth's and Flywhisker's mentors,* she recalled. *I hope they're not blaming themselves.*

Alderheart rested his tail on Cinderheart's shoulder in a calming gesture. "Accusing your kin of treason doesn't help," he told Hollytuft. Turning to Flipclaw, he asked, "Didn't you try to persuade them to come home?"

"Of course I did!" Flipclaw retorted. "I stayed in the Twolegplace for days, catching the odd mouse or snatching bites of that terrible yuck the Twolegs feed their kittypets. I did my best to convince Snaptooth and Flywhisker to return to the Clan, but they wouldn't. Do you think I should have picked them up by their scruffs and brought them back as if they were kits?"

"No cat is blaming you," Ivypool told her son. "We just wish that—"

Whatever she might have said next was lost in the sudden noise of pounding paw steps coming from the thorn tunnel. Lionblaze burst into the camp with Bumblestripe hard on his paws. Both cats' pelts were bushed up, their ears flat and their eyes glaring with wild fury.

What now? Bristlefrost asked herself, her belly beginning to churn with apprehension. They did not look like cats who had just killed their leader's body; she would have expected sorrow, or even guilt, not this uncontrolled rage.

But as he took in the crowd of his Clanmates, Lionblaze came sharply to a halt. "What's going on?" he asked.

"Flipclaw is back!" Fernsong announced.

Lionblaze's gaze swept almost indifferently over the young tom. "Oh, hi, Flipclaw," he meowed. For a moment he gazed around with a hopeful look in his eyes; Bristlefrost guessed he was looking for Snaptooth and Flywhisker. When he found no sign of them, the hope in his eyes died; he didn't ask about them, even though Bristlefrost knew he had been worried about his kits. *He'll question Flipclaw later,* she told herself. *Right now, he has more pressing matters on his mind.*

"What's happened?" Jayfeather asked. "I can scent your anger. Did something go wrong?"

"It couldn't have gone more wrong," Lionblaze replied, his voice a rumble deep in his chest. "Ashfur has escaped his prison in ShadowClan."

A stunned silence met Lionblaze's announcement. Bristlefrost thought that the Clan must be so numb from the shocks they'd received over the past moon that they hardly knew how to react anymore. She herself didn't know what to think. Ashfur was free again to carry out whatever destruction he had planned next—but at least that meant Bramblestar's body still lived. Their leader might yet return.

"Weren't those ShadowClan mange-pelts guarding him?" Cloudtail demanded with a flick of his ears.

"Shadowsight helped him get away," Lionblaze explained. "And . . ." He glanced at Bumblestripe. "We think he was conspiring with Squirrelflight."

Bristlefrost stared at the golden tabby warrior, her whiskers twitching in confusion. At an emergency Gathering the day before, she and Rootspring had watched Squirrelflight beg the other leaders to have mercy on Ashfur to save Bramblestar's body. But the other leaders were sure that killing Bramblestar's body was the only way to get rid of Ashfur's spirit. When they'd left to carry out the grim task, Squirrelflight had snuck off—and Bristlefrost and Rootspring had intercepted her just in time to talk her out of freeing her mate's body. At least, that was what Bristlefrost had understood. Bristlefrost had come back to ThunderClan, but Rootspring had meant to follow Squirrelflight, to comfort her in her grief.

I wonder what happened, Bristlefrost asked herself. *Did Squirrelflight change her mind?*

"Yeah, ShadowClan is holding *Shadowsight* prisoner now," Bumblestripe put in.

"Their own medicine cat?" Cinderheart exclaimed. "Tigerstar's son?"

Lionblaze nodded. "Even Tigerstar can't protect him if he's acted against the Clans to save our enemies."

Bristlefrost found it hard to believe that the young medicine cat would choose Ashfur over the Clans, not after the way Ashfur had deceived him and tried to kill him.

"Shadowsight would never act against the Clans," Alderheart meowed, echoing Bristlefrost's thought. "If he really did help Ashfur escape, he must have had a good reason." His voice shook as he added, "I'm sure of it."

Bristlefrost could almost see the conflict churning through Alderheart as he spoke. It was hard to imagine how he could bear the stress: His father had been driven out of his body, and that body had been condemned to death, while his mother was suspected of defying the Clans in a desperate attempt to save him. Her heart ached for Alderheart. Another cat might have crumpled under the strain, but he still carried on, doing his duty.

"We'll soon know," Lionblaze meowed in reply to the young medicine cat, "because all the Clan leaders, including me, are gathering our strongest warriors. We'll question Shadowsight, and then hunt down Ashfur—and Squirrelflight, if the two of them are together."

"Squirrelflight would never help that vile excuse for a cat." Sparkpelt moved up to stand beside Alderheart, her orange tabby fur bristling in defense of their mother. She glared at Lionblaze, the cat Squirrelflight had chosen to be deputy while she acted as leader.

"That's true." Birchfall backed her up, while his mate, Whitewing added, "Do you have even the *slightest* scrap of proof that Squirrelflight had anything to do with Ashfur's escape?"

"Actually," Bristlefrost mewed, "Rootspring and I saw Squirrelflight in the forest after the Gathering, and she agreed then that she would let the death sentence on Ashfur be carried out. I'm not saying she was happy about it, but she accepted the Clans' decision."

"But don't you think Squirrelflight was just telling you what you wanted to hear?" Bumblestripe asked. "She's argued for so long against allowing Bramblestar's body to be killed—does any cat really believe she just had a change of heart?" Bristlefrost's head whipped around as she glared at him, but Bumblestripe ignored her. His tail twitched menacingly back and forth. "She's a traitor to ThunderClan!" he finished.

"Yeah," Thriftear agreed. "She only cares about Bramble-star, not our Clan."

At her words, the whole Clan broke into a chorus of yowls and caterwauls.

"That's mouse-brained!" Sparkpelt snapped. "My mother has been a loyal ThunderClan warrior since before most of us were kitted!"

"That hasn't stopped her from betraying us now," Leaf-shade snarled back at her.

"She would never do that!"

"She would. I say we should banish her!"

"It's the only way!"

Bristlefrost stood silent in the midst of the uproar, her eyes shut tight, asking herself how her beloved ThunderClan could possibly have come to this. They were talking about banishing the Clan's deputy!

Finally, as the noise died down a little, Ivypool managed to make herself heard. "I believe Squirrelflight must have helped Ashfur escape," she declared. "But she would only have done it to keep Bramblestar's body safe, so that he can return to it. And it's not just because he's her mate. Doesn't every cat want our leader back?"

"I do, for one," Finleap meowed.

"And me," Twigbranch agreed. "I don't agree with Squirrel-flight's actions, but I can understand how she feels. It *would* be wonderful if Bramblestar came back."

"But is that even possible?" Whitewing asked, her tail

drooping sorrowfully. "Bramblestar has been outside his body for so long. Jayfeather, Alderheart—what do you think?"

Alderheart simply shook his head; Bristlefrost could see he was still struggling with conflicting emotions, his claws flexing and retracting, digging into the earth of the camp floor.

"I don't know," Jayfeather growled, his blind blue eyes shining with sorrow. "Nothing like this has ever happened in the Clans before. And since we don't have Bramblestar's body, or his spirit, there's not much use in all of us arguing about it." He hesitated, then added, "But I have to be honest . . . I'm not hopeful."

The Clan was quieter now, despair rolling over every cat like a thick fog. *If even Jayfeather has given up,* Bristlefrost thought, *then it really must be the end for Bramblestar.*

"If Squirrelflight *did* help Ashfur," Cinderheart began after a moment, "then maybe she took him away from Clan territory. That might be for the best, for them both to be far away."

"For the best?" Lionblaze echoed, as if he couldn't believe what the gray she-cat had said. "No, it's outrageous! The only way for ThunderClan to be safe is for Ashfur to be dead, once and for all. I regret losing Bramblestar as much as any cat," he continued, raising his voice to be heard above yowls of protest. "He was like a father to me! But if we're honest, we know that Bramblestar—and probably StarClan, too—is gone forever."

Fear tingled through Bristlefrost from the tips of her ears to the bottoms of her pads. The future that Lionblaze outlined seemed so dark and empty. *How will we cope without Bramblestar and StarClan? How can we call Squirrelflight our leader when she can't receive her nine lives?*

Facing the bleak prospect of ThunderClan without Bramblestar, Bristlefrost struggled to hold on to her earlier certainty that Squirrelflight would never have helped Ashfur. She truly had believed that she and Rootspring had talked Squirrelflight out of interfering in the Clans' plan.

But what if Bumblestripe is right, and Squirrelflight was just telling us what we wanted to hear? She might have let her love for Bramblestar blind her to the evil in Ashfur. Bristlefrost shook her head helplessly. *But she seemed so sincere!*

Now Bristlefrost wished that she had gone with Rootspring when he set out to follow Squirrelflight. If the ginger she-cat had been about to do something desperate, two cats could have stopped her more easily than one.

But she'd left Rootspring to go on alone. . . . If Ashfur—and even Squirrelflight, if she was helping him—had turned on Rootspring, what might they have done to him? Bristlefrost's heart sank; she felt helpless in her anxiety for the cat she cared for so much.

While the argument raged through the Clan, the dawn light had been gradually growing stronger, and now the sun shed a warm yellow glow into the clearing. The assembled cats looked up, blinking, almost as if they had forgotten where they were.

"We need a dawn patrol," Molewhisker meowed. "Lionblaze, shall I lead one?"

"What?" Lionblaze looked distracted. "Yes, okay, go."

Molewhisker gave him a brisk nod and beckoned with his

tail to Cherryfall and Stormcloud. The three cats headed off toward the thorn tunnel; Bristlefrost thought they looked glad to be going.

It was time for hunting patrols to go out, too, but Lionblaze clearly wasn't ready to return to the normal routine of the Clan. "There's something we have to do," he announced. "I want a group of cats to accompany me to ShadowClan. To question Shadowsight, and then go after Ashfur. We need to do it quickly. Which cats will come with me?"

"I will," Bristlefrost responded instantly, thankful for the chance to be active, instead of sitting around in camp worrying. Besides, she wanted to do what she could to help Squirrelflight, and she didn't want to doubt what she believed about the young ShadowClan medicine cat. *If I can talk to Shadowsight, I'll know for sure if he helped Ashfur escape.*

Lionblaze fixed her with a stern look. "Are you able to do what needs to be done?" he asked her.

"Yes, I am." Bristlefrost met the Clan deputy's gaze steadily. "I know how important this is."

For a moment, Lionblaze went on staring at her, as if he could see her very thoughts. Then he gave her a curt nod. "Okay, you can come."

I have to be there, whatever it takes, Bristlefrost thought, while Lionblaze chose the rest of the patrol. *Even if every other cat only cares about chasing down Ashfur, I'll be there to help Squirrelflight.*

"I'll take Bumblestripe, Plumstone, and Leafshade," Lionblaze declared. "And you, Bristlefrost. The rest of you can organize yourselves into hunting patrols."

"But what about me?" Sparkpelt asked. "I want to come with you. Squirrelflight is my *mother*!"

"I can't take every cat," Lionblaze meowed brusquely. "Tigerstar will think we're an invasion."

"But Sparkpelt has a right to be there," Alderheart pointed out. He seemed to have grown calmer now that some definite action was planned. "And so do I. And I think Jayfeather should come, too. Tigerstar won't feel so threatened if you have medicine cats with you."

"I know what you're like, Lionblaze." Jayfeather stepped forward to confront his brother. "No cat better. You tend to think with your claws and then regret it later. I want to make sure that Shadowsight and Squirrelflight get treated fairly."

The golden tabby tom drew himself up, briefly furious, then relaxed and huffed out an annoyed sigh. "All right, if you put it like that . . . but for StarClan's sake, let's get a move on."

He led the way out into the forest and turned in the direction of ShadowClan territory. Bumblestripe strode along at his shoulder, followed by Jayfeather, with Alderheart walking alongside him. The rest of the patrol bunched together after them, and Bristlefrost brought up the rear. She was thankful to be doing something, but her belly felt hollow with dread at the thought of what she might have to face. If Lionblaze didn't like what he heard, even Jayfeather and Alderheart might not be able to calm him down. Shadowsight could be in danger, even in his own territory.

What are we going to find in the ShadowClan camp?

CHAPTER 2

In the ShadowClan camp, Shadowsight huddled miserably in the leader's den. His father, Tigerstar, and his mother, Dovewing, pressed close to him, one on each side. He could feel the beating of their hearts, his nose tickled by the scent of their fear.

They had questioned him throughout the night, but now, as dawn light was beginning to seep into the den, they had fallen silent. Shadowsight could tell that they had not been satisfied with what he had told them. They didn't bother to conceal how worried they were, and how disappointed in him.

Outside in the camp he could hear angry voices, from his own Clanmates and the few warriors from other Clans who had been left to guard him. Shadowsight couldn't hide from the knowledge that the anger was aimed in his direction. Even Puddleshine, his mentor and his friend, had looked stunned and horrified when he'd learned what Shadowsight had done.

"I told you what happened," he began again, feeling compelled to make one last effort to convince his parents that he was telling them the truth. "Ashfur let me see that Bramblestar *isn't* dead. But Bramblestar told me that if we kill his body, he'll die for good. I saw Spiresight, too," he continued desperately when neither Tigerstar nor Dovewing responded. "I think he was trying to tell me something. . . . That, somehow, Ashfur has imprisoned many cat spirits. We *have* to set them free—and how can we do that if Ashfur is dead and can't tell us where he has taken them? How could I let Ashfur die when it means so many other cats will die or suffer?"

Glancing from Tigerstar to his mother and back again, seeing the fear in their eyes, Shadowsight realized that his impassioned plea had made no difference at all.

"You're the cat most likely to die or suffer right now," Tigerstar meowed roughly.

Dovewing rubbed her muzzle against Shadowsight's cheek. "The other Clan leaders are coming to question you," she told him. "We don't want you to go through that. I think you ought to flee, now, quickly, before they get here."

"Leave my Clan?" Shadowsight exclaimed, as shocked as if a tree branch had fallen on him. "No . . ."

"Yes," Tigerstar responded. "The other Clans—even your own Clanmates—are furious that Ashfur has escaped. At the moment, they're not convinced that it's you who is to blame. But if they decide that you *were* responsible, no matter why you did it, they might attack you. You can't admit that you had anything to do with it, or tell the other leaders what Ashfur showed you."

"It was probably a trick of Ashfur's anyway," Dovewing added sadly.

"I *know* what I saw," Shadowsight argued. "I don't care what happens to me, as long as we can somehow put things right. And I'm not going to lie to the other Clans. What Ashfur showed me was not a trick. It really was Bramblestar and Spiresight, and I *have* to tell the other leaders the truth. That's the only way to stop them from making a terrible mistake."

Tigerstar and Dovewing looked at each other over the top of Shadowsight's head. Shadowsight could see their eyes filled with pride in him, but almost at once it faded into sadness. Tigerstar let out a faint sigh. "That won't work," he meowed.

"Please!" Shadowsight begged. "For so long, I thought I had *murdered* Bramblestar, because I told the ThunderClan cats to let him freeze in that snow cave on the moor. If I don't do my best to protect Bramblestar's body now, I'll never be able to change that. Yes, I got it wrong that day: I thought I was speaking for StarClan, but all I did was give Ashfur the chance to come back and terrorize all the Clans. Now I *have* to put it right."

"I understand," Dovewing told him. "But every cat is so angry about everything that Ashfur has done—none of them will even listen to you, let alone believe you."

"Your only choice, if you don't want them to banish you, or even kill you, is to lie," Tigerstar pointed out.

"No," Shadowsight retorted. "I've already told you, I won't do that."

"Then leave before they can question you!" Tigerstar insisted.

"How *could* I?" Shadowsight asked hopelessly. "Where would I go? How is running away any better than being banished?"

Tigerstar rose to his paws and poked his head outside his den. "Tawnypelt!" he called.

The tortoiseshell she-cat entered immediately; clearly she had been just outside, waiting for her son's summons. "So it's come to that?" she asked Tigerstar.

The ShadowClan leader nodded. Then he turned back to Shadowsight. "I knew you wouldn't agree to lie, so I discussed this with Tawnypelt, and we decided that she should travel with you to the Tribe of Rushing Water."

"You remember that I took you there when you were a kit?" Tawnypelt mewed, while Shadowsight gaped at her in shock. "Stoneteller will welcome you. We'll sneak out of camp now, before the Clan leaders get here."

Shadowsight searched his vague memories of his time with the Tribe. He tried to remember the cat called Stoneteller, who his mother had described as kind. But the only images his mind could gather were of sparkling, falling water . . . so beautiful and mysterious. For a moment he was tempted to flee with Tawnypelt and find safety with the mountain cats, so far away from Ashfur and all the trouble he had caused.

He resolutely thrust the temptation away. "But if I can get the others to listen," he meowed, "if the rest of ShadowClan just backs me up, I'll have time to explain, and to convince the other leaders that they have to let Ashfur live. Then we can figure out how to break his hold on Bramblestar and the other spirit cats."

The three warriors in the den with him exchanged a look, passing questions between their eyes for long enough that Shadowsight hoped he had gotten through to them. But when Tigerstar shook his head, Shadowsight felt his heart plummet into his paws. None of them believed that the rest of their Clan would back him. *Are my own Clanmates really as eager to see me pay as ThunderClan is?*

"Sometimes, you can't even depend on your Clanmates," Tigerstar assured him solemnly. "You can only count on your kin."

Shadowsight couldn't repress a gasp of shock. *How can a Clan leader be telling me this?*

Dovewing stretched out her tail and drew it comfortingly down his side. "Go with Tawnypelt," she mewed, "and I promise that your father and I will try to get the Clan to listen to your reasoning. Then, when things calm down a little, you can come home."

Shadowsight looked up at his mother and saw nothing but love in her gentle gaze. He drew in a deep breath. "Okay, then I'll go," he responded. *The Clan might listen to their leader and Dovewing—at least, more than they would ever listen to me,* he thought, but he couldn't hold back the surge of misery that was sweeping through him. *I wonder if I'll ever be able to come home.*

"Then let's be on our way," Tawnypelt meowed. "Cheer up, Shadowsight. It'll be an adventure!"

Shadowsight doubted that he would ever feel cheerful again. He struggled to his paws and followed Tawnypelt out of the den. Tigerstar emerged after them, and let out a commanding yowl.

"Let all cats old enough to catch their own prey join here for a Clan meeting!"

The rest of the Clan immediately began to gather around their leader, leaving Tawnypelt and Shadowsight free to sneak unobserved around the edge of the camp. Shadowsight spotted his littermates, Lightleap and Pouncestep, urging their Clanmates to join the group, guiding them away from him and Tawnypelt.

So they're in on this plan, too, he thought. *I wonder if they doubt me like the others do.*

Tigerstar had leaped up onto the tree branch that overhung his den and was making an announcement about how he expected his Clan to behave when the other leaders arrived. As he approached the tunnel through the brambles that led out of the camp, Shadowsight glanced over his shoulder to take one last look at his Clanmates gazing up at their leader.

As he hesitated, Tawnypelt gave him a prod in the shoulder. "No time to hang around," she meowed briskly. "We have a long way to go."

But as the two of them were about to plunge into the tunnel, Shadowsight froze at the ominous sound of determined paw steps thrumming the ground, swiftly drawing nearer and nearer. Lionblaze emerged from the tunnel, standing nose to nose with Tawnypelt until she reluctantly stepped back to let him enter the camp.

Harestar and Mistystar followed Lionblaze, with a whole crowd of their warriors behind them. Only SkyClan was missing. Shadowsight felt as trapped as if they had thrown him into the bramble enclosure where they had once kept Ashfur prisoner.

"Oh, I can guess what's going on here . . . ," Lionblaze growled, his amber eyes furious as he glared at Tawnypelt and Shadowsight. "You two are trying to escape before the Clans can get to the bottom of all this . . . aren't you?"

Before either Tawnypelt or Shadowsight could reply, Tigerstar leaped down from the branch and came bounding over to thrust himself between his son and the visitors. "Who do you think you are?" he demanded, his shoulder fur bushing out. "Coming into my camp and accusing—"

"I'm a cat who's trying to put right the chaos that *your son* caused," Lionblaze retorted, drawing his lips back in a snarl.

At his words, it seemed to Shadowsight that every cat in the camp erupted into growls and hisses, challenges and arguments flying back and forth like flocks of frightened birds. Even Shadowsight's Clanmates, who were angry enough with him, raced over to support their Clan against the intruders. Shadowsight noticed that the ThunderClan medicine cats, Alderheart and Jayfeather, were trying to calm things down, but no cat was listening to them.

"You're following your own path, as usual," Harestar snarled at Tigerstar. "You're protecting your kit, even though he is our only hope of tracking down Ashfur."

"Yes," Mistystar agreed, baring her teeth as she confronted Tigerstar. "I thought you were as eager as the rest of us to get rid of that StarClan-cursed impostor. But no—you have chosen your own kin over the good of all the Clans!"

"What else can we expect from ShadowClan mange-pelts?" Lionblaze added.

The two sides surged closer, with claws unsheathed; Tawnypelt slipped to Tigerstar's side, joining him to protect Shadowsight. He could see that they were moments away from springing into an attack.

"Stop!" Shadowsight meant the word to be a commanding yowl, but instead it sounded more like the wail of a frightened kit. But it had the effect he wanted: The enraged cats eased away from one another, and their yowls of accusation sank to near silence as they turned to face him.

"I don't need any ShadowClan blood shed on my account," Shadowsight continued. "I'll go willingly."

Tigerstar, his fur still bristling with fury, laid his tail across Shadowsight's shoulders, and Shadowsight's spirits sank as his father led him to the bramble enclosure where Ashfur had been imprisoned. Shadowsight hesitated at the entrance: The impostor's scent, stale but still strong, washed over him, an irresistible reminder of how he had been deceived and manipulated. Tigerstar thrust him inside.

Lionblaze and the other two leaders had followed. "Plumstone, Bumblestripe," the ThunderClan deputy meowed, beckoning with his tail to the two cats he had named, "stay here on guard while we wait for Leafstar and SkyClan. Then we can all decide what we should do together."

Gazing out from the entrance to his prison, Shadowsight saw Lionblaze swing around to confront Tigerstar. "Except for *you*," he growled. "You will not be part of the discussion, since you clearly can't be trusted."

Oh, StarClan! Shadowsight thought despairingly. *This is all my fault, because my father tried to help me.* What else might Tigerstar now lose, along with the other leaders' trust?

Tigerstar's ears flattened and he slid out his claws. Shadowsight felt a flash of fear that his father would attack Lionblaze. But after a moment, he whipped around and began stalking back to his den.

"This is all a huge mistake." The ShadowClan leader tossed the words over his shoulder. "In the future, the Clans will wonder how any cat could have been so flea-brained—if there *are* any Clans left to remember."

Shadowsight was left alone, huddled in the bramble enclosure. The fight had been halted for now, but he knew it would not take much for claws to be unsheathed again.

Things are going from bad to worse, he thought miserably. *Will any cat listen to me now?*

CHAPTER 3

Rootspring half fell, half scrambled down the rocky slope that led away from the Moonpool. Terror throbbed through every muscle of his body, so that he was hardly aware of the dawn chill that penetrated his soaking-wet fur.

I must get back to camp! I need to tell the others what I saw.

But even as the thought crossed his mind, Rootspring wondered whether his Clanmates would ever believe him. He wouldn't have believed it himself if he hadn't seen it with his own eyes: Ashfur grabbing Squirrelflight and dragging her beneath the waters of the Moonpool, where both cats had vanished.

His anxiety mounted as the sun crept up above the hills, reminding him of how much time was passing. He knew he had spent too long vainly searching the Moonpool. Every moment made him feel that Ashfur's escape, his kidnapping of Squirrelflight, was becoming more and more final.

I have to get help!

Reaching the bottom of the slope, with the tough grass of the moorland underpaw, Rootspring was able to pick up his pace until he was pelting along with his paws barely skimming the ground.

He had crossed into ThunderClan territory and was racing alongside the stream that formed the border with WindClan when he spotted a group of cats climbing the hill toward him. Rootspring let out a gasp of relief as he recognized the Sky-Clan deputy, Hawkwing. Mintfur, Macgyver, and Bellaleaf were with him.

"What are you doing out here all by yourself?" Hawkwing asked as Rootspring skidded to a halt in front of him. "You've been missing since the Gathering. Ashfur has escaped. No cat should be out alone."

Rootspring's chest was heaving as he struggled to breathe; for a few heartbeats, he was unable to speak. Hawkwing rested his tail-tip on his shoulder to calm him.

"I'm leading this patrol to look for Ashfur," he continued. "Leafstar means to take another patrol to the ShadowClan camp to confer with the other Clan leaders and find out exactly what happened."

"I can tell you what happened." Rootspring managed to get his breath at last, deeply thankful to have found a cat in charge who could tell him what to do about it. "I went with Squirrel-flight to the Moonpool, and Ashfur appeared and dragged her in. They vanished under the surface, and they didn't come up again!"

He was aware of the other three cats exchanging dubious glances as he spoke, and he guessed that they didn't believe a word of what he was telling them.

"That sounds unlikely to me," Macgyver meowed as he finished his account of his fruitless search of the Moonpool, confirming Rootspring's suspicions. "Maybe you were dreaming, or you got confused. What did you *really* see?"

Rootspring opened his jaws to protest, but Hawkwing forestalled him. "I was there when Ashfur escaped," he told the others. "I certainly believe it's possible that he has taken Squirrelflight as his hostage. That's more likely than Squirrelflight actually helping him get away." Turning to Rootspring, he went on, "Hurry back to camp. You need to catch Leafstar and tell her about this before she gets to ShadowClan. We'll go on to the Moonpool and see what we can find there. Bellaleaf, you'd better go with Rootspring."

"What?" Bellaleaf's whiskers twitched indignantly. "Hawkwing, if you find Ashfur, you're going to need all of us with you."

"It's okay," Rootspring responded, heading downstream again. He didn't want to stand around wasting time while his Clanmates argued. "I don't need an escort!" he called back over his shoulder. "I have to get to Leafstar!"

Rootspring reached the SkyClan camp just in time to see his Clan's leader emerging from the fern barrier. Rabbitleap, Cherrytail, and Harrybrook were with her, as was Rootspring's father, Tree.

"Leafstar!" Rootspring panted. "There's something I have to tell you—about Ashfur."

Leafstar's ears flicked up in surprise. "I have no time now," she meowed. "We're going to ShadowClan territory. You'd better come with us and tell me on the way."

Rootspring padded beside his leader as they headed for the ShadowClan border. "Bristlefrost and I met Squirrelflight after the Gathering," he began. "She agreed that she wouldn't try to save Ashfur when the leaders came to kill him, and I went with her to the Moonpool in case she needed a cat from another Clan to talk to."

Leafstar nodded understandingly. "That makes sense."

"But then Ashfur appeared from out of nowhere and attacked Squirrelflight. Worse, he dragged her—" Rootspring broke off, knowing that this next part would sound crazy to the gathered warriors. But he had to say it. "He dragged her into the Moonpool."

Shocked murmurs came from the rest of the SkyClan patrol at the news.

"Alive?" Leafstar asked, stunned. "Was he trying to drown her?"

"I don't know," Rootspring admitted. "I just know that she was pulled in—and neither of them came out. I couldn't find any sign of them."

"Yeah, and hedgehogs fly," Rabbitleap meowed. "Root-spring, have you got bees in your brain?"

"No, I have not," Rootspring replied indignantly. "I saw it happen, just like I told you."

"But . . ." Leafstar shook her head doubtfully. "Maybe Ashfur pulled Squirrelflight out at the far side of the pool and escaped," she suggested.

"Or maybe he drowned both himself and Squirrelflight," Harrybrook meowed. "He obviously had bees in his brain. That would be sad, but at least it would put an end to this whole mess."

Rootspring forced down rising anger at his Clanmates' disbelief, and made himself speak calmly. "I know what I saw, and I searched the Moonpool. Ashfur took Squirrelflight somewhere I couldn't follow. And he went through the Moonpool to get there."

"We'll have to tell the other leaders about this right away," Leafstar meowed. "Every cat suspects that Squirrelflight helped Ashfur make his escape. But from what you tell me, Rootspring, it's clear that she is his victim, not his accomplice. We need to rescue her."

"Rootspring, are you sure you're not . . . well, imagining this?" Cherrytail asked at last. "After all, you've always seen things a bit . . . strangely."

"And what's wrong with that?" Tree asked, facing up to the tortoiseshell-and-white she-cat. "Remember that Rootspring was the first cat to see Bramblestar's spirit, and alerted us all to what was happening. Is this any harder to believe?"

Rootspring blinked gratefully at his father as Tree defended him. It felt good to have some cat on his side. *And to think I used to be embarrassed that Tree is so weird!*

"There's something in what you say, Tree," Leafstar responded to the yellow tom. She looked deep into Rootspring's eyes, and he held himself straight, determined not to flinch under that searching gaze. Finally, Leafstar gave a decisive nod. "I have confidence in you, Rootspring," she declared. "But we may have some trouble convincing the other Clans."

"In the future, the Clans will wonder how any cat could have been so flea-brained—if there *are* any Clans left to remember."

The words, spoken in a furious snarl, were the first that Rootspring heard as he followed Leafstar through the brambles into the ShadowClan camp. It was Tigerstar who had spoken. Gazing over his leader's shoulder, Rootspring saw him stalking back toward his den, while Lionblaze stood glaring after the dark brown tabby tom. The leaders and warriors from the other Clans were crowded together in the middle of the camp. Rootspring spotted Bristlefrost among the ThunderClan cats and felt a wave of relief.

I wish I could tell her everything that's happened since I last saw her.

"There *won't* be any Clans if we have to rely on you," the ThunderClan deputy growled in response.

Tigerstar halted and spun around. "What did you say?" He strode back across the camp until he was facing Lionblaze. Both cats arched their backs, their claws digging into the ground.

"I said we can't rely on you," Lionblaze replied. "Shadowsight can't be trusted. He's brought terrible danger to *all* the Clans, and your blind loyalty to him is just as bad."

"My loyalty is anything but blind," Tigerstar insisted. "If

you weren't so determined to show off now that you've managed to stumble into the ThunderClan leadership, you *might* be able to see that Shadowsight has been trying to do his best, and show a bit of compassion."

Lionblaze let out a furious hiss at Tigerstar's criticism, bracing his muscles as if he was about to leap into an attack. "What you need is a cat to teach you a lesson," he snarled.

"Lionblaze, no!" Mistystar stepped forward to stand beside the ThunderClan deputy. "Fighting among ourselves won't solve our problems."

"She's right," Jayfeather meowed, dipping his head toward the RiverClan leader. "Are we kits, play fighting while badgers attack our camp? We need to concentrate on what's really important, and that's dealing with Ashfur."

But to Rootspring's dismay, neither leader was listening to the blind medicine cat. Lionblaze flicked his ears as if he were getting rid of a troublesome fly and stretched out his neck until his nose was barely a mouse-length from Tigerstar's. "Shadowsight betrayed all of us," he growled. "The leaders agreed the impostor must die. But he has some kind of *connection*—"

He broke off abruptly as Tigerstar let out a furious yowl and leaped forward, crashing into him and bearing him to the ground. Pinned there by all four of Tigerstar's paws, Lionblaze thrashed helplessly, but couldn't throw him off.

"Say one more word about my son," Tigerstar snarled, "and it will be your last!"

Rootspring thought that the ThunderClan deputy looked surprised that he had been defeated so easily. His pelt bristled with fury, and he let out a snarl of frustration as some of the ShadowClan cats stepped forward to drag their leader off, while Bristlefrost and a couple of the other ThunderClan warriors helped Lionblaze up and tried to block him from attacking Tigerstar.

For all their Clanmates' efforts to keep the two cats apart, Rootspring could see that they were both determined to force their way through them to start their scuffle again. Rootspring worried that the argument would spread to their Clanmates, and soon the whole camp would be filled with a heaving mass of struggling cats, the air echoing with the cries and shrieks of a needless battle.

I have to do something! he thought. Charging forward, he threw back his head and let out a commanding yowl. "All of you, listen to me!"

Every cat froze and turned toward him. Rootspring felt a stab of nerves like a claw piercing his belly to see so many eyes looking in his direction. Then he spotted Bristlefrost gazing at him. Seeing the trust and admiration in her blue-green eyes helped him to calm down. He believed in himself, and in the message he'd come to share.

Once again, Rootspring described how Ashfur had abducted Squirrelflight, and what he had seen at the Moonpool, to make sure every cat knew what was at stake. "We can't let ourselves grow weaker by fighting among ourselves," he finished. "That's exactly what Ashfur wants."

For a few moments all the cats were silent. Rootspring felt slightly encouraged; at least no cat was loudly accusing

him of lying, or of being deceived by Ashfur, even though
he was aware of doubtful glances, and a few of the warriors
muttering among themselves. Bristlefrost's gaze was fixed
on him, and Rootspring once again felt encouraged by the
warmth in her eyes.

At the same time, he could feel tension in the camp, as if
every cat were tightly bound with bramble tendrils. Shadowsight was crouching in the entrance of what had been Ashfur's
prison, while Tigerstar had withdrawn to one side, the cats
of his Clan standing protectively around him. The Thunder-
Clan cats were grouped around Lionblaze, while the other
Clans had slipped into place between them, as if to prevent
them attacking each other again.

Mistystar was the first to speak. "If this is true, then it
changes everything."

"It has to be true." Sparkpelt stepped out from the rest of
her Clan, and let her gaze sweep across the assembled cats. "At
least, the part about what happened to Squirrelflight. That
would explain everything. I know that my mother would *never*
have betrayed the Clans to help Ashfur escape."

"And now that we know what happened, we have to rescue
her." Alderheart padded forward to his sister's side. "We *can't*
leave her in the power of that evil cat. But where could she be,
even . . . ? Has a cat ever gone through the Moonpool?"

"I have." Rootspring was startled to hear Shadowsight's
voice calling from Ashfur's former prison. He looked over
and saw the young medicine cat looking urgently at the
assembled warriors. "In a vision, I . . . I traveled through

the Moonpool into the Dark Forest."

There were gasps from the assembled cats.

"The Dark Forest?" Tigerstar asked, his pelt puffing out around him. "Are you sure?"

"I'm sure," Shadowsight replied. "It met every description I've ever heard of the Place of No Stars. And I found Bramblestar's spirit imprisoned there, and set him free. I also saw a barrier some cat had built that seemed to block a connection to StarClan."

Alderheart was examining Shadowsight thoughtfully. "I remember you telling us some of this," he said. Then his voice tightened. "Do you really think Ashfur took Squirrelflight to the Dark Forest?"

"I do." Shadowsight looked at the ginger tom with sympathy. Rootspring couldn't imagine how he would feel if he learned that his own mother, Violetshine, had been taken to the Dark Forest against her will. "And I know Ashfur. I'm sure this is what he's done. If he can't have Squirrelflight in the living world, he'll try in that wretched place."

Rootspring could see the distress in Alderheart's eyes as he shared an anxious glance with his littermate. Murmurs of sympathy from the other cats showed him that they could see it, too. Sparkpelt leaned closer to her brother, their pelts brushing to support each other.

"Then Squirrelflight is not to blame," Leafstar mewed. "She's in danger."

For a heartbeat Rootspring felt a tingle of optimism that every cat would come together. But his hope was squelched as Lionblaze began to speak.

"If Rootspring is speaking the truth," the ThunderClan deputy began, "then Shadowsight has even more to answer for. Setting Ashfur free has taken Squirrelflight from Thunder-Clan and brought her to the Dark Forest. Will we be able to get her back?" His voice shook a little as he added, "She's spent her life serving ThunderClan, and in many ways, she's held us together through this dark time. Her Clan can't manage to survive without her."

He really does care about her, Rootspring thought. *If Thunder-Clan loses Squirrelflight now, Lionblaze will be leader, but that's not important to him—not if we can get Squirrelflight back.*

Rootspring glanced at Shadowsight. The young medicine cat was flinching as if some cat had raked their claws across his nose. Rootspring felt a rush of protectiveness for his friend, who he believed had only ever been trying to help the Clans. "That's not fair!" he declared, determined to speak up for the young medicine cat. "Shadowsight would never have done what he did without a good reason. He's a medicine cat, and a loyal Clan cat."

"That's true," Tigerstar agreed, thrusting his Clanmates aside to pad forward and stand beside Rootspring. "Ashfur told Shadowsight that he couldn't be killed without Bramblestar dying, too—and Shadowsight says he saw proof that Bramble-star is still alive." He raised his voice to be heard over the exclamations of wonder that came from the assembled cats. "Even more, Ashfur is keeping *other* spirit cats as his prisoners—spirits he has blocked from crossing into StarClan."

Rootspring watched as the cats around him exchanged uneasy glances, clearly wondering what this might mean. The hostility between Lionblaze and Tigerstar seemed to have faded, and every cat seemed more doubtful that Shadowsight could be guilty of treachery after what they had heard.

"That's all very interesting," Jayfeather meowed at last, his blind blue gaze raking the crowd of cats. "So maybe we should stop standing around like a bunch of stunned voles and *go to the Moonpool.* And we'd better get the other medicine cats to join us. Frecklewish, Fidgetflake, Willowshine . . ."

"I'll fetch Mothwing," Puddleshine announced. The former RiverClan healer was now with ShadowClan. "Shadowsight too?"

"Of course Shadowsight," Jayfeather snapped, rolling his eyes as if he was finding it hard to hold on to his patience. "He's the only cat who's been able to cross out of the living world since StarClan disappeared."

"I agree," Mistystar mewed. "Whether we believe Rootspring and Shadowsight or not, it's obvious that *something* happened at the Moonpool. That's the place where we're most likely to get some answers."

To Rootspring's relief, the other leaders agreed with her. His paws itched to be moving, but his anxiety grew as he realized how much time had already been wasted. The sun was well above the tops of the trees; sunhigh could not be far off.

And meanwhile, what is happening to Squirrelflight? he asked himself. *I hope we can figure out what to do, before it's too late for her. . . .*

CHAPTER 4

Bristlefrost flexed her claws with excitement at the thought that after so much arguing, all the Clans had agreed to *do* something. But impatience rose inside her as she realized that the leaders still weren't ready to set out.

"We need fast messengers to go fetch the other medicine cats," Mistystar meowed. "Jayclaw," she added, turning to one of her warriors, "you can get Willowshine, then go straight to the Moonpool."

The tom dipped his head in acknowledgment and disappeared through the bramble barrier.

"Rootspring, go and fetch Frecklewish and Fidgetflake," Leafstar ordered.

As the young tom dashed off, Lionblaze added, "Harestar, can I suggest sending Bristlefrost to WindClan? Your territory is the farthest away, and I think she must be the fastest cat in the forest."

Embarrassed at her deputy's unexpected praise, Bristlefrost still noticed that Harestar looked slightly surprised at the thought of sending a warrior from a different Clan to bring back his medicine cat. But she noticed too that he had brought older Clanmates with him; presumably, he had chosen them for their wisdom and experience rather than their speed.

"Very well," the WindClan leader meowed. "Bristlefrost, if Crowfeather gives you any trouble, tell him I sent you, and that I will explain when I see him."

"Thank you, Harestar," Bristlefrost responded.

As she wormed her way through the brambles that surrounded the camp, she heard argument break out again behind her.

"I think that only the leaders and medicine cats should go," Harestar declared. "We can't have every cat crowding around the Moonpool."

"And what about Tigerstar?" Lionblaze growled. "Should he even come with us? Hasn't he proved that he's untrustworthy when it comes to his son?"

"Who are you calling untrustworthy?" Tigerstar demanded.

The voices faded behind Bristlefrost as she emerged into the forest and began to run. *At this rate, it's going to be dark again before they get to the Moonpool.*

After all the arguing and hostility in the ShadowClan camp, it was a big relief for Bristlefrost to leave it all behind her and just race along. Her muscles bunched and relaxed in a steady rhythm, and her tail flowed out behind her. She reveled in the sensation as the rushing breeze surged through her fur and plastered it to her sides.

Bursting out of the trees, she continued along the lakeshore, splashing through the stream that had once been the border between ShadowClan and ThunderClan but now passed through SkyClan territory. The ThunderClan border markers were fresh as she crossed into her own Clan, but she didn't pick up the scent of any of her Clanmates. She didn't see any cat until she stood panting on the bank of the border stream with WindClan territory on the far side.

I wonder if I should just cross and head for their camp, she asked herself as she got her breath back. *I don't want to waste time waiting for a patrol to give me permission.*

Bristlefrost had almost decided to continue when she picked up the scent of WindClan cats and spotted a patrol heading downstream toward her through the trees. Breezepelt was in the lead, with Crouchfoot and his apprentice, Songpaw, following close behind.

Of course it's Breezepelt I run into! Bristlefrost groaned inwardly. The black tom was probably the most unwelcoming cat in the whole of WindClan—except for maybe his father, Crowfeather, the deputy.

"What are you doing here?" Breezepelt demanded as he padded up to face Bristlefrost on the opposite bank of the stream.

Bristlefrost bit back a rude reply and dipped her head politely. "I need to visit your camp," she meowed. "I have a message for Kestrelflight."

"What?" Suspicion leaped into Breezepelt's amber eyes. "What business does a ThunderClan warrior have in the WindClan camp?"

"I told you, I have a message for your medicine cat. Hare-star sent me."

Now Breezepelt sounded even more suspicious. "Why would our leader send a ThunderClan cat?"

"Because the message is urgent, and I'm fast," Bristle-frost replied. *It's a good thing I stayed on this side of the stream, or I'd be tempted to claw his stupid ears off.* "Now, may I please speak to Kestrelflight? It's very important."

But Breezepelt still seemed unimpressed. "That's not good enough," he responded. "You need to tell me what it is that you want to talk to Kestrelflight about."

Bristlefrost paused, annoyed that the WindClan tom was holding her up when Squirrelflight was in increasing danger with every heartbeat that passed. She was aware too of how crazy the truth might sound. But she had no choice: Breeze-pelt was only doing his duty, and there was no time to come up with a story that would satisfy him.

Besides, the Clans need to work together now.

"We're gathering all the medicine cats," she told Breeze-pelt, "because we think that Ashfur has taken Squirrelflight through the Moonpool to another place—maybe to the Dark Forest. Shadowsight got there in a vision by going through the Moonpool."

Breezepelt flinched at the mention of the Dark Forest. "Do you and the others mean to venture there to save Squirrel-flight?" he asked, his suspicious attitude falling away.

"I'm not sure," Bristlefrost admitted. "I think that's what the medicine cats are meeting to decide. All I know is, my

Clan leader and deputy are missing, and they need help. If I have to go into the Dark Forest to get them, then that's what I will—"

"You must have bees in your brain if you're thinking like that," Breezepelt interrupted. "You have *no idea* what that place is like. You weren't even born the last time the Dark Forest haunted the Clans, and I'd bet a moon of dawn patrols that you can't even begin to imagine it."

Privately, Bristlefrost thought the WindClan warrior might be right. She had heard enough stories from the elders to have an idea of how horrific the Dark Forest was, and how dangerous the spirit cats were who had been banished there, but listening to stories wasn't the same as actually being there. However, she refused to show Breezepelt any fear or hesitation, and met his gaze levelly as she responded.

"The safety of all the Clans might depend on this—and right now, that's the only thing that matters."

Breezepelt hesitated for a moment longer, then gave her a curt nod. "Okay, you can come over."

Bristlefrost leaped over the stream and followed Breezepelt to the edge of the trees and up the long slope of moorland that led to the WindClan camp. Crouchfoot and Songpaw, who had listened to the conversation round-eyed with shock, brought up the rear.

WindClan camped in a hollow near the top of the moor, surrounded by gorse bushes. Bristlefrost looked around her with interest as Breezepelt led her down the slope to the center of the camp. Dark holes gaped around the edges; Bristle-frost guessed they were abandoned rabbit burrows. Boulders were scattered around the hollow, and more gorse bushes had rooted themselves in the sandy soil. *Some of them must form the WindClan dens,* Bristlefrost guessed.

Weird . . . If I had to sleep there, I'd get thorns in my fur every night. I wonder if that's what makes Breezepelt so prickly, she added to herself, suppressing a snort of amusement. *If I lived in this camp, I'd spend half my time grooming my pelt!*

"Wait here," Breezepelt ordered Bristlefrost, then darted off and disappeared behind a large boulder at the far end of the camp. A moment later he reappeared with his father: the Clan deputy, Crowfeather.

Another difficult cat, Bristlefrost thought. *Great StarClan, this is really my lucky day!*

"Greetings, Bristlefrost," Crowfeather began. His tone was polite but cool. "Breezepelt tells me that you want to speak to Kestrelflight. Before you do that, I need to know why."

"Harestar sent me," Bristlefrost replied. "He said he would explain later."

Clearly dissatisfied, Crowfeather twitched his whiskers. "I'll need more than that, I'm afraid."

Bristlefrost's whole pelt tingled with impatience. Time kept slipping away, all while Squirrelflight was in Ashfur's power. But to her relief, Breezepelt began to repeat what she had told him, before she could say something she might regret to the uncooperative WindClan deputy.

Crowfeather's attention seemed to sharpen at his son's mention of Squirrelflight, and when Breezepelt finished his story, he gave a brisk nod.

"Very well," he meowed. "You can speak to Kestrelflight. But I'm coming with you."

Bristlefrost was so pleased to be given permission that she didn't protest as Crowfeather led her through a crack in a massive boulder. A couple of tail-lengths from the entrance, the crack widened into a shallow cave; the floor was covered in reeds and a shaft of light from a chink in the rocks overhead showed Bristlefrost a narrow recess where Kestrelflight was sorting herbs.

The medicine cat looked up as Crowfeather and Bristlefrost emerged into his den. "Bristlefrost!" he exclaimed in surprise, dusting scraps of leaf from his forepaws. "What brings you here?"

As quickly as she could, Bristlefrost explained what had happened, and how the leaders had called for a meeting of the medicine cats at the Moonpool. "You must come with me now, Kestrelflight," she finished. "It may be our only chance of saving Squirrelflight."

"Of course I'll come with you," Kestrelflight meowed, "but I'm not sure what good it will do. The medicine cats haven't been able to contact StarClan at the Moonpool for moons now, much less pass through it to somewhere else."

He rose to his paws, ready to leave, but Crowfeather did not move, and Bristlefrost realized that he looked deeply troubled.

"Maybe we've got it all wrong," he suggested. "Has any cat considered the possibility that Squirrelflight *wanted* to go with Ashfur? They were Clanmates for a long time; who knows what their connection might be?"

Bristlefrost sensed her pelt growing hot with outrage at the WindClan deputy's words. "Ashfur stole Bramblestar's body!" she exclaimed. "And Ashfur tried to murder *your* kits that Squirrelflight raised, let's not forget! Do you think she'd have a single word to say to that . . . that piece of crow-food?"

"Perhaps not," Crowfeather replied. "But we all know that Squirrelflight's relationship with Bramblestar has always been troubled. Look at how she defied him to help the Sisters. Or even further back . . ." For a moment Crowfeather hesitated, then went on with a bitter edge to his voice. "Squirrelflight lied to Bramblestar about whose kits she was raising. They didn't speak for moons after he learned the truth."

Bristlefrost shook her head, not wanting to get caught up in debating actions that were ancient history. "But I *know* that Squirrelflight loves Bramblestar," she asserted, determined to defend her Clan deputy in spite of her discomfort. "The only reason she cares at all about Ashfur is to make sure that Bramblestar has a body to return to." Taking a deep breath, she added, "There's no way she's working with Ashfur to hurt the Clans. I'd bet my life on that."

Crowfeather stared at her, unspeaking, for so long that Bristlefrost was afraid she had failed to convince him. Then she let out a purr of relief as the WindClan deputy gave a brisk nod. He headed out of the den, gesturing with his tail for Kestrelflight and Bristlefrost to follow him.

Out in the open, Crowfeather called to a group of cats sharing tongues beside the fresh-kill pile. "Hootwhisker!"

A young tom with dark gray fur shot to his paws. "Yes, Crowfeather?"

"I have to leave for a while. You're in charge while I'm gone."

The gray tom's eyes widened and he puffed out his chest proudly. "Sure, Crowfeather. You can rely on me."

"Does that mean you're coming with us?" Bristlefrost asked, not sure whether she was glad or sorry about that.

"I am. Ashfur might still be lurking around up there by the Moonpool. Kestrelflight will need more than one warrior with him." Crowfeather's whiskers twitched irritably. "Where *is* Kestrelflight, anyway?"

As he spoke, the medicine cat emerged from his den, a leaf-wrap of herbs in his jaws. "Sorry, Crowfeather," he mumbled. "I thought these might be useful. If we find Squirrelflight, she may be injured."

"You could be right. Okay, let's go."

Crowfeather led the way up the slope out of the hollow and through the barrier of gorse bushes. Once on the open moor, he halted and turned to Bristlefrost. "You might as well go back to ThunderClan," he meowed. "Leave the medicine cats and the more experienced warriors to deal with this. You've done your part."

Bristlefrost flattened her ears, outraged by this attempt to get rid of her. *Like I'm going to take orders from a WindClan cat!* "You just said that Kestrelflight needed more than one warrior with him," she pointed out. "So *I'm* coming to the Moonpool with you, too."

Crowfeather gave her a doubtful look, the tip of his tail twitching in annoyance. Bristlefrost waited for him to repeat his order, but in the end all he did was shrug and turn toward the moorland slopes that led up to the Moonpool.

Bristlefrost followed, relieved that he hadn't tried to prevent her from coming. She was sure that whatever was about to happen, Squirrelflight would need some cat on her side. *And I'm not sure how many cats—especially the cats from the other Clans—really are.*

Sunhigh was long past by the time Bristlefrost and the WindClan cats toiled up the rocky hillside toward the Moonpool. Bristlefrost's belly was growling; the mouse she had shared with Thriftear at dawn now seemed a long time ago.

Pushing her way through the thornbushes at the top of the hill, Bristlefrost realized that she and her companions had to be the last to arrive. All the other medicine cats had already followed the spiral path down to the edge of the Moonpool, while the Clan leaders remained crowded together just inside the line of bushes.

Bristlefrost noticed that Tigerstar wasn't there; his deputy, Cloverfoot, was representing ShadowClan. *It must have taken them a while to convince Tigerstar to go along with that,* she thought.

Sparkpelt was there, too, looking deeply worried about what had happened to her mother, and at the edge of the group, Bristlefrost spotted Rootspring and his father, Tree. *I suppose they were chosen because they can see spirits,* she thought.

Bristlefrost padded along the top of the hollow to join the two SkyClan cats, dipping her head in greeting as she sat beside them. Seeing Rootspring, and his welcoming gaze, already made her feel optimistic, as if a ray of sunlight were warming her pelt.

Back in the ShadowClan camp, she had watched him intervene in the fight between Tigerstar and Lionblaze. *He was so brave!* Knowing that he and cats like him were determined to stop all the Clans falling apart—so much so that he would get between two fighting cats who were older and far more senior than him—gave her hope.

Besides, with Rootspring next to her, Bristlefrost felt much less awkward among so many important cats.

"I've tried to connect to the land to tell me where Squirrelflight is, like I learned from the Sisters," he told her. "But I'm not having any luck."

Bristlefrost nodded sympathetically. "I'm afraid that wherever Squirrelflight is, it's not in the living world," she replied.

Rootspring sighed. "I fear you're right."

Crowfeather went to join his Clan leader, while Kestrelflight headed down the spiral path to meet the other medicine cats beside the Moonpool. Some of them, Bristlefrost noticed, had also brought bundles of herbs, which lay neatly on the ground beside them.

Mothwing beckoned Kestrelflight into the group. All the medicine cats shared the same puzzled expression as they spoke together in low voices; Bristlefrost angled her ears and could just pick up what they were saying.

"How can a *living* cat pass through the Moonpool?" Frecklewish wondered aloud. "Even if it leads to StarClan's hunting grounds, that seems impossible."

Alderheart nodded agreement. "Cats have visited StarClan and the Dark Forest before," he pointed out, "but only in dreams, or when they were very close to death. Never in their own bodies."

"The Dark Forest cats were able to come into the living world in real bodies at the time of the Great Battle." Mothwing shuddered, her voice sounding deeply troubled. "StarClan cats did that, too."

Jayfeather looked just as disturbed as the golden tabby she-cat. "It must be possible to cross between the worlds of the living and the dead," he meowed, giving his pelt a shake as if he were trying to get rid of ants crawling through it. "We just need to figure out how."

Bristlefrost noticed that Jayfeather's fur had been spiking a little ever since the first mention of the Dark Forest. *I've seen him do that in camp, too,* she realized. *Whenever our Clanmates mention that awful place . . . not that they do, very often.*

Until recently, just as Breezepelt had warned her earlier, she hadn't really understood what the Dark Forest could be like. The Great Battle had taken place many moons before she was even born. So many cats' names had lived in her imagination, especially the names of the cats who had died bravely defending ThunderClan, but they had never felt any more real to her than spirits. Now it seemed as though spirits were more threatening than anything else she could imagine.

"Suppose we try one last time to reach StarClan," Puddle-shine suggested, his gaze flitting from one of his fellow medicine cats to the next. "I know it's not night, but if we touch our noses to the water, like always, then maybe . . ."

"Maybe hedgehogs will fly!" Jayfeather lashed his tail. "How many times have we tried and failed? Why should this time be any different?"

For all his fierce words, there was a tremor in his voice. Bristlefrost thought that it might have scared her, if she hadn't been feeling so unsettled already.

"It can do no harm to try," Willowshine meowed, and the rest of the medicine cats murmured agreement.

Jayfeather let out an ill-tempered snort. "Have it your own way. Don't blame me when it doesn't work."

The medicine cats settled into position around the Moon-pool, crouching on the very edge with their necks stretched out so that they could touch their noses to the surface. They closed their eyes.

A shiver passed through Bristlefrost as she witnessed the ceremony that, until recently, had been the secret ritual of the medicine cats. *Oh, StarClan, please come to them!* she prayed, half expecting to see the sides of the hollow suddenly filled with the starry forms of their ancestral spirits.

"While the medicine cats are doing that, we ought to search the area," Harestar interrupted Bristlefrost's thoughts. "We might find some evidence of what happened."

The rest of the cats spread out around the top of the hollow. Bristlefrost paced along the edge, not sure what it was that she was supposed to be looking for, until she reached the place where the stream gushed over the rim of the rocks and cascaded into the pool below.

"That's where Ashfur dragged Squirrelflight into the water." Bristlefrost started as she realized that Rootspring had padded silently up to her side. He pointed with his tail. "Just there, where the waterfall slides over that mossy boulder. But I can't see any traces now."

"Do you wretched mange-pelts mind!?" Jayfeather's exasperated hiss, intensified by his dread, rose up from the pool below. "It's hard enough to concentrate—we don't need you lot stomping around like horses, and chattering like kits let out of camp!"

"Sorry, Jayfeather!" Bristlefrost mewed.

Together with Rootspring, she crept back along the edge of the hollow until she reached her starting point at the top of the spiral path. The other cats were gathering there, too. None of them had found anything that might help them understand where Ashfur had taken Squirrelflight, or how they might follow her.

The sun was slipping down the sky, casting long shadows over the water, by the time the medicine cats stood up. Bristlefrost felt a thrill of hope tingle through her pelt, until she saw the forlorn looks on their faces.

"Did you see anything?" Leafstar asked, though her despairing tone told Bristlefrost what answer to expect.

"Not a thing," Kestrelflight replied. "We still can't reach StarClan. They're as silent as ever."

A heavy, tense hush fell over all the cats. As the twilight deepened, Bristlefrost felt as though all hope was dying with it, as if the Clans were descending into darkness. *I'll never see Bramblestar or Squirrelflight again.*

At last Sparkpelt broke the silence, her voice quivering with desperation. "Maybe if we go *into* the Moonpool, we'll be able to see a path?"

"We can't do that!" Puddleshine objected at once.

"Yes, this is a place for medicine cats," Jayfeather added. "You shouldn't even *be* here."

"You're the cat who suggested we should come," Sparkpelt retorted swiftly. "And this is no different from the time we all broke the ice. This is an emergency: We have to do things we wouldn't usually think of, if they might help."

"I went into the water when I first saw Ashfur drag Squirrelflight in there," Rootspring meowed. "I didn't find anything. I'm not much of a swimmer, though."

Jayfeather grunted, flicking his whiskers in annoyance, but the other medicine cats gazed up admiringly at Rootspring. "I think that was pretty brave," Bristlefrost told him, leaning closer to whisper into his ear. Rootspring blinked in surprise and let out a pleased purr.

"Suppose the RiverClan cats try?" Mistystar suggested. "We have no trouble swimming, and we might find something."

"I'll come, too," Mothwing announced. "I'm no longer a

RiverClan cat, but I can still swim."

Mistystar and Willowshine exchanged a sad glance at her words, but neither cat objected. Bristlefrost felt a throb of sadness in her belly to see how much they clearly missed their former medicine cat. Mothwing had refused to return to RiverClan after Mistystar had refused to also take back Icewing and Harelight, two cats who had fought on the side of the rebels against the impostor—and against RiverClan. Bristlefrost knew that Mothwing loved RiverClan, and she admired her strength in standing up for the cats who'd fought Ashfur. For now, she was a ShadowClan medicine cat.

"I'm still not convinced this is a good idea," Jayfeather insisted. "If the Dark Forest is at the end of this path, exactly what do you plan to do when you get there? The Dark Forest isn't to be taken lightly. You don't just *stumble into* it."

Mistystar flicked her tail dismissively. "We must find Squirrelflight—who knows how long we have? I'd say you've been outvoted." The RiverClan leader bounded down the spiral path to join the medicine cats, and all three plunged into the Moonpool together.

Bristlefrost watched the water settling where they had vanished, not daring to meet any cat's gaze. She didn't think she could bear to see the vain hope that was fluttering in her chest reflected in their eyes. *I'm trying to stay optimistic, but that would destroy it.*

Moments stretched out until Bristlefrost began to feel that the RiverClan cats must have found something, because surely no cat could hold their breath underwater for so long.

Then one head broke the surface, followed almost immediately by two more. The three cats swam to the edge of the Moonpool and hauled themselves up onto the bank.

"Well?" Jayfeather asked impatiently. "Did you find anything? Spit it out!"

Mistystar took two or three gasping breaths before replying. "The only thing I can spit out is water. There's nothing down there . . . nothing."

Groans of disappointment came from the rest of the cats. As she watched Mistystar and the two medicine cats shaking the water from their pelts, Bristlefrost felt as though the last chance of rescuing her leader and her deputy had just vanished.

"Maybe we *shouldn't* be trying to follow Ashfur and Squirrelflight," the RiverClan leader went on at last. "I'm not suggesting she was working *with* Ashfur, and I know what Rootspring says he saw, but isn't it possible that Squirrelflight went through with Ashfur *on purpose*?" she hastily asked.

Alderheart shook his head, a look of outrage on his face. "If she wasn't working with Ashfur, I can't imagine why. And she would never work with that cat!"

"Well, look at it this way," Mistystar mewed, shaking her head. "I've known Squirrelflight for a long time, and I know she would gladly sacrifice herself for the good of her Clan—for the good of *all* five Clans. Maybe she decided it was worth losing her life to make sure Ashfur couldn't do any more harm."

For a moment, Bristlefrost wondered if that could be true. She was sure that Squirrelflight *would* lay down her life to save the rest of her Clan, if it came to that.

But then Rootspring spoke up at her side. "It's not just about Squirrelflight."

"That's right," Shadowsight agreed, from where he stood by the Moonpool with the other medicine cats. "When I confronted Ashfur, I saw his eyes disappear, to be replaced by Bramblestar's, and then Spiresight's. Bramblestar said it was still possible for him to return to his body. I think Spiresight was *trying* to tell me that Ashfur has other cat spirits trapped somewhere in the Dark Forest..."

"That could explain what happened in SkyClan." Rootspring's eyes widened with understanding. "When we held the ceremony to try to speak to the spirits of the dead, we saw many cats, more than have died in the Clans—and they all seemed to be in great pain."

Even though several of the assembled cats had been present at the ceremony, they still exchanged frightened glances at Rootspring's reminder. "Have we lost StarClan because Ashfur is capturing the spirits of the dead?" Cloverfoot demanded.

No cat could answer her. Eventually Harestar gave a frustrated lash of his tail. "So what *can* we do?" he asked. "It's all very well to decide that we won't abandon Squirrelflight and Bramblestar, but so far we haven't found a single clue to tell us how to follow them."

"I wonder . . ." Frecklewish blinked worriedly. "Maybe Squirrelflight was able to travel through the Moonpool because she was with the spirit of a dead cat, even though he was in a living body."

"Quite likely," Jayfeather mewed crisply. "But that doesn't help us much, does it? Not many dead cats around here to show *us* the way."

Shadowsight stepped forward, ducking his head shyly. "As I said, I was able to visit the Dark Forest," he began. "I've explored a bit. And, for better or worse, no cat has spent as much time with, or knows Ashfur, like I do."

Jayfeather narrowed his eyes. "So what?" he asked.

Shadowsight fluffed his pelt. "I can go after them," he explained. "I know I can help. Someone just has to teach me how to safely reach the Dark Forest."

CHAPTER 5

Shadowsight watched as understanding leaped into the other cats' eyes. He was volunteering himself to go into the Dark Forest. He could feel their tension swirling around the Moonpool like a dense, damp mist.

"You can't just stroll into the Dark Forest as if it's any other place!" Jayfeather yowled suddenly, flicking his tail over Shadowsight's ear. "It isn't just a territory to be wandered into. It has powers all its own. It can turn a good cat bad."

"That's why it should be me," Shadowsight meowed insistently. Although his voice was quiet, the gaze of every cat turned toward him. "I'm the only one who knows what the Dark Forest is like. And I'm prepared for what awaits me once I get there."

Puddleshine shook his head. "That may be true," he admitted. "But I hope you're not thinking of taking deathberries again."

"Deathberries?" Mothwing snapped. "Have you got bees in your brain? No cat is going to try that, ever again. It's far too dangerous."

"I know that!" Shadowsight protested. Using deathberries

had been stupidly reckless, and he had been lucky to survive. "I promise I won't even think about it."

Mothwing gave him a stern glare. "You'd better not."

"Then how can any cat get there?" Frecklewish asked.

"Shadowsight isn't the *only* cat who knows what the Dark Forest is like," Harestar replied. "When we were having all that trouble with the place, some cats were able to dream themselves across." He paused, giving his chest fur a couple of embarrassed licks, and Shadowsight remembered hearing that when the WindClan leader had been a warrior called Harespring, he had been one of those deceived by the Dark Forest cats.

"It helped if you could focus on the darkness inside you," Lionblaze murmured, looking uncomfortable. *Perhaps remembering his own time in the Dark Forest,* Shadowsight thought, holding himself straight, determined not to flinch under the ThunderClan cat's unfriendly regard.

"We can't take entering the Dark Forest lightly," the golden tabby tom went on. "If a cat must go, should it really be Shadowsight?"

"Why shouldn't it be?" Frecklewish retorted, moving closer to Shadowsight and giving him an encouraging glance. "He *has* done it before, and he's willing to try again now, in spite of the dangers."

Shadowsight felt warmed by the support of the SkyClan medicine cat, but Lionblaze seemed unimpressed. He took a breath, apparently struggling to hold on to his patience. "Sure, Shadowsight has done it before. But that only means it *can* be done—not that it can only be done by him. Those of us who remember the Great Battle know that *any* cat can dream themselves into the Dark Forest, if they can focus on their darkest thoughts."

Cloverfoot stared at the golden warrior with a bemused head tilt. "Does that mean you think we should send in warriors who know the place?"

"Not exactly," Lionblaze replied, his mew shaky, his eyes flaring in what looked like fear, for just a moment. "Just that every cat should know what they're getting into. Besides, has any cat considered that Shadowsight might only be volunteering to escape the punishment he deserves?"

"'Deserves'?" Cloverfoot glared at Lionblaze, baring her teeth in the beginning of a snarl. "If Shadowsight is telling the truth, he doesn't deserve any punishment at all. He deserves the thanks of every cat in the forest!"

Shadowsight blinked in surprise at his deputy's vehement defense of him. After so long feeling that every cat was against him, even in his own Clan, he felt bolstered by the realization that at least some of them were on his side.

"Besides that," Jayfeather snapped, "going to the Dark Forest, even for a short time, is no way to *escape* punishment. If Shadowsight has already been there, he knows that very well."

Shadowsight nodded seriously, grateful to the blind cat for pointing out the obvious. *Maybe they'll realize that I'm talking sense and let me go.*

But he soon discovered that it wouldn't be as easy as that. "I'm not sure," Mistystar mewed, her doubtful glance flicking from Shadowsight to Jayfeather and back again. "Whether Shadowsight will be safe or not, can we really trust him to find Squirrelflight? If it weren't for him, Ashfur wouldn't have escaped, and Squirrelflight would be safe here with her own Clan. Shadowsight has chosen Ashfur over the Clans, by setting him free."

Another argument bubbled up around Shadowsight at the RiverClan leader's words.

"And if he hadn't, Bramblestar's body would be *dead*," Bristlefrost yowled, seemingly unable to keep silent any longer. "Shadowsight did the right thing."

"We only have his word for that," Harestar snapped, while Lionblaze fixed Bristlefrost with a glare from narrowed eyes.

"Shadowsight prevented the leaders from carrying out their decision. If he were a ThunderClan cat, I would exile him quicker than I would kill a mouse. Can any cat trust him again?"

Alderheart turned a look of outrage on his acting leader, but before he could speak, Jayfeather rested the tip of his tail on his shoulder. "Don't be mouse-brained, Lionblaze," he rasped. "Would you really try to punish a medicine cat for doing what he thought was the right thing to do?"

Shadowsight stood in the midst of them, listening to them talking about him as if he weren't there. As the moments slipped by, he felt more and more uneasy. Some cats were on his side, but most of them still suspected him, and their hostile tone told him that it was not just Lionblaze who was looking for a reason to exile him.

Or worse, he told himself with an inward shudder. *But I can't blame them. They're right. None of this would be happening if it weren't for me.*

He noticed Cloverfoot watching him with an appraising gaze. When he met her eye, she nodded at him and turned to the others. "We mustn't forget that entering the Dark Forest is dangerous—not just to your body, but to your mind," she mewed. "You must focus on the darkness inside you to get there. And, as many cats have said, the Dark Forest can turn a good cat bad."

Lionblaze growled. "Then maybe we *should* send Shadowsight—he doesn't have far to go."

Shadowsight flinched, and Cloverfoot shot Lionblaze an icy glare. "He's *willing*," she pointed out. "And Shadowsight has always had special talents . . . he's no stranger to dark forces, and he's survived his encounters with them without losing himself. Perhaps he *would* be the right cat to send."

The collected cats grew silent, each glancing over at Shadowsight with some combination of admiration and fear.

"We could try, anyway," the ShadowClan deputy meowed. "He could get the lay of the land, and look for any clues to what happened to Squirrelflight. Shadowsight, could you do that?"

"Yes, I—" Shadowsight replied, only to be interrupted again, this time by Lionblaze.

"I've already said I don't trust Shadowsight," the golden tabby warrior growled.

"So let me do it." Mothwing spoke before Shadowsight had

a chance to defend himself, raising her voice to be heard over the other cats' exclamations of surprise. "If you think Shadowsight could do it—no offense, but he's barely more than an apprentice—then surely I can, too." She gave one forepaw a nonchalant lick. "I'm tough; I can face the Dark Forest. And if something should happen to me there, I have complete faith in my fellow medicine cats to bring me back."

Some cats nodded in approval, but Jayfeather quelled them with a hiss of annoyance. "I hoped it would not come to this," he snapped, "but if any cat is going into the Dark Forest to save Squirrelflight, it should be me. I have a stronger connection to her than you, Mothwing—and, like Shadowsight, I've been there before."

"That's true," Cloverfoot mewed with an approving nod.

"Certainly Jayfeather is a better choice than Shadowsight," Harestar added.

Shadowsight stared at his paws. *How do I make them see I'm the best choice?* As he hesitated, several other cats murmured agreement, and then Willowshine stepped forward.

"I'll go."

"Why?" Jayfeather, having made up his mind, seemed annoyed that another cat was trying to take his place. "Why you?"

"The cats who think it's hard to trust Shadowsight are right," Willowshine replied calmly. Shadowsight began to bristle at his fellow medicine cat's criticism, then forced his fur to lie flat again. "He let Ashfur escape," Willowshine continued, "which means that if we're going to send a medicine cat, it should be someone else. And it's exactly because I'm *not* a Clanmate or kin of Squirrelflight that I should be chosen."

"That doesn't make any sense at all," Sparkpelt protested. "Some cat should go who cares about her."

"Ashfur could use that kind of connection against them," Willowshine pointed out. There was a slight edge to her tone, Shadowsight thought, as if she had only just managed to stop herself from adding *mouse-brain*. "Besides, if things don't go well, whoever enters the Dark Forest will have a difficult decision to make: to get out while they can, instead of maybe doing something stupid for Squirrelflight's sake. The cat who goes in needs to stay level-headed, and not let their feelings get the better of them."

"There's sense in that," Cloverfoot commented.

"And I do admire Mothwing's bravery—well, Mothwing, I admire everything about you," Willowshine continued, "but you've never been able to contact StarClan, and that makes it unlikely that you could travel into the Dark Forest. No," she finished decisively, "it has to be me, or no cat."

The buzz of comment that followed the small gray tabby cat's words died away as Mistystar padded up and faced her medicine cat. Shadowsight waited tensely for her reaction. "Willowshine, I know how brave you are," the RiverClan leader meowed, "but I suspect you haven't thought this through. You're our Clan's only medicine cat. What will your Clanmates do if something goes wrong and you never come back?"

Willowshine dipped her head respectfully to her leader. "I

have no intention of dying," she responded. "But, if the worst happens, perhaps Mothwing will consider returning to her rightful Clan." She shot a meaningful glance toward her former mentor, but Mothwing only turned her head away.

For a moment, silence fell; Shadowsight could see that every cat was thinking deeply about Willowshine's suggestion.

As if they can't see how mouse-brained it is . . . Shadowsight wanted to speak up, but he wasn't sure it would help his case. So few of the cats here trusted him.

At last, Puddleshine spoke. "Perhaps Willowshine has a point."

The rest of the cats—medicine cats and warriors— exchanged approving glances while they meowed their agreement. Shadowsight's heart thumped in his chest as if it were a rock trying to break its way out, and he could no longer hold his tongue.

"You can't be serious!" he yowled. "What's happening now has never happened before," he reminded them desperately, "and I'm the only cat who knows what Ashfur can do! Willowshine is a brave cat, but she won't be able to—"

"He's right about one thing: You should prepare, Willowshine," Jayfeather meowed. "Speak to a cat who has dreamed themselves into the Dark Forest—Harestar, for a start."

"*I've* been there," Shadowsight protested. "And not long ago. The Great Battle was *seasons* ago! Besides, I know Ashfur better than any cat in the forest, except for Squirrelflight."

Jayfeather dipped his head. "That's not entirely true," he pointed out. "Many of us were alive when Ashfur was among the living. Many of us called him Clanmate."

Shadowsight flicked his ear. "Yes, but he hadn't truly revealed himself then," he insisted. "You know the cat he was pretending to be, but I know the evil cat he *is*. He deceived me and made me believe he was giving me messages from StarClan. And even when we found out how evil he was, I had to listen to him the whole time I was his healer." He shuddered. "Every word was poison, like snake venom dripping into a pool, but it's helped me understand him."

He broke off as Willowshine padded up to him and rested her tail on his shoulder. Her steady gaze silenced him. "I understand what you mean, and I appreciate your concern," she mewed, "but the decision has been made. I'll be glad of your advice, about the Dark Forest and about Ashfur, but either you give me all you can, or you should leave now."

Shadowsight saw the determined look in her green eyes and realized that he was not going to win this argument. *Maybe it's arrogant of me to believe that I'm the only cat who could understand Ashfur,* he thought, suppressing a sigh. *After all, Willowshine is a clever cat, and Mothwing really respects her.*

Finally, he bowed his head. "All right," he meowed. "The thing you have to understand about Ashfur is, he doesn't care about the Clans. . . ."

Shadowsight opened his eyes and raised his head, blinking blearily around him. For a moment he couldn't remember where he was. Then he took in the rocks and the waterfall, and the pale surface of the Moonpool as dawn broke over the hills.

His memories rushed back: of the arguments the night before, and the decision to let Willowshine try to cross into the Dark Forest. She had been eager to make the attempt right away, but Harestar had objected.

"It's getting dark, and we've all had a long day," he pointed out. "I think the warriors should hunt, and then when we've eaten we can get some rest."

"We can't rest while Squirrelflight is in danger!" Sparkpelt protested. "Every moment might count."

"No, I think Harestar is right," Cloverfoot meowed. "How can we face something this important when we're all exhausted? Willowshine especially needs to be fresh and rested before she takes this big of a risk."

"But I have to go to sleep if I'm to dream my way into the Dark Forest," Willowshine pointed out. "I can't do that if I'm fresh and rested."

"You can if I help you relax," Mothwing told her. "But you won't be able to endure the Dark Forest if you're worn out. You have to be ready for what you might find, what you might have to battle. Remember, if you're injured in the Dark Forest, you carry that injury back into the real world."

Willowshine's eyes widened. "Oh. You're right, then—I'd better be rested."

There was still some grumbling, especially among the ThunderClan cats, until Lionblaze spoke up. "Well, my belly thinks my throat's torn out. Let's go and hunt."

He led the way up the spiral path, while Mothwing turned to the other medicine cats. "We need to talk. Not you," she added to Shadowsight. "I think it's best if you stay out of this."

Shadowsight felt a hot flash of humiliation in his chest at Mothwing's dismissive tone as the rest of the medicine cats gathered around her. He willed himself not to react, or to protest, and after the heat faded away, he felt grateful for the chance to rest and share a vole with Puddleshine after the hunters returned.

At last he had settled down to sleep, glancing across to where Willowshine was grooming herself, slowly and deliberately. *Maybe this delay will make her realize what a massive risk she's taking. There's still time for her to reconsider.*

Now, as the dawn light strengthened, every cat was beginning to stir, rising to their paws, giving their pelts a shake, and arching their backs in a good long stretch. Glancing around, Shadowsight spotted Willowshine and Mothwing standing together at the edge of the Moonpool; he padded over to join them.

"Willowshine, do you remember what I told you?" he asked. "Are you prepared to deal with Ashfur?"

He was hoping that Willowshine had changed her mind, only to be disappointed as she replied.

"Yes, I think it's all very clear," she meowed briskly, with an acknowledging dip of her head. "He doesn't frighten me. I'll be fine."

"I discussed this with the others." Mothwing angled her ears toward her fellow medicine cats. "We think it might help if you focus your thoughts on RiverClan cats who have died recently. They might be able to help you make the crossing."

Willowshine nodded thoughtfully. "I could try. Softpelt died in the battle against Ashfur. I know that she will help me if she can."

"Good," Mothwing mewed approvingly.

The other medicine cats began to gather around; even the Clan leaders and warriors joined them, picking their way down the spiral path to speed Willowshine on her hazardous journey.

"Remember that you're going just to gather information," Mistystar told Willowshine. "Find out where Ashfur is keeping Squirrelflight, and how many cats he has helping him—if he has any at all. If you see anything useful, we can work out how to send in warriors later."

Jayfeather gave a derisive snort. "I'm sure there'll be no shortage of volunteers for that mission."

Shadowsight wondered whether he had expected the warriors to flinch away from what was certainly medicine-cat business, but at once, an eager murmur spread among the gathered cats.

"I'd be proud to go," Cloverfoot announced, raising her head confidently.

"So would I," Sparkpelt added, equally confident.

"Maybe, but you shouldn't rush in so eagerly," Jayfeather warned them. "I admire Willowshine's bravery, but we should all think very hard about reentering the Dark Forest—and how to deal with what we find there. You can dismiss my concern as the ramblings of an old, grumpy cat—"

"Surely not!" Alderheart muttered under his breath.

"—but I know what I'm talking about," Jayfeather continued, ignoring the interruption. "We can't know what will happen next, but I'm sure of one thing: It's not going to be easy."

Silence followed Jayfeather's announcement. As he gazed around at the other cats, Shadowsight realized that they were beginning to understand the daunting task that was ahead of them, and the dangers they were going to have to face if they wanted to defeat Ashfur and bring back StarClan.

Eventually Willowshine broke the silence. "That's enough," she meowed. "I'm aware of the risks, and what I have to do. There's no point in hanging around any longer."

Mothwing nodded. "Let's get started, then." Carefully she dragged over a large leaf with a clump of poppy seeds lying on it. "Lick those up," she instructed Willowshine. "Once you've taken them, you should sleep until around sunhigh." As Willowshine dipped her head over the leaf, Mothwing added, "This is your last chance to back out."

Willowshine's only response was to open her mouth and lick up the poppy seeds with one swipe of her tongue.

Shadowsight watched, his heart pounding in his ears. He only hoped he had told Willowshine enough to keep her safe.

CHAPTER 6

Rootspring stood watching as Willowshine curled herself into a ball with her tail wrapped over her nose. Dread shivered through him from ears to tail-tip; he felt as if he were being slowly engulfed in icy water.

What if Willowshine can't find her way back to the living world?

Creeping closer to Bristlefrost, he whispered into her ear. "Maybe we should stop this."

Bristlefrost shook her head. "It's too late," she responded. "All we can do now is watch and wait. Besides, I don't think they would listen to us."

For a while the gathered cats crouched in tense silence, their gaze fixed on Willowshine's sleeping body. Rootspring thought it was as if they were waiting for a sign. His own heart fluttered in his chest as he watched Willowshine carefully, remembering what the older cats had told them about carrying injuries sustained in the Dark Forest with you into the living world. *What would that even look like?* Would a slash suddenly appear across Willowshine's flank, or a bite on her ear? Rootspring shuddered. He had no idea what Willowshine was experiencing in the Dark Forest, but he felt that after what

Ashfur had done to Squirrelflight, he must be capable of anything.

Still, Willowshine looked peaceful. The sun came up and the sky took on the clear blue of a beautiful greenleaf day; the surface of the Moonpool glittered under the bright rays.

But the growing warmth and light couldn't banish Rootspring's feeling of uneasiness. *I know that something is wrong.* Did Willowshine look . . . too peaceful? He looked closer.

Is she breathing?

An icicle of fear stabbed through his blood, and he opened his jaws to warn the other cats. But before he could speak, a high-pitched yowl rang out, seeming to echo across the water.

A shapeless mist began to rise from Willowshine's still body, slowly forming into a translucent image of the medicine cat. The spirit cat looked at her inert body with horror. The heart-wrenching yowl was coming from her.

She's dead! And her spirit is stranded! As Rootspring glanced to and fro in rising panic, he realized that no other cat could see or hear her—not even his father, Tree.

"Willowshine?" he gasped. But the spirit didn't respond, and only moved closer to her body, over which Mothwing was crouched.

The older medicine cat suddenly looked up, alarm in her amber eyes. "She's not breathing—something's wrong! We've got to bring her back—now!" she meowed urgently.

"I *knew* that this was a mistake!" Jayfeather muttered, as he hurried to Willowshine's side.

"It's too late," Rootspring murmured. Willowshine was

already dead, but even her spirit seemed not to understand that.

In the chaos, he wasn't sure anyone heard his words—except Tree, who looked up with alarm.

Puddleshine joined the other medicine cats, and all three huddled around Willowshine's body, desperately trying to revive her.

"Press on her chest to restart her breathing!"

"What happened? Did something hurt her in the Dark Forest?"

"Seems that way," Mothwing replied through gritted teeth, clearly focused on reviving Willowshine.

"What about trying a juniper berry?"

Rootspring tore his focus from the medicine cats to watch Willowshine's spirit vainly trying to rejoin her body. Over and over again, she flung herself at it, but each time, she flew through the still form like a wisp of smoke. "It won't work . . . ," he murmured, but no one heard him, least of all the spirit cat. And a part of him wondered if what he said was true. If she somehow managed to jump back into her body, could she revive herself, as they hoped Bramblestar would do?

Then, as she prepared to try once more, she suddenly froze, hovering over her body and the frantic medicine cats. Her ears pricked as if she could hear a sound, though Rootspring couldn't pick up anything.

"Mothwing! Jayfeather!" he called out, suddenly regaining his voice. "Willowshine is here. I see her . . . and she's seeing . . ."

What is she seeing? He wished he knew. But it didn't matter; the medicine cats were too busy trying to save Willowshine's life to pay attention to what Rootspring was trying to tell them. He guessed that they couldn't even hear him over the commotion they were making.

In the midst of the noise and panic, with more cats gathering around, Rootspring heard a desperate snarl from Willowshine's spirit. "Leave me alone!" She paused as if she was listening to something, until another yowl burst from her. "Never! Let me go!"

At that same moment, Rootspring saw Willowshine's spirit form being dragged away from where her body lay, though he could not see who or what had her in its grip. Struggling wildly, she was hauled backward toward the Moonpool, then plunged down into it, her legs flailing until she vanished under the surface of the water.

Icy horror gripped Rootspring like a massive claw. *This is worse than anything I could have imagined!*

"She's gone!" he yowled, just as Mothwing lifted her head and let out a wail of grief, saying the same words as Rootspring.

"She's gone!"

But Mothwing only means that she's dead, Rootspring thought. She hadn't seen Willowshine's spirit disappear into the Moonpool. She hadn't seen something *drag* her there.

Looking stunned and sick, Mothwing went on pouncing on Willowshine's chest, as if she was determined to bring her back, even though she must have known it was too late.

Eventually, Jayfeather used his head to push her aside.

"It's over," he meowed, his normally sarcastic tones softened by grief. "She was killed in the Dark Forest. Willowshine is dead."

"It's worse than that," Rootspring interjected. "I saw her spirit emerge from her body. She tried to rejoin it, but it didn't work—and then she was dragged by something into the Moonpool!"

Jayfeather turned his head sharply, his blind blue gaze fixed on Rootspring as if he could see him as well as any other cat. "What? What do you mean?" he demanded.

Rootspring explained what he had seen and heard. "It looked like Willowshine was fighting with something," he finished. "Like she was being *taken*. But I couldn't see what did it."

Jayfeather's blind eyes rounded as he seemed to take that in. "This is worse than we thought," he murmured. "Ashfur may have powers we've never seen before—not even during the Great Battle."

The medicine cat's statement was followed by silence. Rootspring imagined that every cat was having trouble understanding the danger they faced. *Will we ever get Squirrelflight back? Or Bramblestar, or Willowshine?*

"Are you all happy now?" Shadowsight pushed forward to the center of the crowd of cats around Willowshine's body. The normally gentle young medicine cat looked furious, his eyes blazing and his pelt bristling until he looked twice his size. "Willowshine has sacrificed her life for a mission that

I should have taken. I told you not to underestimate Ashfur. Now RiverClan has lost their only medicine cat."

Mothwing, already sunk in grief, turned a hurt look on the ShadowClan cat. She seemed to realize what that meant for the Clan that Rootspring knew she still loved, despite her exile.

"She died almost as soon as she fell asleep," Mothwing muttered. "She barely had a chance. Something *knew* she was there."

The assembled cats exchanged uncomfortable glances. "But how?" Bristlefrost asked. "The Dark Forest is big . . . isn't it?" At a few nods, she went on. "What are the chances that something was waiting in exactly the right place when Willowshine passed through?"

Rootspring heard a growl of annoyance, then looked over at Jayfeather. "Unless they knew she was coming," he suggested with a scowl.

"How would they know?" Rootspring asked. "Is Ashfur *watching* us somehow?"

Mothwing sat up, a sudden clarity in her eyes. "Maybe he doesn't have to," she meowed. "Willowshine reached out to Softpelt in her thoughts, remember—to guide her." She looked around at the other cats, who were nodding. "Maybe Ashfur intercepted that message? Maybe it gave him warning that a Clan cat was crossing over."

There was silence for a moment, each cat trying to think this through. Rootspring felt sick.

"Now it's even clearer to me that I have to be the one to do this," Shadowsight went on. "I will not allow any other cat to die." He strode toward the Moonpool.

But before Shadowsight could reach it, Jayfeather leaped into his way and faced him, glaring at him from his clear, blank eyes. "Don't you dare!" he spat. "Don't you understand this was a mistake?"

"Jayfeather's right," Rootspring agreed, padding up to join Shadowsight and brushing his tail along his friend's side in an effort to calm him. "No other cat will go into the Dark Forest. It's way too dangerous—even for a cat with your abilities." Shadowsight opened his jaws to argue, but Rootspring swept on. "Something killed Willowshine almost immediately when she entered the Dark Forest. We have our theories, but we don't know why—not for sure. Who's to say that the same thing won't happen to whichever cat we send in next?"

"So what do you expect us to do?" Shadowsight demanded, sounding not at all soothed by Rootspring's words. "Sit back on our haunches and let our friends fend for themselves in the Dark Forest?"

"Yes," Rootspring responded, forcing his voice to be as steady as he could. "Until we can work out how to get there without risking any cat's life, that is exactly what we're going to do."

A few *mrrows* and murmurs of agreement followed his words. Only Mothwing, deep in her grief, looked on silently.

CHAPTER 7

Sunhigh was a little way off when Bristlefrost and her Clanmates
returned to the ThunderClan camp. The bright day seemed
to mock the darkness of grief in her heart. RiverClan had lost
their medicine cat, and ThunderClan was no nearer to recovering their leader or their deputy. And as the day wore on,
Bristlefrost realized that any hope of peace in the Clan had
gone with them.

As soon as she and the others reached the stone hollow,
the rest of the Clan crowded around, demanding to know
what had happened. Bristlefrost had expected that Lionblaze
would tell the story, but to her surprise the Clan deputy had
waved his tail at her.

"Tell them," he choked out, as if he couldn't bear to put the
terrible scene into words.

Bracing herself, Bristlefrost forced out the words to describe
the meeting at the Moonpool: how the leaders and medicine
cats had discussed what to do to rescue Squirrelflight, and the
argument about which cat should be the one to try to enter
the Dark Forest. It felt as if she were living the ordeal all over

again. Her Clanmates gasped in horror as she told them how Willowshine had died.

"But how did some Dark Forest cat get to her that quickly?" Poppyfrost cried.

Several other cats echoed her words. "Maybe you misunderstood what happened," Twigbranch suggested. "Things can be confusing at the Moonpool."

Bristlefrost wasn't surprised at her Clanmates' reaction. *I don't think I would believe it if I hadn't been there to witness it,* she thought.

"Willowshine dreamed her way into the Dark Forest," she repeated. "But she never woke up. She died, and the medicine cats couldn't revive her." Murmurs of unease greeted her words, her Clanmates staring at her in utter dismay. *And I haven't even told them the most unlikely part yet.* "Rootspring said it looked like something got hold of her spirit and dragged her into the Moonpool," she continued.

"Yeah, and hedgehogs fly!" some cat mewed derisively.

Bristlefrost couldn't feel offended. "I know how crazy my story must sound. But I trust Rootspring," she insisted. "He would not lie. I realize that doesn't make the truth any easier to accept, though. I didn't know Willowshine all that well, but I respected her as much as any cat—especially when she volunteered for a mission that she knew would be dangerous."

As she spoke, Lionblaze stepped forward; there was fury in his eyes, and Bristlefrost realized that it was anger, not grief, that had kept him silent until now.

"Bristlefrost," he meowed, "tell our Clanmates whose idea it was for some cat to even enter the Dark Forest."

Bristlefrost hesitated before replying. "It was Shadowsight's suggestion," she responded, "but he—" She intended to add that Shadowsight had meant to go himself, until Willowshine had insisted that she should be the one.

But Lionblaze interrupted her. "Shadowsight should be punished," he growled. "Harshly."

"Oh, Lionblaze, no!" Whitewing protested. "He's just a harmless medicine cat."

"Harmless?" The golden tabby warrior let out a derisive snort. "Look at what he has done, to all the Clans! It was the *harmless medicine cat's* idea that led to Bramblestar's death, and let that filthy impostor into our leader's body. Shadowsight was the one who had the false vision about the codebreakers that almost caused the Clans to fall apart. And it was Shadowsight who nursed Ashfur back to health and let him escape, which led to Squirrelflight being kidnapped. We're never going to get Bramblestar back," he snapped, "and Shadowsight is the reason why. I should have killed—" He broke off suddenly; Bristlefrost thought he realized that he had said too much.

Ivypool, standing at his shoulder, gave him a gentle prod with one forepaw. "You 'should have killed' who, Lionblaze? Killed the impostor when you had the chance? Or did you mean, you 'should have killed' Shadowsight?"

Lionblaze shook his head, staring down at his paws. "I know how ugly that sounds," he began, not meeting his Clanmates' gaze, "and I don't relish the idea of any cat's death. But the truth is, if Shadowsight or the impostor he's protecting were dead, we would all be better off."

Silence followed his statement, until Spotfur pushed forward to confront him. "Outbursts like that show why you're not ThunderClan's true leader, Lionblaze."

Lionblaze blinked at her, clearly taken aback. "What do you mean by that?" he asked, sounding genuinely bewildered, as if he couldn't believe that his own kit was challenging him. "Squirrelflight appointed me her deputy, and now that she's gone, it's right for me to follow her as leader."

"But that's not the point," Spotfur told him. "Since we lost touch with StarClan, and the real Bramblestar disappeared, no cat has been *chosen* to lead us. Not since Bramblestar succeeded Firestar. And that includes Squirrelflight."

"But she—" Lionblaze began.

Spotfur ignored her father's attempt to interrupt. "And *that* means that there are many Clanmates with just as much claim to the role of deputy—and now stand-in leader—as you have, Lionblaze."

Bristlefrost realized how much bitterness must have been building inside Spotfur, for her to attack her father so vehemently. But she didn't have time to think about that. As if Spotfur's words had unleashed a flood, like ice melting in newleaf, a clamor broke out among the ThunderClan cats.

"Ivypool would be a better leader! She's Firestar's kin, too."

"Yeah, or Mousewhisker!"

"Whichever cat leads us, they need to be a warrior who will

deal with Ashfur once and for all!"

Lionblaze finally managed to make himself heard, raising his voice above the outcry in a frustrated yowl.

"I may not have been chosen by StarClan, but what other choice is there? I can't believe any of you would disagree."

Bristlefrost could see hurt in his amber eyes, and sensed that the fight was going out of him. *He's a great warrior,* she thought, reflecting on the events of the last couple of days. *But he's got such a grudge against Shadowsight, it's affecting his judgment.*

No cat paid any attention to Lionblaze's protest. The clamor continued while sunhigh passed and the sun began to slide down the sky. Some cats were trying to get support for themselves, or their choice of leader, while other cats wanted to make another plan to rescue Squirrelflight.

A few of the warriors—Whitewing, Birchfall, and Lily-heart among them—withdrew to the side of the hollow, where they anxiously discussed what had happened to Willowshine, and wondered if their chance of rescuing Squirrelflight had evaporated for good.

Bristlefrost hovered on the edge of the argument, not knowing what she or any cat could say or do to pull the Clans together again.

Then, in the midst of the wrangling, a deep, authoritative voice rang out from the direction of the thorn tunnel. "What in the name of StarClan is going on here?"

The caterwauling faded abruptly into silence. Bristlefrost whipped around to see an old but powerful gray tom standing at the camp entrance, raking the crowd of cats with a disapproving yellow glare.

"Graystripe!" Bristlefrost gasped. "You're back from your wander!"

Graystripe paced slowly into the center of the clearing. The force of his gaze was so strong that no cat even stepped forward to greet him.

"Is this what ThunderClan has become while I've been away?" he asked, his voice rumbling deep within his chest. "A bunch of bickering kits, vying for power? I've been trying to solve the Clan's problems. But it looks as if you're trying to make them worse."

No cat could answer. The silence seemed to Bristlefrost to stretch out for moons, until Flipclaw padded forward, dipped his head to Graystripe in profound respect, then touched noses with him. "Greetings, Graystripe," he mewed. "How did things go at the Moonstone?"

"Not well," Graystripe replied simply.

"So you didn't reach StarClan?"

Graystripe took a deep breath, seeming to think that over, then shook his head. "Never mind that. I thought I was returning to Clanmates and warriors. Where is Squirrelflight?"

Some of the Clan were so shamed by Graystripe's scolding that they couldn't reply, while others began to tell him everything that had happened since he had left. But every cat was talking at once, their voices growing louder and louder as they tried to make themselves heard.

Graystripe shook his head in exasperation, then let out a yowl. "Silence!" When the noise had died away, he turned to

Bristlefrost and fixed her with an expectant gaze. "You—spit it out," he meowed.

The gray warrior's command made Bristlefrost feel a tingle of nervousness all down her spine. When he had left ThunderClan, Graystripe had been an elder who had seemed uncertain about his place in the Clan, and upset by the damage that the impostor had done. But while he had been away, something had clearly happened to him. He now looked more like a warrior in his prime, and an air of complete authority had settled around him.

He's such a powerful cat! However did I miss that?

As calmly as she could, Bristlefrost told the story yet again, about how Ashfur had escaped from his prison in the Shadow-Clan camp and kidnapped Squirrelflight. She related the most recent events at the Moonpool, too: the effort they had made to rescue Squirrelflight from the Dark Forest, which had led to Willowshine's death.

Graystripe listened with grim patience, simply nodding his head at even the most unbelievable parts of the story. Bristle-frost didn't know what he had experienced while he was away from the Clans, on his wander, but it seemed to have left him utterly unshakable.

"Thank you for telling me, Bristlefrost," Graystripe meowed when she had finished. "If cats are traveling to the Dark Forest again, things are very bad indeed. I'm not sure you younger cats understand what you're dealing with. But let's sort out the problems in this Clan first." Glancing around, he added, "I see that the fresh-kill pile is low. Maybe tempers are running high because you're all hungry. That's a bad combination with fear and idle paws."

"Well, it's been difficult . . . ," Lionblaze began, clearly embarrassed at the disorder in the camp under his leadership.

"Warriors cope with 'difficult,'" Graystripe told him sternly. "We should send out a few hunting patrols right away. And what about RiverClan?" he continued, as several warriors began to organize themselves into groups. "If Willowshine is truly dead, then they've lost their only medicine cat. They'll need some help, and we have *two* medicine cats. . . ."

Alderheart nodded, seeming to understand what the gray warrior intended. "I'll go, as soon as I collect some herbs to take with me." He disappeared behind the bramble screen into his den.

Bristlefrost watched admiringly as Graystripe sent out the hunting patrols and ordered the apprentices to take what prey remained on the fresh-kill pile to the elders. The rest of the Clan was calming down, recovering their sense of purpose.

"Graystripe, you should be our leader!" she blurted out. "At least until Bramblestar or Squirrelflight comes back."

Graystripe blinked in surprise, as if the thought had never occurred to him. He opened his jaws to respond, but Jayfeather cut him off before he could speak.

Oh, no! Bristlefrost groaned inwardly; she already felt embarrassed by her outburst. *Now Jayfeather will say something gruff and sarcastic, and the arguing will start again.*

But to her amazement, Jayfeather's tone was approving. "I think that would be a wise choice. After all, Graystripe, you were once deputy to Firestar, perhaps the greatest leader our Clan has ever known. If you wouldn't satisfy StarClan, no cat would."

"But what about Lionblaze?" Bumblestripe protested. "He was Squirrelflight's deputy."

The question hung awkwardly in the air, as every cat's gaze shifted to the golden tabby. Bristlefrost could feel their tension as they waited for him to explode in anger.

Slowly, Lionblaze padded forward to face Graystripe and lifted his gaze to meet the old tom's. "Bristlefrost is right," he meowed. "It should be you, not me."

Bristlefrost let out a breath of relief. Already she could feel the difference in the camp, the renewal of hope that Graystripe's presence had brought to the Clan. If he could calm Lionblaze and unite every cat under a single voice, then perhaps ThunderClan would survive long enough to get their true leader back.

"Thank you for your confidence," Graystripe responded. "All I want to be is your *temporary* leader, until we can set things right again. And Lionblaze, I should like you to continue as temporary deputy. Together we will keep the Clan safe while we work out how to get Bramblestar and Squirrelflight back." With a snort of amusement, he added, "StarClan knows, I'm really too old for this, but I promise you I'll do my best."

"So what should we do next, Graystripe?" Lionblaze asked.

"The first thing I want to do is go to SkyClan and talk to Rootspring," Graystripe replied. "I want to know more about what's happening in the Dark Forest. If he was the last cat to see Squirrelflight, I want to know everything he knows about her disappearance. And about this strange way that Willowshine's spirit disappeared into the Moonpool."

"Do you want to go now?" Lionblaze asked. "It's getting late."

Bristlefrost realized that the light was reddening toward sunset; twilight would be gathering before a patrol could reach the SkyClan camp.

Graystripe shook his head. "No, you're right. Besides, I have already traveled a long way today. My paws are dropping off, and my belly thinks my throat's torn out. I need to eat and rest before I'm fit to tackle the Clan's problems."

Glancing around, he continued, "Lionblaze, Jayfeather, Bristlefrost, you can come with me. You seem to know most about what's been going on, so be ready at dawn tomorrow. And you, Sparkpelt—you can watch over the Clan while we're away."

Sparkpelt almost jumped out of her fur in surprise. "Me?" she asked.

"Yes, you." Graystripe's eyes gleamed kindly. "As Squirrelflight's daughter, I know you'll do your mother proud."

"Oh, I will, Graystripe, I promise!" Sparkpelt assured him fervently. "I'll be glad to do anything if it means we'll get closer to saving my mother."

"Good." Graystripe waved his tail toward Bristlefrost. "I have some questions I need to ask you," he meowed. "I want to make sure I understand everything that has happened while I have been away."

"Sure, Graystripe," Bristlefrost responded.

"Why don't you bring some prey up to Bramblestar's den?" Graystripe suggested. "Bring some for yourself, too. Then we can have a good talk and decide what it is that we need to do about that mange-pelt Ashfur."

CHAPTER 8
❧

Shadowsight was gathering elder leaves from a bush that grew near the pool at the bottom of the slope leading up to the Shadow-Clan camp. His paws moved slowly as he sought the youngest, freshest leaves and neatly stripped them from their twigs; most of his attention was inward, as he relived what had happened earlier that day.

He couldn't forget the terrible scene at the Moonpool, when Willowshine had died in her attempt to reach the Dark Forest, and his fellow medicine cats had tried in vain to revive her. He shuddered at the story Rootspring had told: how Willowshine's spirit had tried over and over again to return to her body, until something had seized her and dragged her under the surface of the water.

Some cat really needs to go back to the Dark Forest, he thought. A cold sensation of guilt and misery wrapped around him, as if his pelt were slowly turning to ice. *But it should have been me. Is it my fault that Willowshine died? Should I have tried harder to make every cat see that it had to be me?*

The questions bombarded his brain like hailstones pounding on the ground, but he could not answer them.

As he began to gather up his bundle of leaves, he spotted his father, Tigerstar, approaching through the trees, with his mother, Dovewing, padding alongside.

"Shadowsight!" Dovewing exclaimed, bounding forward to touch her nose to his. "It's good to see you out and about again."

Shadowsight dipped his head in acknowledgment, thankful that since that morning the leaders had agreed to relax the restrictions they had placed on him. But his gaze flicked anxiously to his father as Tigerstar strode up to join them. "Is everything okay today?" he asked, worried that his parents were out of camp, yet didn't seem to be on an ordinary border patrol or a hunt. "Ashfur hasn't—"

"There's no sign of Ashfur," Tigerstar assured him. "Dovewing and I have been keeping an eye on the borders, and checking our patrols. Everything is quiet."

"And you're back doing your duties as a medicine cat," Dovewing purred. "I know it won't be long before the others trust you again."

"Trust me?" Shadowsight echoed, feeling as bitter as the taste of dock leaves. "I'm still a prisoner in ShadowClan; they're just trusting me not to run. They know as well as I do that Willowshine's death has trapped me here. I would never forgive myself if I abandoned the Clans now. So they're allowing me to work—under supervision."

He cast a glance over his shoulder, directing his mother's gaze to where Puddleshine and Mothwing were standing underneath a nearby tree, clearly watching his every move.

"I don't know what they think I'm going to do," he continued resentfully. "Pick the wrong herbs, or bring Ashfur back from the Dark Forest? I don't intend to do either. Whatever happens now, I have to stay and endure it." Hopelessness threatened to overwhelm him, and he looked down at his paws. "I deserve that."

"What happened to Willowshine wasn't your fault," Tigerstar insisted. "She knew the risks. And though I may be wrong to say this—I'm glad it wasn't my son who died. I'm not sure I could have stood to lose you."

"Oh, nor could I . . ," Dovewing murmured, giving Shadowsight a lick around his ears.

Thankful for his parents' support, Shadowsight felt the icy bonds of wretchedness and guilt begin to thaw a little. But he still couldn't help wondering whether they—and the whole of his Clan—wouldn't be better off without him.

For the rest of that day Shadowsight was kept busy with basic apprentice tasks, like sorting herbs and throwing out the withered ones, or laying freshly gathered herbs out to dry. Whenever he looked up from his task, he would spot either Puddleshine or Mothwing keeping an eye on him.

In the late afternoon, while Puddleshine was napping and Mothwing was foraging for herbs, Shadowsight was startled by the arrival of Icewing in the medicine-cat den.

"It's nothing, really—I just think I have a small bone stuck in my teeth," she said quietly. "I knew I was eating that mouse too quickly."

Shadowsight nodded warmly. "You must be accustomed

to fish," he said lightly. Icewing and Harelight had joined ShadowClan with Mothwing when Mistystar had refused to take them back for fighting against the impostor. "Though don't they have *more* bones? Why don't you come over here and I'll take a look?"

Icewing moved closer and opened her jaws. Peering in, Shadowsight located a small shard of bone lodged in one of her back teeth, and began to pry it out with his claws.

"This is awkward, I know, but it will only take a moment," he told Icewing.

Soon the shard popped out, and Icewing groaned with relief and closed her mouth. "That's much better, thank you," she said.

Shadowsight nodded, waiting for Icewing to head out, but she lingered. "Is there something else?" he asked.

Icewing stared at him for a moment, then looked awkwardly at the ground. "There are rumors," she said, "that at the Moonpool last night, you volunteered to go to the Dark Forest to search for Squirrelflight."

Shadowsight flicked his whiskers, feeling strangely embarrassed. "I did," he admitted.

Icewing met his eye. "You're very brave. But the Dark Forest is a dangerous place. Did you know that my son, Beetlewhisker, was killed there?"

"No," Shadowsight gasped. He had heard stories of the Great Battle, but had never put together that Icewing's son was among the casualties. "I'm so—"

"You don't need to say you're sorry," Icewing interrupted,

tilting her head to one side. "I just want to make sure you understand what the risks are. Brokenstar left my son in the Dark Forest to rot. If you die in the Dark Forest, you die in real life. Your loved ones will never see you again. Do you comprehend that?"

Shadowsight didn't know what to say. He knew that it was a huge risk, but someone had to stop Ashfur and set this right.

"I know some cats in ShadowClan don't trust you, but I believe you are a good cat, Shadowsight," Icewing added with a tip of her head. "Don't make Tigerstar and Dovewing suffer as I have. Thank you for your help."

With those words, she was gone, leaving Shadowsight staring after her with a head full of questions.

Finally, the sun dipped down below the trees, and the scarlet light of sunset faded from the forest. Shadowsight let out a sigh of relief as he headed for his nest. He curled up, grateful for the comfortable moss and bracken, but not expecting to get much sleep. His thoughts still scurried around in his brain like panicked mice, too active to let him rest. Instead, closing his eyes and listening to his fellow medicine cats' steady breathing, he let his mind wander.

I know it's a risk. But somehow I need to make right what happened.

Shadowsight wanted more than anything to go into the Dark Forest to save Squirrelflight. Then he might feel that Willowshine's life hadn't been lost in vain. But how was he supposed to reach the Dark Forest? Dream himself in, as Willowshine had tried?

Dreaming herself in had turned out to be dangerous for

Willowshine—but then, the Dark Forest itself was danger-ous. Shadowsight remembered what Mothwing had suggested about Willowshine calling out to Softpelt's spirit: *Perhaps that was her mistake. So I won't call out to any spirits.* Shadowsight breathed in and out, feeling surprisingly pleased with this plan. *I'll just focus on something dark, the way cats dreamed themselves in before.*

Every hair on his pelt tingled with optimism. *Maybe I can reach the Dark Forest that way.* He had never tried, but that didn't mean it wouldn't work. *If I dream myself in from here . . . no one can stop me.*

Shadowsight decided there was no time like the pres-ent to give it a try. The camp was dark and quiet, with most cats already in their nests, Puddleshine and Mothwing were asleep, and there were no sick cats to look after. *It doesn't get more perfect than this.*

Shadowsight slowed his breathing, calmed his mind, and fixed his thoughts on a figure, blurred at first, then growing sharper into a form that was all too familiar.

Ashfur.

Even though the evil cat had disguised himself in Bramble-star's body, Shadowsight could picture quite clearly the menacing look in his eyes and his slouched, furtive demeanor whenever he knew that no cat but Shadowsight was watching. Worst of all, he remembered the sound of Ashfur's voice hiss-ing in his ear. *And he's tormenting Squirrelflight right now. . . . No! I have to stop him!*

Shadowsight focused on him, to let the usurper draw him into the Dark Forest. He remembered that Harestar had described how thinking dark thoughts could create a path into the evil place.

And there are no thoughts darker than my memories of Ashfur!

Bracing himself for a confrontation, he bent all his thoughts on bringing him to the wicked cat. But instead of sensing Ashfur, and his malevolent presence and intent, Shadowsight's mind was swamped by true darkness, as though a thick fog were passing over his eyes. All he could feel was a sense of desolation. A hopelessness, more powerful than anything he had experienced before, seemed to take over his whole being, like a wound through which all optimism and enthusiasm were bleeding out of his body. The feeling was so overwhelming that his paws were urging him to flee.

But where would I run?

After a long, terrible pause, the fog that had filled Shadowsight's vision began to clear, revealing a desolate forest with bare trees and no hint of prey, suffused by a pale, sickly light. He felt that he was alone, but he could hear the faint sound of something scurrying through the dead leaves that covered the forest floor. Or maybe it was just the cold wind blowing through his shivering pelt.

It worked. This has to be the Dark Forest, Shadowsight thought with a shudder. It seemed even more frightening, closer to decay, than the first time he had visited. He could easily imagine that a cat like Ashfur could make his home here. And now that he had crossed over into the nightmarish territory, he felt an odd sense of certainty that Ashfur was nearby, even though he couldn't see him.

But when Shadowsight began to take a step forward, the fog that he had seen before returned, swamping his vision and getting into his lungs. A fit of coughing shook him as he tried to expel the dampness from his chest. Even though he was standing upright, he could feel the ground and the soft bedding of his nest beneath his flank, where he was lying in the medicine cats' den. He knew that he was going to be wrenched out of this vision and back into the real world.

I need to focus. . . .

Though all his senses screeched out against it, and he shook with fear as if he were standing against a high wind, Shadowsight gritted his teeth and sent his mind out again, searching for Ashfur. He knew that the evil cat's presence would anchor him in the Dark Forest.

After a few long moments, the fog cleared again, and the sight of the desolate forest returned. Shadowsight held on to his sense of Ashfur as he began to move through the trees, feeling a tingle of fury that he had failed the first time.

I'm trying to achieve something here, he thought; the tingling intensified. He remembered with annoyance how his consciousness had tried to pull him out: *How small-minded and stupid! I have something important to do . . . can't any cat see?*

With a shudder, Shadowsight realized that these thoughts didn't feel like *his.* He remembered Jayfeather's warning at the Moonpool, that the Dark Forest could turn a good cat bad. Could the Dark Forest, and the cat who lurked there, be affecting him?

Could it turn me into a cat like Ashfur?

The thought was alarming enough that it disrupted Shadowsight's concentration. At that moment he felt a churning of fear in his belly, but not the sickly feeling in his chest, as if he were about to vomit. Somehow that told him that the fear wasn't his own. And it wasn't Ashfur's, either.

So where is it coming from?

Shadowsight's thoughts and emotions were becoming so tangled that he couldn't sustain his concentration. The Dark Forest wavered around him, and he found himself back in the medicine cats' den. The transition was so sudden that for a couple of heartbeats he couldn't recognize the familiar surroundings.

When his racing heart had slowed, and he was sure that he was safely back in the real world, Shadowsight pondered what he had just experienced. He had reached out for Ashfur and found him, but what had happened right at the end, before he was dragged back? Whose fear was he picking up?

It had to be Squirrelflight's, Shadowsight thought. *That's why I went, to bring her back . . . it makes sense she would be in my thoughts. And that's why I wasn't able to stay in the Dark Forest. But if I can steel myself to focus on my sense of Ashfur. . . .*

He remembered briefly the strange, ruthless thoughts he was having in the Dark Forest. *The Dark Forest can turn a good cat bad. . . .* He shuddered. *But I have to risk it . . . to save Squirrelflight.*

Shadowsight padded over to Mothwing and Puddleshine, and prodded them until they woke.

"What in the world are you doing?" Mothwing asked, blinking blearily at him. "It's night, and time to sleep!"

"There's something I need to tell Tigerstar and Dove-wing," Shadowsight explained. "And you said you had to be with me at all times." *See how you like that!* he added to himself, unable to repress a pulse of satisfaction.

"What, now?" Puddleshine groaned.

"Yes, now. It's important."

Puddleshine hauled himself out of his nest and shook scraps of bracken from his pelt. "Then I suppose we'd better go. And StarClan help you if it's just some nonsense you've dreamed up!"

In Tigerstar's den, Shadowsight stood before his parents, while Puddleshine and Mothwing flanked him, one on either side. Tigerstar had risen to his paws, his eyes narrowed suspiciously as he gazed at his son. Dovewing stayed curled up in their nest, her gaze filled with anxiety.

"So, what's worth waking us at this time?" Tigerstar demanded.

"I've realized something," Shadowsight explained, his voice steady as he faced his father.

At once Tigerstar exchanged a skeptical glance with Dove-wing, not bothering to hide his disbelief, though he said nothing.

"I know you don't trust me yet," Shadowsight continued, "and I've given you plenty of reasons to doubt me. But this time, I know I'm the right cat to enter the Dark Forest. I can dream my way in, just as warriors did during the time of the Great Battle. And if it works, I can bring Squirrelflight back."

Dovewing looked more worried than disbelieving. "But what about Willowshine?" she mewed, her voice quivering a little. "She died doing the same, didn't she? What would protect you?"

"I understand Ashfur," Shadowsight replied, drawing himself up straight, "for better or worse."

Irritation flashed behind Tigerstar's eyes. "So this wasn't worth waking us up," he growled. "I'm not willing to let you risk—"

"It's not a risk," Shadowsight meowed calmly. "I've just tried it, and here I stand. I can *do* this, Tigerstar. I'm not sure exactly why, if I'm being honest, but I think it's something about my history with Ashfur. Maybe I know too much about him for him to target me."

Tigerstar fell silent, staring at him with an expression that Shadowsight couldn't identify. Was it wonder? Or fury?

After a few moments, his father spoke. "So do it here," he growled more softly. "So your mother and I and Puddleshine and Mothwing can keep an eye on you."

"No, I have to go to the Moonpool," Shadowsight responded; he felt a flutter of nervousness in his belly, because he knew that neither Tigerstar nor Dovewing was going to like that. "It's where the connection to the Dark Forest is strongest, and it's the last place Squirrelflight was seen. I'll have a better chance of it working there."

"Absolutely not," Tigerstar growled, a flash of fury in his amber eyes. "The Moonpool is where Willowshine lost her life. You should stay clear of it for the time being—at least until the cats in the other Clans stop thinking about how it was your idea for a cat to go into the Dark Forest."

"Your father is right," Dovewing agreed. "If what you want to do can only work at the Moonpool, then maybe it's too dangerous to try at all."

"But I know I can—" Shadowsight tried to protest.

"Shadowsight, I won't argue with you about this," Tigerstar interrupted. "The answer is no. It will always be no. It's too dangerous at the Moonpool right now."

"Okay." Shadowsight's head drooped in disappointment, though inwardly he still asked himself if he really meant to obey his father. "I'm sorry I bothered you."

As they headed back to the medicine cats' den, Shadowsight felt Puddleshine touch his shoulder with the tip of his tail.

"Cheer up," his former mentor advised him. "It's all for the best. What if you met Ashfur up there? We'll find another way that isn't so risky."

But though Shadowsight settled in his nest again, he still couldn't sleep. He knew with his whole heart that he had to go to the Moonpool, and he had to go right away. He respected his father and usually followed his orders. *But this time, I just can't. Not now, when I finally know what I have to do.*

As quietly as he could, Shadowsight uncurled himself from his nest and padded softly toward the entrance to the den. But before he reached it, he felt a thorn drive into his pad, from where he had been sifting through the bedding earlier that day. Startled by the sudden pain, he let out a short yowl.

Immediately Mothwing raised her head, blinking blearily

at him. Shadowsight froze, hoping that she might fall asleep again, but instead her amber gaze sharpened. "Where do you think you're going?" she asked.

Despair surged over Shadowsight like an icy wave. *It had to be Mothwing who woke up! I might have been able to convince Puddleshine, but Mothwing has never really trusted me since she came from RiverClan. She's the cat who persuaded the rest to make me an apprentice again, because of the way I was connected to Ashfur. She's the last cat who'll help me now.*

Briefly frozen in shock, Shadowsight couldn't think of an effective lie. "I'm going to the Moonpool," he confessed, keeping his voice low so as not to arouse Puddleshine, too.

He expected that Mothwing would look annoyed and respond with something sarcastic, but instead, in the dim light of the den he could see that her amber eyes were full of sorrow.

"Isn't it bad enough that we lost Willowshine?" she asked. Shadowsight could detect a tiny quiver in her voice. "Are you determined to have us lose you, too, trying to get to that awful place?"

Shadowsight was racked with guilt to have dredged up Mothwing's pain at losing the cat who had been her apprentice. "You have to trust me," he mewed. "I'm sure about what I have to do, though I admit it will be difficult." He raised his head, stiffening his resolve. "But I'm going, whether you want me to or not. You can't stop me—this is too important, for all the Clans."

"And it doesn't matter that your father forbade you to do that?"

"It matters," Shadowsight admitted, "but it doesn't make any difference. Medicine cats don't have to obey their Clan leader if they have good reason. You know that, Mothwing. And I promise you, there's no better reason than this."

Mothwing let out a long sigh. "Fine," she whispered. "If you insist on being a mouse-brain, I'm coming with you. If we leave now, we might make it to the Moonpool before too many cats realize we're gone."

For a heartbeat Shadowsight gaped in amazement that Mothwing had given in so easily. "Okay," he murmured at last; Mothwing sounded so determined that he knew there was no point in insisting on going alone.

Mothwing gave him an approving nod. "If I'm with you, you might not get into so much trouble," she pointed out. "And if you're in danger once you've crossed over, I might be able to wake you in time to pull you out."

That makes sense, Shadowsight realized. "Thank you," he meowed.

Mothwing led the way, creeping out of the camp through the dirtplace tunnel so that no cat would see that they were leaving. As they headed out into the forest, Shadowsight waited for his pads to begin tingling with the familiar feeling of nerves, as if fear were crouching in the shadows like a massive creature that had chosen him as its prey.

But the feelings did not come. Somehow, he was certain that this was going to work.

CHAPTER 9

The moon was sinking in the sky when Shadowsight and Mothwing climbed the last rocky slope and thrust their way through the bushes to stand looking down at the Moonpool. Shadowsight gazed at the glimmering surface and could hardly believe that such a peaceful place had recently been the focus of so much terror and grief.

On the weary journey from ShadowClan territory, the two cats had scarcely spoken. There still seemed nothing to say as Shadowsight led the way down the spiral path, feeling his paws slip into the hollows left by other cats so long ago.

When they reached the water's edge, Mothwing turned to Shadowsight, her head tilted. "If this doesn't work," she meowed, "Tigerstar will probably want to kill both of us."

Shadowsight shrugged. "If this doesn't work, I'll be dead anyway," he pointed out. "And if we don't try at all, we'll be in the same terrible situation we're in now. So we might as well get on with it. Good luck with telling Tigerstar, if I don't come back."

As he spoke, he forced himself to sound confident, but nerves were tumbling around in his belly like a litter of play-fighting kits. The certainty he had felt when they set out had drained away like water on parched earth. He knew this was the best chance any cat had of getting into the Dark Forest and coming out alive, but the closer he came, the less sure he felt that he would be able to save Squirrelflight, or even save himself.

I'm a medicine cat, not a trained warrior. Oh, StarClan, I want to be brave, but will I really know what to do? All he could think about now was how unlikely they were to succeed, and how dangerous this endeavor was. *But I mustn't let fear get the better of me,* he added to himself, giving his pelt a shake. *I'll need all my confidence if I'm going to outwit Ashfur.*

Mothwing peered at him more closely, and when she spoke, it was to give voice to the fears he was trying to repress. "Even though your body isn't going to the Dark Forest, your spirit will still be at risk. And surely, the longer it's away from your body, the harder it will be to return."

"I know," Shadowsight responded, forcing himself to speak calmly. "And I accept the risks. Squirrelflight has risked her life more than once, for the sake of all the Clans. The least I can do is risk mine, this once, for her."

"I admire your courage," Mothwing told him, "but you have no idea what will be waiting for you in the Place of No Stars. There could be a welcome party that won't be all that welcoming."

"I'm ready for anything the Dark Forest can throw at me," Shadowsight insisted, trying to ignore the uncomfortable churning in his belly.

"You're a brave cat, for insisting on this when you don't have to do it." Mothwing stretched forward to touch her nose to Shadowsight's ear. "I admit I'm surprised—and impressed."

Shadowsight blinked up at her, touched that his harshest critic was at last showing him some respect. "Thank you," he murmured.

"If I think you're in trouble," Mothwing meowed, "I'll do my best to rouse you and pull you out. No, don't argue," she added, as Shadowsight opened his jaws to protest. "That will be *my* judgment as a medicine cat."

"Okay," Shadowsight agreed reluctantly.

"I wish you luck," Mothwing continued. "You'll definitely need it, where you're going. And if you're determined, you should take all the precautions you can to make sure you go unseen by any cat who might be lurking around. The Dark Forest is full of unscrupulous cat spirits—if they were good cats, they wouldn't be there, would they?"

"I know that," Shadowsight mewed, twitching his whiskers in impatience to be on his way.

Mothwing ignored the interruption. "There's no way for you to know who you can and can't trust," she went on. "Even if the cats there aren't fighting on Ashfur's side, they're all full of wickedness from their ears to their tail-tips. They may attack you or bully you just for the fun of it. If you're going to get out of there alive, you'll have to move like a ghost. Do you think you can do that?"

Shadowsight let out a little snort of amusement. "I'll be a spirit," he pointed out. "So it shouldn't be that hard."

Mothwing took a pace toward him and jabbed one paw into his chest, none too gently. "Listen, you'd *better* get out of there alive. If you don't, Ashfur's not the cat you'll have to worry about—I am."

Her words were curt, but there was warmth in her amber gaze, and Shadowsight understood that she had spoken harshly because she cared about him. For some reason, his apprehension eased; he found it wasn't hard to clear his mind and release the burdens of fear and uncertainty.

Shadowsight sat back on his hindquarters and tried to focus on his destination. He let his darkest thoughts flow through him: all the times he had been deceived by Ashfur; the evil cat's contempt for him and the way he had manipulated him. He allowed the image of Ashfur's crafty eyes and furtive demeanor to drift into his mind. He let a low growl rumble in his throat as he thought over and over again, *I'm coming for you.*

Soon Shadowsight felt a tugging on his pelt, as if a strong wind were pulling him instead of pushing. A lightness followed it; he felt free, but also exposed. *And so cold . . .*

Once again, as he had expected, a thick fog passed over his eyes. With it came the hopelessness and desolation that drove out all his optimism and enthusiasm, and wrestled with his confidence and bravery.

When Shadowsight had begun to feel that he couldn't bear the sense of oppression for a heartbeat longer, the fog cleared and revealed the Dark Forest: as barren and menacing as he remembered it from his last brief visit. The place was so terrible that the last thing he wanted was to focus on the vision, and all the feelings of terror and self-doubt that came with it.

He imagined Ashfur was somewhere close by, and Shadowsight forced himself to hold on to his certainty of the evil cat's presence, if he wanted to stay in the Dark Forest. He needed that, though; he knew that Squirrelflight could only be saved by his confronting Ashfur, once and for all.

And I will.

Concentrating, Shadowsight stepped forward, trying to hold on to everything hideous: Ashfur, his surroundings, the spongy feel of the Dark Forest ground beneath his paws. He knew he had to ignore the vague hint of the real world beneath his hindquarters, where he sat beside the Moonpool with . . .

No!

The vision around Shadowsight began to shimmer and fade; he knew it was because he had been thinking of a real-world cat. Instead, he had to be fully present here, in this macabre territory. Squirrelflight, Bramblestar . . . every cat in the Clans was depending on him getting this right.

But it was no use. The Dark Forest vanished like morning mist under a hot greenleaf sun and he found himself once again beside the Moonpool. Mothwing was looking down at him, concern in her amber eyes.

"Didn't it work?" she asked.

Shadowsight let out a long, frustrated sigh. "Oh, it worked," he replied. "I was there—but I couldn't stay there. I lost concentration, and I found myself back here."

"Did you see Ashfur?" Mothwing was staring at him intensely.

"No," Shadowsight said. "I could *feel* him there, but . . . that may have just been me."

Mothwing nodded. "Good." Some of the tension seemed to leave her body. "He wasn't waiting for you, the way he was for Willowshine."

"No," Shadowsight replied. He remembered what he had told his parents . . . that he knew too much about Ashfur to be disposed of like Willowshine had been. He wasn't sure why, but he knew, somehow, that this was true.

Ashfur had had plenty of opportunities to kill him already. Whatever the evil cat had in store for Shadowsight, it would be much more complicated than a quick death.

He shuddered and tried to turn his thoughts back to the present. His claws raked the stone at the edge of the pool; his failure tasted as bitter as traveling herbs. "I can't seem to stay in the Dark Forest. All those other cats managed it, before the Great Battle, so why can't I?"

"You can," Mothwing responded. "You've already proved that. Maybe all you need is a bit more practice. Now lie down, relax, and try again."

"I suppose . . ." Shadowsight let himself slump down onto the stones, then curled up and closed his eyes as if he were going to sleep. He felt Mothwing's tail stroke soothingly along his side.

Once again Shadowsight focused, gathering all his hatred and fear of Ashfur and ignoring the pull of the real world.

What is this doing to me? he asked himself as the darkness soaked into him like rain drenching his pelt. *Am I becoming more like Ashfur? Am I losing part of myself?*

But Shadowsight had to thrust those thoughts away. He needed all his courage to fight against misery and despair as the thick fog engulfed him, until the horrific view of the Dark Forest became vivid once again, and he steeled himself to stay present there.

Paw step by paw step, he ventured deeper into the forest, trying to remember every time he veered around a tree or leaped over a gully so that he could find his way back later. He turned around a narrow ledge that led down a rocky hillside, then headed straight through a tangle of vines and into a bog, musty and damp, where stinking water welled up around his paws. On the far side was a dried-out riverbed, and beyond it a cliff face, with dark holes gaping at the foot.

His pelt bristling with apprehension, Shadowsight stepped forward, peering into the darkness of the first cave. He cocked an ear toward it and took a deep sniff, but he could find no trace of Squirrelflight or Ashfur, even though he could sense the evil tom's presence more and more.

The second cave he checked felt so oppressive that he felt an almost uncontrollable urge to get out of it, but as he headed for the entrance, he heard the sound of loud, clumsy paw steps just outside.

Instinctively Shadowsight backed up. He didn't know who that cat was, or whether they could be trusted, but he remembered what Mothwing had told him, that a cat must surely be bad to have ended up there in the Dark Forest.

I mustn't be seen. The last thing I want is to be caught here, in this awful place.

But at the thought of Mothwing and the need to escape the Dark Forest, Shadowsight's surroundings began to waver, as if he were looking at them through water. He caught a glimpse of Mothwing's outline, her ears pricked against the sky paling toward dawn.

Not now! Shadowsight clung desperately to his focus on Ashfur, and to his relief the Dark Forest grew solid again, the sound of paw steps dying away.

Shadowsight stuck his head out of the cave and saw a sleek gray she-cat heading into the distance. He had no idea who the cat was, and she hadn't seen him. But just as he was breathing a sigh of relief, the cat halted, half turning her head.

Oh, no! I've been spotted.

For a few moments Shadowsight froze, uncertain whether to flee and hope to outpace the Dark Forest cat, or to retreat further into the ominous depths of the cave. As he stood there, irresolute, he could hear the rush of water as it cascaded down into the Moonpool. His surroundings began to flicker and fade. He was losing all sense of a connection to Ashfur as the real world tugged at him.

Shadowsight struggled to regain his focus on the evil tom, but he couldn't; panic sparked beneath his pelt as he stared at the she-cat. *Who is she? If she means to hurt me, I could be killed here, and that means I would be gone forever. . . .*

Then, to his surprise, Shadowsight saw his surroundings

grow solid again. The sound of the waterfall faded. *Of course!* he thought. *Nothing will keep me here better than my fear of this horrible forest!*

Relieved that he was securely fixed in the dark world again, Shadowsight peered out at the gray she-cat, waiting until, after a few heartbeats, she padded on. Once he was sure that she was really gone, he stepped outside the cave. He was ready to continue his explorations of the dreadful territory when a loud, anguished yowl sounded in the distance. Its echoes seemed to shake the barren tree branches.

That's Squirrelflight!

His fear of being seen completely forgotten, Shadowsight raced toward the sound.

CHAPTER 10

❧

Rootspring padded slowly down a dark tunnel. All his senses were alert, but he had no idea what he was doing there, or what he expected to find. All he knew was that he felt restless, as if something was not quite right.

He was not sure how long he had spent walking into darkness, when somewhere ahead he heard an eerie yowling. Light flared up in front of him, and he spotted Shadowsight outlined against it; his friend was stretching out his paws, his claws extended and his eyes wild.

Rootspring let out a startled gasp. *He needs me! I have to help him!* He began to run, his paws thrumming on the ground, yet however hard he tried, he seemed to draw no closer to Shadowsight. Then, with no warning, a dark chasm opened up between them. Rootspring tried to stop himself, but he was too late. For a heartbeat he teetered on the edge of the yawning gap, then let out a terrified screech as he plummeted down, down into blackness.

Opening his eyes, Rootspring found himself thrashing about in a nest of moss and bracken.

"For StarClan's sake!" A grumpy voice spoke near his head.

"Do you have to make that racket? Any cat would think we're being attacked by badgers."

Rootspring raised his head to see Macgyver glaring at him as he rose and shook scraps of moss from his pelt. "Sorry," he muttered.

He realized that he was lying in his own nest in the warriors' den. Panting with relief, he told himself that he'd only had such a weird dream because he was disturbed by everything that had happened the day before at the Moonpool.

Yet he had brought his unsettled feeling with him into the waking world. It was the way he had felt at the failed Sisters ceremony, when angry spirits were reaching out to him. *Oh, StarClan, don't tell me that Shadowsight is dead!*

Glancing around, Rootspring realized that thin rays of daylight were shining through the gaps in the roof of the den. Most of his denmates had already left; apart from Macgyver, now sliding out of the den with an irritated flick of his tail, only Plumwillow, who had been on night watch, was still curled up in her nest with her tail wrapped over her nose.

Worried that he had overslept, Rootspring bounded to his paws and pushed his way into the open, giving himself a rapid grooming as he gazed around.

Outside in the camp, everything looked like an ordinary day. Leafstar was sitting at the entrance to her den, deep in conversation with her deputy, Hawkwing. Wrenpaw was pushing a ball of moss toward the elders' den; she tore off a scrap and rolled it into a smaller ball for Beekit and Beetlekit, who were frisking about near the nursery, proudly watched by their mother, Nectarsong.

No cat seems to have noticed I was still asleep, Rootspring thought with relief. *I'd better go hunt.*

But as Rootspring headed for the tunnel entrance, the fern fronds waved wildly and several cats made their way into the camp. Dewspring was in the lead, with Mintfur just behind him; Rootspring assumed they had been the dawn patrol. Following them were several ThunderClan cats: Lionblaze, Bristlefrost, and Jayfeather. Bringing up the rear was a handsome gray tom Rootspring had never expected to see again; his eyes stretched wide with astonishment as he recognized him.

Graystripe!

Rootspring immediately felt cheered to see that the ThunderClan elder had returned from his travels, because he knew that Bristlefrost had been worried about him. Instinctively his gaze flicked toward her, and she gave him a tiny nod, her pleasure obvious in her shining eyes and quivering whiskers.

Whenever he saw Bristlefrost, Rootspring felt the same tangle of emotions, as if he were trying to find his way through twisting ivy and bramble: Her presence made him happy, but he was saddened too when he remembered that they couldn't have a future together. Neither of them could leave their Clan, which meant they could never be mates.

This will stop hurting at some point, Rootspring supposed, *but today is not that day.*

Mintfur raced across the clearing to alert Leafstar, who

rose to her paws and padded forward to meet the Thunder-Clan patrol. "Greetings, Graystripe," she purred. "It's good to see you back in the forest again."

Graystripe dipped his head politely. "Greetings, Leafstar. I'm glad to be home, but there's no time for cats to fuss over me. When I returned yesterday, I found ThunderClan in chaos, and Squirrelflight missing. Lionblaze has agreed to step aside and allow me to act as leader until we can recover her."

Leafstar blinked, her whiskers twitching in astonishment. "That . . . makes sense," she mewed.

Rootspring, who had slipped quietly up to listen, assumed that his leader meant it made as much sense as anything else these days. But he knew that ThunderClan had struggled to find a warrior who would command the same respect as Bramblestar. Without StarClan to confer nine lives and a new name on Bramblestar's replacement, Rootspring thought that Graystripe would be a good enough choice to lead them for now.

Though he is awfully old . . .

Then Graystripe turned his gaze on Rootspring, who was startled by the power in his eyes. It felt kind of weird to be noticed by an elder of another Clan. He had heard that Gray-stripe had once been deputy to the great Firestar; Rootspring suddenly felt his paws shaking, and dug his claws hard into the ground.

This cat isn't just any elder. He's . . . amazing!

"I've come here because my Clanmates have told me an utterly unbelievable story," Graystripe began. "They say that you are claiming that the false Bramblestar escaped his prison and dragged Squirrelflight into the Moonpool—while she was still alive."

"Yes, that's true." Rootspring was unable to keep his voice from quivering, and had to force himself to meet Graystripe's gaze.

"It's a very strange story," Graystripe responded, with a skeptical twitch of his ears. "I've been alive for many seasons, yet I've never heard of a cat disappearing into the Moonpool."

"Yes, I know it's really strange," Rootspring admitted. "But it *is* what I saw. And since Ashfur came back, a lot of things have been happening that have never happened before—at least, I don't think they have."

Graystripe narrowed his eyes, and Rootspring felt himself being examined by that piercing gaze, like a beetle on a thorn.

After a moment, Graystripe nodded curtly and turned to Leafstar. "With your permission, I'd like your young warrior to take me to the Moonpool," he meowed, "and tell me exactly what he saw. So I can examine the pool for clues to what happened. You must understand that ThunderClan is desperate to get Squirrelflight back."

Leafstar dipped her head in acknowledgment. "I have great respect for Squirrelflight," she told the gray warrior. "SkyClan will do anything it can to help. Rootspring, are you ready to go?"

Instinctively Rootspring's gaze flew to Bristlefrost, who was listening with a look of eager anticipation. "Yes," he replied. "I'm ready."

Rootspring's paws ached as he and the ThunderClan patrol slipped through the bushes. He had enjoyed every paw step of the journey as he padded beside Bristlefrost, talking to her about Graystripe's return. A tingle of excitement thrilled through him every time their pelts brushed against each other. He noticed that his father, Tree—who had returned from hunting as the patrol was on the way out of camp, and invited himself along—was giving them an approving nod.

Rootspring wished fervently that love between cats of different Clans were as easy as Tree seemed to think it should be. The Sisters, too, hadn't been able to see the problem. Nor, it seemed, could any cat who wasn't Clanborn. Rootspring heaved a deep sigh. They did not—*could not*—understand the loyalty that Clan cats felt toward their Clans.

Soon they stood looking down at the Moonpool. Rootspring's fur began to bristle with apprehension. Two cats were already there! Mothwing crouched at the water's edge with her paws tucked under her, and Shadowsight, apparently unconscious, lying beside her.

"What's going on?" Graystripe muttered.

He led the way at a swift pace down the spiral path toward the water. Following him, Rootspring still felt how strange this was. He could remember when only medicine cats were allowed to be here. That seemed a very long time ago now, back when things were normal.

"Please tell me he hasn't taken deathberries again!" Rootspring blurted out as he reached the water's edge. Cold horror swept over him at the thought that Shadowsight might have accidentally taken too many and poisoned himself to get back into the Dark Forest. He knew how desperate Shadowsight was to return, but surely he wasn't bee-brained enough to go back to such a dangerous method, which every cat had been forbidden to use?

Mothwing looked up at the newcomers. "No, of course not," she told them. "Do you think I would have let him do that? Shadowsight has dreamed himself into the Dark Forest, like many cats before him. I'm just here watching over him; I think he'll be fine."

Rootspring was relieved by the medicine cat's words. If he'd been asleep for a while, that meant no cat had ambushed him like they had Willowshine. Still, he knew that Shadowsight was at risk every moment he was in the Dark Forest. *I know Shadowsight has dealt with Ashfur before, but can he really protect himself from such an evil cat?*

Graystripe took a pace forward to examine Shadowsight's body more closely, and Rootspring saw that he had a concerned look in his yellow eyes. "I wonder if he really knows what he's getting himself into," the gray warrior murmured.

At that moment, Rootspring heard the sound of paw steps and glanced up to see Tigerstar and Dovewing racing down the spiral path to halt, panting, at the bottom.

"Where's Shadowsight?" Tigerstar demanded. "He was

missing from his den this morning—and so was Mothwing."

Reluctantly, Rootspring stepped back so that the Shadow-Clan leader could see his son, stretched out at Mothwing's side. He knew how furious Tigerstar would be when he discovered what Shadowsight had done.

Tigerstar's fur bristled up and his eyes widened in horror. "No—not again!" he choked out.

Mothwing rose and dipped her head to the Clan leader. "Keep your fur on, Tigerstar," she meowed. "Shadowsight isn't hurt. He has sent his spirit into the Dark Forest."

Tigerstar didn't look much relieved to hear that, while Dovewing let out a piteous little mew. "And you let him?" Tigerstar snarled. "After that was exactly what I told him *not* to do?"

"I'm sorry, Tigerstar," Mothwing meowed calmly; Rootspring thought she didn't sound particularly sorry. "But there are times when medicine cats have to make their own decisions about what is best for their Clan."

The ShadowClan leader let out a furious snort, while Dovewing leaned closer to him, though whether she was seeking comfort or giving it, Rootspring couldn't tell. Then both of the ShadowClan cats seemed to realize the presence of the others for the first time.

"Graystripe—is that you?" Tigerstar sounded annoyed, rather than pleased, that the gray warrior had returned. "And Leafstar. What are you all doing here?"

"I could ask you the same question," Graystripe retorted drily. "According to what Bristlefrost told me, Shadowsight was being held prisoner in your camp."

Tigerstar glared at the ThunderClan elder. "Not anymore. Shadowsight has returned to his medicine-cat duties. What concern is it of yours?"

Graystripe flicked his ear. "I'm just trying to understand. . . . Every cat was very concerned about Shadowsight's role in all of this, but this morning you learned he was missing and decided to run here, to the Moonpool, before alerting the other Clans?"

"I'll let them know, all in good time. Besides, Shadowsight is my son," Tigerstar growled, glaring at the gray warrior. "And you have never led a Clan, so what would you know about the decisions a Clan leader should make?"

"I'm leading ThunderClan right now," Graystripe informed him.

"Perfect!" Tigerstar let out a snort of amusement. "It's your turn, is it? Maybe you'll last a whole quarter moon. Or maybe you should step back and let the real leaders—the ones chosen by StarClan—take care of this."

Graystripe returned glare for glare; when he spoke, there was the hint of a snarl in his voice. "I led ThunderClan for moons when Firestar was away on his quest to find SkyClan— long before you were even kitted. So how about a bit of respect?"

Tigerstar turned his head away, unable to meet the gray warrior's gaze.

"Graystripe, you know that I don't share Tigerstar's opinion of you," Leafstar began, clearly hoping to calm tempers with her gentle voice, "but he does make a good point. The other leaders should be alerted to what Shadowsight is doing."

"Certainly," Graystripe agreed. "And maybe we should discuss asking the Sisters for help again. I'm told they're still nearby. I understand that their ceremony to find Bramble-star's spirit didn't end well, but they might know something we don't about traveling between the worlds."

"I'll fetch Harestar," Tree offered.

"And I'll go to RiverClan to fetch Mistystar," Lionblaze added.

Mothwing turned to him, a sorrowful look in her amber eyes. "Last night would have been Willowshine's vigil," she mewed. "Mistystar may be sleeping."

"Yes, the timing is unfortunate," Leafstar sighed. "But we need all the leaders here to make this decision. Go, both of you."

As Lionblaze and Tree climbed the spiral path, Root-spring stared down at Shadowsight's sleeping form. After a few moments he realized that he was looking for some sign of injury or trouble with breathing, just as he had with Willow-shine. *But it's all right. Shadowsight is still sleeping peacefully, for now at least.* Rootspring couldn't help wondering what his friend's wandering spirit was seeing. A moment later, Bristlefrost pad-ded over and sat next to him.

"I hope Shadowsight is okay," she murmured.

Rootspring nodded. "I'd be scared out of my fur to enter the Dark Forest alone. And Shadowsight isn't a trained war-rior. . . . We know that if he gets injured there, he gets injured in real life." *And if he gets killed* . . . But Rootspring couldn't bring himself to say the words out loud.

Bristlefrost's eyes shone with empathy. "But Shadowsight has always been brave," she reminded him.

Rootspring nodded. It was true. Now there was nothing to do but wait for the other leaders to arrive. Rootspring could feel tension stretching among Tigerstar, Graystripe, and Leafstar, but eventually all three of them settled down at a safe distance from one another.

Exhaustion suddenly overwhelmed Rootspring; his disturbed rest and the long trek to the Moonpool had taxed his strength. Gradually he began to drift into sleep, but as soon as unconsciousness claimed him, he found himself once again padding down the dark tunnel. The same light flared up in front of him, with Shadowsight outlined against it.

The young medicine cat's fur was bristling up, and his eyes were wild. His forepaws stretched out toward Rootspring, claws extended, and he screeched, "Beware!"

Rootspring startled awake. Around him, several of his companions were sleeping, or talking together in quiet voices. From the corner of his eye he spotted light gathering on the surface of the Moonpool; turning his head, he saw a glowing form emerge from the water and stare straight at him.

Am I still dreaming? he asked himself.

At the same moment, he recognized Willowshine—or Willowshine's spirit.

The luminous form bounded across the surface of the pool and halted in front of Rootspring. "Come quick," she meowed.

"Only you can save Squirrelflight."

Rootspring let out a gasp of astonishment. "Me?"

"*Only* you."

As Rootspring hesitated, Willowshine lashed her tail and let out a hiss of impatience. Lunging for Rootspring, she snapped, "Come on! You have to help me!" As soon as the words were out, she grabbed him by the scruff.

She grabbed me? Rootspring felt a chill of horror sinking through his pelt as far as his bones. *Spirits can* touch *me now?*

Even worse, Willowshine began pulling him toward the Moonpool.

"Wait!" Rootspring yowled. The noise startled Bristlefrost awake; she stared at him with wide eyes. "I don't—I can't swim!"

But that didn't matter. Willowshine gripped him fast and plunged into the water, dragging Rootspring with her. As he thrashed helplessly, water gushed into his mouth and ears. He stared up at the surface; the last thing he saw was the shocked face of Bristlefrost, distorted by the water, staring down at him.

CHAPTER 11
❧

Bristlefrost stared into the Moonpool, shocked to the tips of her claws; she could hardly believe what she had just seen. Rootspring had suddenly lunged toward the pool and dived in, but it had looked as if something was forcing him to do it. His neck had been bent, as if he was being dragged into the water by some other cat she couldn't see. He had let out a frantic yowl: "I can't swim!"

When the first shock had ebbed, Bristlefrost didn't hesitate. Scrambling over the stones that edged the Moonpool, she plunged in, barely hearing the startled cries of the gathered cats.

With water splashing up around her, Bristlefrost tried to paddle back and forth across the pool, searching desperately for Rootspring. But she couldn't see any sign of him. *Did he sink?* she wondered, remembering the first time they had met, when he'd fallen into the lake as an apprentice, and she'd rescued him. *He was so frightened then. . . . Oh, Rootspring!* Her heart felt torn in two with the thought that he could be suffering or scared.

But Bristlefrost didn't really know how to swim, and soon

she felt herself sinking deeper into the chilly water of the Moonpool. *Who would have thought it could be so deep?* She still couldn't find Rootspring, and within a few heartbeats she realized she was out of air, and the surface seemed so far away.

Horror clutched her chest like a massive claw. She kicked out with all four legs, struggling to propel herself upward, but around her the light was dying, and she could feel life leaching out of her.

Is this how it will end? It seems so . . . so pointless, after everything that I've been through.

Suddenly a dark shape exploded into the water. Bristlefrost felt a sharp tug on her scruff as some cat dragged her body to the surface. The other cat tossed her out of the Moonpool; she landed hard on the stones surrounding it, the impact forcing some water from her lungs.

Coughing and spluttering, she turned her head to see Mothwing leap out and land beside her.

"Stupid drypaws," she muttered. "If you can't swim, you *can't swim.*"

The medicine cat pressed strong paws down on Bristlefrost's chest, over and over again, while Bristlefrost coughed up more pool water.

Eventually Mothwing stepped back. "Can you sit up?" she asked.

"I think so." Bristlefrost felt really groggy, but she pushed herself up and sat looking around her while water streamed from her thick gray pelt. "Thanks, Mothwing," she croaked out. "Did you see Rootspring?"

Mothwing shook her head, a serious look on her face. "No," she replied. "There was no sign of him. It's like he's disappeared altogether."

"Just like Squirrelflight."

The voice was Jayfeather's; for the first time, Bristlefrost realized that the other cats were all gathered around her, their faces full of concern. Mistystar and Lionblaze were there, too; they must have arrived while she was taking her nap.

"But Squirrelflight was dragged into the water by Ashfur," Leafstar meowed. "At least, that's what Rootspring said he saw."

"Rootspring was dragged in, too," Bristlefrost explained. "Anyway, I think so. He looked like he was being forced, and he was arguing with some cat—or some *thing*."

No cat seemed to know what to do. While they were discussing their next move, Bristlefrost rose and gave her pelt a good shake to dry it off. She was feeling stronger with every heartbeat, ready to do anything she could to find Rootspring, if only some cat would tell her what.

As she hovered at the edge of the group, listening to the argument, Bristlefrost spotted movement at the top of the spiral path: Harestar was emerging from the bushes, followed closely by Tree. Leafstar noticed the newcomers, too, and padded to the bottom of the path to wait for them.

"Tree, there's something I need to tell you," she began, her voice heavy with anxiety.

Tree glanced around, suddenly apprehensive. "It's Rootspring, isn't it?" he meowed. "Where is he?"

Sadly Leafstar explained to Tree how his son had been dragged into the Moonpool and disappeared. Bristlefrost's heart ached for him as she saw horror and confusion spreading over the yellow tom's face.

"I've never heard of a spirit being able to do that before," Tree responded when Leafstar had fallen silent. "We all know what happened to Squirrelflight, but no spirit has ever been able to touch me, let alone force me to do anything." He paused, then added more hesitantly, "I do remember how angry they were at the ceremony we held to find Bramblestar. It was disturbing. If one of those spirits got its paws on Rootspring . . ."

He shivered, and Bristlefrost saw true fear in his eyes.

Leafstar touched her tail to Tree's shoulder for a moment, then gave her pelt a shake. "Now that all the leaders are present," she mewed briskly, "we can discuss whether to ask the Sisters for help."

"Yes, I'm sure that's the right thing to do," Tree agreed, his voice cracking with fear and despair. "The Sisters might be the only cats who can help now. They are Rootspring's kin, after all."

Leafstar nodded. "And the Sisters know Squirrelflight, too, because she and Leafpool spent some time with them. But does any cat know where they might now be found?"

"ThunderClan knows," Graystripe replied, "because Daisy has been staying with them for a while." At the exclamations of surprise that followed his words, he added, "It's a long story, and this isn't the time. The Sisters are camping just beyond

ThunderClan's border. There's a hollow with a spring between two boulders, and gorse and elder bushes all around it."

"I think I know where that is," Leafstar responded. "I'll go and talk to them. The Sisters know me, and trust me."

"Good." Graystripe turned to Lionblaze. "You go with her—it might help to have some cat from Squirrelflight's Clan."

As the two cats headed off, Lionblaze called over his shoulder, "We'll stop off in the ThunderClan camp and pick up Mousewhisker. He went with Daisy to the Sisters' camp, so he knows exactly where it is."

Graystripe nodded in acknowledgment as Lionblaze followed Leafstar up the spiral path.

The sun had set, and twilight was thickening into night. A whole day had passed since Bristlefrost and the others had traveled to the Moonpool, and they were no nearer to rescuing their Clanmates. Shadowsight still lay beside the pool, with Mothwing sitting close by, all her attention on his unmoving form.

I hope he's okay, Bristlefrost thought. *He's been in the Dark Forest for so long. When the elders told us about the cats who traveled to the Dark Forest before, it sounded like it was only overnight, during their natural sleep. But this is going on much longer. And Rootspring . . .* She couldn't bear to think what he might be going through.

The rest of the cats were still discussing what they might do now, even though it seemed that nothing could be done—not until the Sisters arrived.

"We're wasting our time here," Graystripe pointed out at last. "It's late, and we can't all sleep beside the Moonpool. Maybe we should go home and get some rest, and things will look clearer in the morning."

There was a murmur of assent; Bristlefrost thought that most of the cats were relieved that some cat had put into words what they were all thinking.

"I have to stay and take care of Shadowsight," Mothwing pointed out.

"And we're certainly not leaving," Tigerstar added, wrapping his tail around Dovewing's shoulders. "Not until we know that our son is okay."

Tree nodded. "That goes for me, too."

Graystripe rose to his paws, ready to lead the remaining cats out of the hollow. Bristlefrost tensed, afraid that the gray warrior would order her to leave with them. But when he turned to her, it was to meow, "You stay as well. I'd like a ThunderClan cat here."

"Thank you, Graystripe!" Relief flooded over Bristlefrost. She would have found it so hard to leave, when Rootspring was still in such deadly danger. And what if Shadowsight woke up? Bristlefrost wanted to be right here when that happened—the first to know.

"I'm glad you're here, Tigerstar," Tree meowed when the rest of the cats had left. "And you too, Dovewing. When you have a kit, protecting them is the only thing that matters."

"That's true," Tigerstar agreed; Bristlefrost heard his voice warming, as if he was growing more friendly toward Tree, since they both had kits in the Dark Forest. "I admit I'm worried," the ShadowClan leader continued, "but I have to accept what Mothwing tells me: that Shadowsight would have found his way into the Dark Forest whatever happened. He was determined."

"He gets that from his father," Dovewing murmured.

"And which cat left her Clan to be with the cat she loved?" Tigerstar retorted.

The two ShadowClan cats exchanged an affectionate glance. Bristlefrost wondered if they were trying to make each other feel better, to distract each other from their desperate anxiety about their son. She felt a pang of envy in her heart: They had been born in different Clans, exactly like her and Rootspring, yet they had ended up together.

Could that ever happen for us? she wondered.

"I can trust Rootspring," Tree went on. "He's intelligent and brave, and he'll do whatever he can to help Squirrelflight and Shadowsight in that awful place. He'll fight if he has to—I just hope he won't have to."

"Oh, so do I!" Bristlefrost agreed fervently. Tree gave her an understanding glance, and Bristlefrost knew he must be able to see all the love in her eyes as she gazed back at him.

Just then she was alerted by the sound of rustling from the top of the hollow, and stared upward as cat after cat emerged from the bushes. Bristlefrost recognized their muscular bodies and healthy, gleaming pelts. Her paws tingled with optimism at the thought that now something might be done to save Rootspring and Squirrelflight.

"It's the Sisters!" she exclaimed.

One of the newcomers stepped forward to where the path led down to the water. Bristlefrost recognized Snow, a large white she-cat with blue eyes.

The Sister dipped her head respectfully. "May I come down?" she asked.

It was Mothwing who replied, looking up from where she still kept watch over Shadowsight. "Yes, come."

Snow paced down the spiral path, and Tree rose to his paws to meet her at the bottom. "Snow, you have to help us," he meowed, desperation in his voice. "My son is lost in the spirit world, and Tigerstar's son is, too. We don't know what to do to get them back."

Tigerstar was fixing the Sisters with a dubious glance, and made no move toward Snow. Bristlefrost felt like giving him a good claw around the ears, but she knew you couldn't do that to a Clan leader, especially when he was the leader of a different Clan. But she made no attempt to hide her exasperation as she drew closer to him.

"Rootspring and Shadowsight are both my friends," she began, "and right now, they're all that stands between us and Ashfur's evil plans. Surely we should use every possible chance to keep them safe? Even if that *does* mean trusting the Sisters."

The doubt in Tigerstar's eyes faded to confusion, as if he didn't know what to think anymore. "Fine!" he spat at last. "But you'd better believe I'll watch them like a hawk!"

"You need to rest," Dovewing mewed gently, rubbing her muzzle against Tigerstar's shoulder. "We should go back to

ShadowClan and tell every cat what has been happening."

"Go back?" Tigerstar echoed. "Leave Shadowsight here?"

"Shadowsight is getting the best possible care," Dove-wing pointed out. "Mothwing will stay here, watching over him. And while I trust Cloverfoot to keep things running smoothly, our Clanmates must be wondering where their leader is, and what's become of Shadowsight."

Bristlefrost could see how torn Tigerstar was between his realization that his mate was right, and his instinct to stay close to his son. "I can be a messenger," she suggested. "If anything happens to Shadowsight or Rootspring, I'll come right away and tell you."

"That's a good idea," Mothwing meowed, rising from her place beside Shadowsight and padding closer. "I'll send Bristlefrost if there's any news. For now, there's no reason for you to be here."

Still uncertain, Tigerstar looked up once again at the Sisters crowded together at the top of the hollow. "The Moonpool is a sacred place," he growled. "Are we really okay with a group of rogues moving in?"

Bristlefrost saw Snow's shoulder fur begin to rise at the word *rogues*, though she said nothing.

"If it comes to that," Mothwing retorted drily, "there was a time when you wouldn't have been allowed here, Tigerstar."

"We'll make camp nearby," Snow assured the ShadowClan leader. "We don't want to disrespect the sacred place of the Clans. Besides, it will take time for us to make contact with the spirits and work out what can be done."

"Come on." Dovewing gave Tigerstar a prod. "It will be fine."

Reluctantly, Tigerstar rose to his paws and followed Dovewing up the path; Snow padded after them. When the ShadowClan cats had disappeared through the bushes, the Sisters withdrew too, leaving Bristlefrost alone with Mothwing and Tree.

Almost without thinking, she let her paws lead her to the edge of the Moonpool, and stared down into the depths. *I wonder what's happening down there.*

Bristlefrost wished that she could feel something, some hint that Rootspring was okay wherever he had gone. But the calm surface, glimmering in the light of moon and stars, gave nothing away. All Bristlefrost could do was hope that Rootspring and Shadowsight were safe.

CHAPTER 12

As Shadowsight raced through the trees, he could still hear the yowling of the distressed cat, but he couldn't pinpoint exactly where it was coming from. Somehow the direction seemed to change, so that he felt that he was running in circles. He was beginning to suspect that the Dark Forest was playing tricks on him, when without warning a pale blur shot out from behind a tree, barreled into him, and slammed him to the ground.

Panic surged over Shadowsight, but he struggled not to show it in the face of a possible enemy. The cat—if it *was* a cat—held him pinned down with his face pushed into the debris of the forest floor, so he could hardly breathe, much less see what had attacked him.

"Who are you?" he choked out.

"I could ask you the same thing," a voice growled into his ear. "What are you doing here?"

Shadowsight realized that even though his assailant had him at their mercy, they had chosen to question him instead of ripping him to pieces. Maybe the only way he might escape was if he cooperated. "I'm looking for a living warrior who was brought here by mistake."

"A living warrior?" The voice sounded slightly less hostile. "So *that's* what's going on, is it?"

The body on top of Shadowsight moved back, allowing him to get up, shake the stinking debris off his pelt, and turn around. He was looking at . . . *Wait, what am I looking at?*

In front of him was the outline of a cat, but the shape seemed to blur and fade at the edges, and sometimes it winked out altogether. In its most solid state it was a skinny white tom, with a scar that began at his neck and snaked around his belly.

Shadowsight felt his muscles tense. On his previous visit to this fearsome place, in a vision, he hadn't encountered any other cat. Suddenly he became aware that this was the *Dark Forest*, the territory he had grown up hearing stories about. He had always assumed that his older Clanmates had exaggerated the dangers, either to give him a scare or simply to make a good story. Now he knew that it was real, and worse than he had ever imagined.

Gazing at the cat who had attacked him, Shadowsight remembered how concerned Jayfeather had been when Willowshine was about to dream herself into this terrible place. The blind cat's words echoed in his mind. *The Dark Forest can turn a good cat bad.* And a cat would have to be pretty bad to be sent to the Dark Forest in the first place.

Mothwing warned you about that, mouse-brain. Maybe you should have paid more attention, he scolded himself.

What if he hurts me? Shadowsight wondered, eyeing the skinny white tom. *I'll be hurt in real life. . . .*

"Hi. I'm Snowtuft," the white tom meowed.

"I'm Shadowsight." Shadowsight paused, waiting for some signal from the tom. *Can I trust him? Can I tell him the truth?* But almost as soon as he had the thought, he realized he had no choice. *If I want to save Squirrelflight, I need to find out whatever I can.* So he asked, "Can you tell me what's going on in the Dark Forest?"

Snowtuft twitched his whiskers. "Funny. I was going to ask you the same thing," he replied. "Things have been changing recently. I've seen a strange cat here who comes and goes; I thought he might be a StarClan cat, because he has sparkles in his fur. But I have no idea how he got here." He shrugged.

"Have you noticed anything else?" Shadowsight asked.

Snowtuft blinked worriedly. "Since that cat appeared, I've noticed that the forest is shrinking. Parts of it I used to know well have faded into mist, and if I walk into the mist, I feel light-headed."

"That's awful," Shadowsight mewed, suppressing a shiver. "And you think this strange cat is behind it all?" *It must be Ashfur,* he thought to himself. *Of course he is!*

"Yes, I'm sure of it," Snowtuft responded. "Some of the other cats here have started to work for him. He promises them great things in the future if his plan succeeds."

"But you didn't join him?" Shadowsight wondered if he could trust a word this cat was telling him. *This could be a trap.* He knew how persuasive Ashfur could be in the living world; how else could he have convinced the Clans to exile their codebreakers? *He's so strong-willed, and this cat looks too feeble to resist him.*

Snowtuft shook his head emphatically. "Not for anything. That is one evil cat. And I haven't told you the worst yet," he added. "Some of the other cats have just . . . disappeared. They don't vanish all at once, they sort of . . . fade." He shuddered. "I'm scared that I'm fading, too."

Shadowsight thought he might be right to worry, remembering how blurred Snowtuft's outline had been when they first met. He seemed more solid now, just as the forest itself had firmed up around Shadowsight.

Shadowsight realized that at that moment, he felt more securely present in the Dark Forest than ever before. He no longer had any sense of lying beside the Moonpool with Mothwing watching over him.

It could be the talk we're having. We could be making each other seem more real.

Good. Now it's easier to concentrate on my mission here.

Then a bolt of panic struck Shadowsight, as fierce as lightning; it was all he could do to stop himself from fleeing. He was thinking of what the older cats had told him: *The Dark Forest can turn a good cat bad.*

Surely that began with not being able to sense the real world anymore.

What if I'm fixing myself here, and I can never get back?

"I'm sorry that's happening to you," he told Snowtuft, forcing his voice to be strong and steady. He was more inclined to believe the skinny tom; his obvious fear suggested he was telling the truth. "I'm a living cat," he went on, "so I don't know much about what happens here."

Snowtuft's eyes widened with interest. "A living cat? Yes, I'm familiar with that. You must be dreaming."

"I am . . ." Shadowsight's voice trailed off; he was still not entirely sure he could trust the Dark Forest cat. "Things are very bad in the Clans," he continued, "and the StarClan cat you noticed is the reason for that, too."

Snowtuft nodded, though his interest was clearly fading. Shadowsight guessed that troubles of living Clans must seem very remote to the Dark Forest cat, and Snowtuft's next question confirmed his suspicion.

"Do you know how many seasons have passed since I died?"

"No, I've never heard your name," Shadowsight replied. "Which was your Clan?"

"I was a ShadowClan cat."

"Oh, I'm from ShadowClan too," Shadowsight purred, instantly feeling more friendly toward the white tom. "Our only elder just now is Oakfur. Did you know him?"

Snowtuft blinked at him, uncomprehending. "Who is Clan leader?" he asked.

"Tigerstar," Shadowsight told him, and added proudly, "He's my father."

"Oh, I knew Tigerstar!" Snowtuft exclaimed, a gleam in his eyes. "He was a great cat. He could have been leader of the whole forest if it hadn't been for that stupid kittypet Firestar." He suddenly looked confused. "I thought that he was dead. I saw him here. . . ."

Shadowsight suppressed a shudder, realizing that Snowtuft was praising the *first* Tigerstar. *What kind of cat looks up to* him?

"Er . . . this is a different Tigerstar," he meowed. "The cat you remember died many seasons ago. I wasn't even born then."

Snowtuft let out a heavy sigh. "Time moves strangely in the Dark Forest. I might have been here for a hundred moons, or only one." He stared down at his paws for a moment, before raising his head again to meet Shadowsight's gaze. "I don't usually talk to other cats," he went on. "Since the battle, I can only hear them, or catch a glimpse of them, slinking through the forest. So I don't learn anything about the living world from them. But one thing I do know: Cats who lived in certain parts of the Dark Forest are gone, and sometimes the forest itself is gone, too. The boundaries are closing in. I don't know what is happening, but I'm afraid that I won't exist much longer, either." He sounded weary, as if he was resigned to his fate.

Shadowsight's sympathy for the lonely, apprehensive cat was growing; he was finding it hard to suppress it and concentrate on why he was really there. The ground beneath his paws felt a little more solid now, as though his connection with Snowtuft was fixing him more securely in the Dark Forest. "Do you remember why you came here?" he asked.

For a moment Snowtuft seemed to be struggling with memory, his gaze dark and inward, then shook his head. "I don't remember much about my life," he confessed. "I vaguely remember that I wasn't the nicest cat. Well, if I had been, I wouldn't have ended up here, would I? When I was alive, I know I cared a lot about power. But what does that power mean now?" He shrugged. "Nothing. When you spend forever slinking through a dark and dying forest, alone, you realize how little power you ever had."

"You said you knew the first Tigerstar," Shadowsight continued. "That battle you mentioned . . . was it the Great Battle, between the Dark Forest and the living Clans?"

"Yes, I remember that," Snowtuft replied. "I fought at Tigerstar's side. But I don't want to talk about it anymore," he added, his lips drawn back into a snarl. "Just shut up about it, okay?"

Shadowsight was startled; after that first attack, the Dark Forest cat had been even-tempered . . . but not anymore. He glanced at the fearsome scar that snaked from Snowtuft's throat to his belly, and wondered whether that had something to do with his reluctance to talk about the battle.

"Okay," he responded. "Suppose you show me around the Dark Forest? I need to get some idea of what this starry cat is doing."

"Oh, I can show you that," Snowtuft meowed, his aggressiveness disappearing. "Follow me."

He led Shadowsight around a sprawling bramble thicket, past a massive tree where ivy tendrils sagged among the bare branches, and then along a narrow gully with no stream at the bottom, only dry, sharp stones. As he followed, Shadowsight wondered how much time was passing, how long it was since he had stood in the living world. It felt like a good amount of time, but was it a quarter moon? Or only a tail flick? He remembered what Snowtuft had said about time moving strangely in the Dark Forest, and he couldn't decide which was more terrifying: time moving more slowly, or it moving more quickly. Too slowly and he might need to spend an eternity here; too quickly and he could reenter a new world when he woke up. Fear bubbled inside him like bile from rotting crow-food; he had to grit his teeth and focus on his mission, to stop himself from wailing like a lost kit.

Finally Snowtuft halted. "What do you think of that?" he asked.

Moving past him, Shadowsight saw that the gully opened out into a shallow valley with rocky slopes on either side. The trees were thinner here, and he should have been able to see a long way. But the end of the valley was blocked off by roiling gray fog, as if a storm cloud had dropped down into the forest.

"That's . . . bizarre," Shadowsight mewed after a moment when he was too shocked to speak.

Snowtuft shuddered. "It's closer now than it was the other day," he meowed, his tone taut with nervousness. "And this isn't the only place where it's happening. It's like the fog is rolling in from all sides—it's making the Dark Forest smaller." Turning to Shadowsight, he went on with desperation in his voice. "I need help. I know I wasn't the best cat when I was alive. All of us Dark Forest cats have done things we shouldn't have. That's why we're here. But surely I have the right to exist? Something is destroying my home, and I don't understand why."

"I don't know—" Shadowsight began.

"You seem like a smart cat," Snowtuft went on, ignoring the interruption. "Will you help me?"

Shadowsight hesitated. He knew he ought to refuse, but everything in his medicine-cat training was telling him not to turn his back on this terrified cat.

"I'm here to find a living cat," he responded at last. "I have to put that first. But if I can help you as well, I will."

Snowtuft let out a grunt. "Thanks. I suppose in my position, I can't be choosy."

As Snowtuft spoke, the yowling of a distressed cat broke out again. Though they had traveled a long way so that Shadowsight could see the wall of fog, the noise seemed closer than before.

"There!" Shadowsight exclaimed. "I'm sure that's the cat I'm looking for. But when I tried to follow the sound, I seemed to end up farther away than ever."

Snowtuft didn't look surprised. "It's weird, the way sound travels in the Dark Forest," he meowed. "But I'm used to it by now. Follow me, and I'll get you there."

The white tom led Shadowsight back up the gully, and up a slope covered with dead bracken. The brittle fronds broke as the two cats brushed through, the scraps clinging to their pelts.

Beyond the bracken, the trees massed together more closely. Snowtuft wound his way confidently among them until he reached a thicket of gnarled brambles that stretched up several tail-lengths above the cats' heads. The leaves hung limply from the tendrils, smelling of decay.

Another yowl split the air from the other side of the thicket.

"This way," Snowtuft whispered. "But keep down."

Shadowsight followed him around the thicket, creeping with his belly fur brushing the ground. On the far side, he realized that they were approaching the edge of a clearing, screened by clumps of rank grass.

Across the clearing, Shadowsight spotted two cats. "Ashfur and Squirrelflight!" he gasped.

Snowtuft slapped his tail across Shadowsight's muzzle. "Quiet, mouse-brain!" he muttered into his ear.

Ashfur and Squirrelflight were facing each other, their backs arched and their hackles raised. They were so intent on each other that they hadn't noticed Shadowsight and Snowtuft.

Shadowsight stared at the evil tom, welcoming the feelings of anger and violence that his presence stoked inside him. Again, the Dark Forest seemed to come into focus with devastating clarity. *The Dark Forest can turn a good cat bad,* Shadowsight remembered, and he realized that his own hate was anchoring him even more deeply in the Place of No Stars. But he pushed the thought away.

He was trying to accomplish something.

I'm here, Shadowsight thought at his nemesis, the cat who had brought the Clans he loved to near ruin. *It started with me, and it will end with me.*

I'll do whatever it takes to save Squirrelflight, and the Clans.

CHAPTER 13

Rootspring plunged deeper into the Moonpool, struggling to free himself from Willowshine's grip on his scruff. He choked as water surged into his mouth and ears.

I'm drowning!

He was so caught up in panic, like a fly trapped in a spider's web, that he hardly noticed when Willowshine pulled him through a dark tunnel at the bottom of the pool. He could breathe again now, but the air seemed different, *darker,* so that everything around him looked blurred. Sensing that at least he wasn't underwater anymore, Rootspring collapsed at the foot of a huge gnarled tree.

Eventually he realized that Willowshine was sitting beside him, waiting for him to recover. Hauling himself up to sit next to her, Rootspring looked around and finally understood what was happening to him.

"Am I in the Dark Forest?" he asked.

Willowshine nodded. "Sorry." Her eyes were narrowed to tiny slits.

"Are your eyes okay?" Rootspring asked.

"Sort of," Willowshine told him. "It's just that the light is so dim, I'm having trouble seeing. The mist hurts my eyes."

Rootspring blinked, wondering why his eyes were fine, once he'd gotten used to the weird light, then decided with an inward shrug that it must be because he was still alive. The thought gave him a tingle of relief, even though it was swiftly swamped by dread and fear.

"Anyway," the medicine cat went on more briskly, "I didn't mean to scare you, but it was the only way to get you here. You're the only living cat I can communicate with, and even though I'm dead, I'm still a RiverClan cat, on the side of the Clans. I know things now that can help save them, and I need your help. Do you understand?"

"Of course. I'll do anything to save the Clans," Rootspring assured her, feeling a tingle of hope in his pads. "Tell me everything you've learned."

"I will," Willowshine meowed, rising to her paws. "But first of all, we need to locate Ashfur. Let's go."

Rootspring rose and followed the medicine cat, deeply uneasy as they trekked through the bare trees and dying undergrowth. The air was filled with a sickly scent that spread over his tongue and made him want to vomit.

He couldn't help wondering what it meant for him to be here. *I'm still alive, right?* he asked himself apprehensively. *I'll still be able to get back to the Clans . . . and see Bristlefrost again?* It took a massive effort for him to put his worries out of his mind and concentrate on his mission here.

"Have you seen Shadowsight?" he asked Willowshine.

The medicine cat shook her head. "Should I have? Is he okay?"

"I hope so," Rootspring responded. "It's sort of a long story. He dreamed his way in last night, so he should be around somewhere."

I wonder what's happened to him, he added to himself. *Has he found out the same stuff as Willowshine?*

The dead RiverClan cat was padding along cautiously, her slitted gaze scanning the clumps of rotting bracken and withered bramble thickets for any sign of Ashfur. She seemed to be concentrating too hard to give Rootspring any of the information she had promised.

"Willowshine, what—" he began.

He broke off with a startled squeal as Willowshine barreled into him and thrust him into the shelter of a fallen tree. "Quiet, mouse-brain!" she hissed as he took a breath to protest.

Willowshine crouched down beside him and peered over the top of the tree trunk. Following her gaze, Rootspring spotted two cats slowly winding their way through the undergrowth. The cat in the lead was a powerful tortoiseshell-and-white she-cat with a broad face; her fur was clumped and tattered, as if it had been many moons since she had bothered to groom herself. A thrill of pure horror shivered through Rootspring as he realized he could see the forest through her body, as if her spirit was fading away to nothing.

"Who *is* that?" he whispered.

"The tortoiseshell is Mapleshade," Willowshine replied,

breathing the words into Rootspring's ear. "Believe me, she's not a cat you want to tangle with. The tom with her is Silverhawk. I came across both of them in the Great Battle."

Rootspring's gaze flicked to the gray tom who was padding along at Mapleshade's shoulder. As the two cats drew closer, he could hear what Silverhawk was saying.

"I don't like it," he grumbled. "Who does this Ashfur think he is, coming here and giving us orders, like we're his Clan?"

Ashfur! They were talking about the evil cat who'd started all this. Did that mean . . .? Was Ashfur *recruiting* Dark Forest cats to work for him?

Mapleshade opened her jaws to reply, showing a mouthful of snaggly teeth. "I don't like it either. I don't take orders from any cat, much less a ThunderClan flea-pelt. Not unless it suits me."

Rootspring and Willowshine ducked down, pressing themselves into the slimy debris of the forest floor, as the two Dark Forest cats stalked past the fallen tree where they were hiding.

"Let's follow them," Willowshine whispered once they had passed. "They were talking about Ashfur—maybe they'll lead us to him."

Rootspring didn't want to get closer to either of the cat spirits—especially the fearsome Mapleshade—but Willowshine was already slipping out of hiding and creeping along in their paw steps.

She's right, Rootspring thought. *It's Ashfur we need to find. And if these cats can lead us to him, they're our best bet—even if they are terrifying!*

A few fox-lengths ahead of him, Silverhawk was still complaining. "Ashfur hasn't even told us what it's all about," he meowed. "What does a StarClan cat want, here in the Dark Forest?"

"Nothing good," Mapleshade responded. "Personally, I don't care what he wants, and I doubt he's going to get it, but if he does what he's promised us, that's good enough for me."

"But will he?" Silverhawk muttered. "*Can* he?"

"Well, he's the only cat to die and make it back to the Clans in a living body," Mapleshade pointed out. "Imagine that! Imagine the *power* we could have . . . the revenge we could take. It's worth putting up with him for now, if he can do the same for us." She halted to arch her back in a long, luxurious stretch. "I could take over the body of a nice young she-cat—that would do me just fine. Imagine getting to taste real fresh-kill again! Imagine raking your claws across some cat's pelt, and drawing real blood!"

Rootspring drew in a horrified breath. *All my Clanmates, all the brave cats from the other Clans, driven out of their bodies to let the Dark Forest cats live again? And which cat would Mapleshade choose, to give herself a second chance at life? Oh, StarClan, please not Bristlefrost!*

"I suppose you're right," Silverhawk admitted. "Anyway, I need to go this way. I'll see you back at the island, Mapleshade."

To Rootspring's dismay, the two Dark Forest cats split up, Silverhawk heading straight, while Mapleshade veered aside and began to claw her way up a rocky slope.

"Fox dung!" Willowshine hissed.

"What did he mean, 'back at the island'?" Rootspring asked.

"No time to explain," Willowshine mewed. "You follow Mapleshade; I'll take Silverhawk."

"But—" Rootspring began to protest, but he was too late. Willowshine was already slipping cautiously through the undergrowth, hard on the paws of the gray tom. There was nothing for Rootspring to do but head up the slope after Mapleshade, trying to set his paws down silently, while he darted from the cover of one rock to the next.

The cat spirit padded on purposefully for a long time, while Rootspring followed, his heart pounding in his chest as he expected her at any moment to glance over her shoulder and spot him. *Please don't see me. Please don't hear me.* He'd seen and heard enough from Mapleshade just now to know that he didn't like his chances against her in a fight . . . and that was not even taking into consideration that whatever she did to him here, he'd carry on his body in real life forever. *If* he survived the attack.

Don't think about that. Just follow her. Finding Ashfur is your only chance of ending this.

He had no idea where she was going; she seemed to be trekking around in circles.

Though I must be imagining that. This forest is so confusing.

Eventually Mapleshade led Rootspring down a narrow path that snaked its way through a stretch of rotting plants; Rootspring winced as the stinking leaves trailed over his pelt.

The air here seemed even more oppressive than in the rest of the forest, so thick and humid that he found it hard to breathe.

Emerging on the other side, he saw a cliff face ahead of him; at the bottom of the cliff gaped the dark opening of a cave. Mapleshade suddenly put on a spurt, bounded up to the opening, and disappeared inside.

Rootspring halted, crouching down behind a moss-covered rock. The last thing he wanted to do was follow Mapleshade into that black hole. His whole pelt shivered even at the thought of it.

But I must, he thought. *This cave would make the perfect lair. Ashfur could be in there, and he might even be holding Shadowsight prisoner.*

Forcing his paws to stop trembling, Rootspring padded up to the cave entrance and slipped inside. For a few heartbeats he crept along in darkness, feeling his pelt brush against the wall on either side, wondering what would happen if he met Mapleshade coming the other way. He could scarcely make out his own thoughts over the pounding of his heart.

Gradually he began to see gray light strengthening in front of him. The passage widened into a large cave, with chinks in the roof where the pallid light of the Dark Forest could filter through. Several passages led off in different directions.

Now, which way did Mapleshade choose?

Rootspring raised his head for a deep sniff and parted his jaws to taste the air, but he couldn't pick up any trace of Mapleshade's scent. *Do Dark Forest spirits even have a scent?*

He was about to choose the nearest tunnel when he heard a scraping sound and saw showers of dust cascading from the cave roof. A moment later a bigger hole opened up, letting more light flood in, and a huge rock thumped down on the cave floor, close enough to Rootspring that he was covered in the debris that the impact threw up.

"Great StarClan, what's happening?" he squealed, springing back and blinking rapidly to clear the grit from his eyes.

For a moment shock kept his paws frozen to the floor. More of the cave roof began to crumble away; a sound like thunder filled the air as stones rained down and choking clouds of dust billowed around Rootspring. More terrifying still, he saw gray fog bulging out of one of the passages at the far side of the cave, swelling until it filled the whole space and advancing with unbelievable speed toward him.

Rootspring spun around and fled.

Bursting out into the open air, he paused for a heartbeat, coughing and drawing rasping breaths into his chest. Then he looked back to see the whole cliff face falling in as the fog engulfed it, and gray tendrils of fog reaching out for him as if it were alive and able to sense him.

He ran on, barreling through the patch of rotting vegetation, leaping over rocks, and dodging around trees in his desperate need to escape the fog. He thought that he could hear cats, too, their paws thrumming against the ground as they chased him.

I can't keep going like this for much longer, he thought despairingly.

But gradually the noise of the pursuing cats died away behind him, and when Rootspring looked back, he couldn't see the dreadful enveloping fog any longer. He dared to slow his pace, his heart pounding and his breath coming in short gasps.

Now what do I do?

All around him stretched the dying trees of the Dark Forest; fungus grew from their trunks, giving off an eerie glow. The ground was dotted here and there with clumps of withered bracken or sprawling thickets of bramble. There was nothing to tell Rootspring where he should go.

"Willowshine!" he called. His voice sounded feeble, quenched by the stifling air. "Willowshine!"

There was no response. All Rootspring could do was pad on, hoping that sooner or later he would find something that would show him what he should do next.

He lost all sense of time: In the Place of No Stars there was nothing to tell him how long he had been trudging through the trees, nothing but his growing weariness. After a while he thought he could hear sounds in the distance up ahead; he halted, pricking his ears, and made out the faint yowling of cats.

Rootspring knew that any cats he was likely to meet here would be dangerous, but he didn't feel he had any choice. *I can wander around here until I collapse from exhaustion, or I can find out who those cats are and what they're doing.*

More cautiously now, Rootspring padded forward, the cat voices growing louder with every paw step. Finally he emerged from the trees at the top of a shallow slope, which led down to the edge of a dark lake. Rootspring stared at it curiously. What he had thought at first was black water looked more like

pure darkness, as if night had gathered itself together and settled into a hollow. The sight of it scared him to the tips of his
claws, but it held a horrible fascination, too, that he couldn't
ignore.

Crouching down as if he were stalking prey, his belly fur
brushing the ground, Rootspring ventured down the slope.
He had almost reached the shore of the lake when he spotted another cat close by, hunched in the shade of a clump of
bracken. He drew a massive breath of relief as he recognized
Willowshine.

"Hi," he mewed, padding up to her.

Willowshine jumped as if a fox had sunk its fangs into her
tail. "Rootspring!" she gasped.

"Yeah, it's only me," Rootspring responded. "No need to
look so surprised."

"You scared me out of my fur!" Willowshine snapped.
"And have you *seen* yourself?"

Rootspring glanced down to see his fur still clogged with
dirt from the collapsing cave. "You'll never guess what just
happened to me," he meowed, taking a pace back and giving
his pelt a good shake.

"Well, there's no time to tell me now," Willowshine told
him. "We have stuff to do. This lake—"

"It's so weird . . . ," Rootspring murmured.

He took a couple of steps toward the lake and tentatively
reached out a paw, but before he could touch the surface, a
thrill of fear rippled through him and he flinched, drawing
back. "What happens if you fall in there?" he asked. He had

a feeling it would lead to a fate much worse than drowning.

But Willowshine wasn't paying attention. "Look over there," she meowed.

Following her gaze, Rootspring spotted an island: a stretch of mud barely rising above the black waves. A few rotting trees grew there, and cats were swarming all over it.

Spirit cats! Rootspring realized, seeing that he could make out the outline of the trees through their bodies.

His heart quickened as he recognized some of them. Too excited to think better of it, he called out to them: "Sandy-nose! Stemleaf!" But no cat seemed to hear him. "Rosep—"

"Have you got bees in your brain?" Willowshine growled, grabbing Rootspring and thrusting him back into the shelter of the bracken, where they flattened themselves behind the thick fronds. "Do you *want* Ashfur's cats to find us?" Pointing with her tail, she added, "Look!"

Rootspring glanced in that direction and spotted a dark gray tabby tom slinking around the edge of the lake. He halted every few paw steps and peered curiously into the trees.

"That's Darkstripe," Willowshine explained. "He's a Dark Forest cat, and he was with the first Tigerstar from the very beginning, when they were both members of ThunderClan. Long before we were born, of course, but he's still violent and unpredictable. He can do a lot of damage—you don't want to challenge him."

"But what's he doing here?" Rootspring asked. He could see a narrow, muddy path leading from the island to the shore. "Is that the only way in or out?"

"Looks that way," Willowshine mewed.

Rootspring watched tensely as Darkstripe went on scanning the trees for a few more moments, then relaxed when the striped tom reached the end of the path and settled down beside it.

Feeling safer, for the time being at least, Rootspring turned his attention back to the island and the spirit cats. Some of them were pacing restlessly, while others had flopped down in the mud. They all seemed miserable and helpless, as if they had given up all hope.

"It looks like he's holding them prisoner," Rootspring meowed. When Willowshine looked at him, stunned, Rootspring explained, "Darkstripe. But why . . ." He looked back at the island, mentally counting each cat he could glimpse. "Is that every cat . . . ?" Rootspring began.

"Every cat who died after we lost contact with StarClan, and then some," Willowshine replied. "And you're right, they look trapped."

"Like they can't move on," Rootspring mused, looking from one miserable face to the other. *They shouldn't be here,* he thought mournfully. *They should be in StarClan—every one of them.*

Then he remembered something: When the Sisters had held their ceremony to locate Bramblestar's spirit, they hadn't found him. But they had summoned a force of spirit cats, all of them wailing at Rootspring, begging him for help. *As though they were trapped.*

Rootspring turned to Willowshine with a sudden certainty. "I know what's happened. Darkstripe isn't holding them prisoner—he's working for Ashfur in the hopes of getting back to the living world, just like Silverhawk and Mapleshade. And Ashfur has been collecting these spirits, holding them here."

Willowshine didn't outwardly react, but her voice reached a high pitch as she whispered, "That's terrible!"

Rootspring nodded, watching the island. He remembered what Shadowsight had said, about how he believed Spiresight was trying to warn him of something as he fought against Ashfur's control.

"I'm afraid he might be able to . . . control them," Rootspring went on. "Ashfur, I mean. I have reason to believe he can control the spirits with his mind."

Willowshine turned to him. "If that's true, we don't have much of a chance," she mewed softly.

Rootspring nodded, not sure what to think. "I hope I'm wrong. Is Bramblestar there, too?" he asked, the idea suddenly occurring to him. "Could the *real* ThunderClan leader be imprisoned on that island? Maybe that's why I haven't seen him for so long, and why he hasn't made contact with any other cat."

Willowshine looked thoughtful for a moment. "I don't see him," she replied at last. "But it's certainly possible. That's why I wanted to fetch you, Rootspring. I knew you would help."

Her narrow gaze flicked from Rootspring to the island, then back again. Clearly she was waiting for him to do something.

Rootspring, too, gazed at the island. *It's horrible . . . ,* he thought, his claws working in and out at the thought of being imprisoned among the mud and rotting trees. If his theories were correct, then Ashfur's plans for the living Clans were darker than he ever could have imagined. *If he can control the spirits . . . what does he mean to do with them?*

Rootspring swallowed hard, imagining. There were no good answers to his question. Could Ashfur mean to use the spirits against the living, forcing the Clans to witness their lost loved ones being used and abused? Or, worse—he gasped at the thought—could he be planning to use them to *fight* the living?

It only made sense. Ashfur didn't have enough Dark Forest cats to defeat the living ones. Of course he would want to use the spirits.

Rootspring shook his head, remembering stories he had heard about the Great Battle against the Dark Forest cats, before SkyClan had ever come to live beside the lake. These spirits would make foes just as terrifying if Ashfur led them into battle. And could the living cats even summon up the will to fight their stranded friends and kin? Rootspring trusted himself to fight with his all against Ashfur, or even the Dark Forest cats, but he tried to imagine what it would it be like if he had to fight Needleclaw. Or Violetshine? Or—the thought knocked the breath out of him—Bristlefrost?

I won't have to, he reminded himself, forcing himself to breathe, *because none of the cats I love have died recently. But so many others have . . .*

"Well?" Willowshine startled him from his grim musings, prodding his shoulder with one paw. "What next?"

What next? Rootspring echoed silently. He couldn't bring himself to share his thoughts with Willowshine. She *was* a spirit—if she fell under Ashfur's control, who would he force her to attack?

No, he couldn't go down this path. He had to stay focused. *What can I do to stop him?*

But no answer came.

"Well?" Willowshine asked again.

He suddenly felt very small and foolish. The dead medicine cat was clearly counting on him, and he had absolutely no idea what to do.

CHAPTER 14

The night was still and quiet. Bristlefrost sat beside the Moonpool, gazing down at the sleeping form of Mothwing; she and Tree had insisted that the medicine cat get some rest, and promised that they would keep watch over Shadowsight. The young cat looked as if he were sleeping, too; his chest was rising and falling, proving that he was still alive, and his spirit would be able to return to his body. Bristlefrost felt a warm sense of relief that nothing terrible seemed to have happened to him yet.

She only wished that she could feel as reassured about Rootspring. She couldn't imagine what he must be going through. Until recently, it had never occurred to her that any living cat would venture to the Dark Forest again—much less for their *body* to be dragged there along with their spirit. *I have to be positive,* she told herself, scraping her claws over the stones at the edge of the pool. *I can't let myself think the worst. I have to imagine Rootspring coming back, safe and sound. . . .*

"I never thought I would lose Rootspring this way."

Bristlefrost started at the sound of Tree's voice, and realized that the SkyClan cat had padded up silently behind her.

"You scared me out of my fur!" she exclaimed, turning to look up at him.

Tree tilted his head in apology. "Coming to the Clans as an outsider," he went on, "I had to prepare myself for the possibility of losing my son in battle. But not like this, not to the Dark Forest, or to StarClan. If StarClan even exists . . . I haven't been terribly vocal about this, you know, but if I'm being honest, I'm still not sure."

"That must be against the warrior code," Bristlefrost responded instinctively, "not to believe in StarClan."

"Is it?" Tree stared listlessly into the Moonpool. "Good thing I got over it, then. Wouldn't want to be one of those dreaded codebreakers."

Bristlefrost couldn't suppress a snort. It was so strange, being stuck here with the father of the tom she loved—the tom she would be mates with, if only such a thing were possible. It was strange even before you considered Tree's strangeness. And Tree was, in and of himself, very strange.

Tree stared at the space between his paws, his eyes closed for a moment, his expression serious again. "Lately, I've wondered if I might lose my son because he decided to join another Clan."

He flashed a knowing look at Bristlefrost. She looked away, briefly, clearing her throat.

"Actually," she began, "Rootspring and I decided that we can't have a future as mates. I can't leave ThunderClan, and he can't leave SkyClan. It's impossible for us ever to be together."

She couldn't quite keep her voice steady on the last few words; the pain struck her again, sharper than thorns.

Tree blinked in surprise. "Did you really decide that?" he asked. Bristlefrost nodded. "But you're both so young!" he protested. "When cats are as young as you and Rootspring, that's the time to believe in love wholeheartedly. You do love my son, don't you?"

"Yes." Bristlefrost's voice broke, and she couldn't go on. Even the thought of Rootspring made her wince; she didn't want to dwell on her feelings for him right now. *This is so hard. . . . I don't want to break the warrior code—and yet, at the same time, I do!*

"I can tell," Tree mewed gently. "And I can tell that Root-spring loves you, too. Real love is hard to hide."

Bristlefrost couldn't find words to respond.

"You must care about your Clan very much, if you're choos-ing it over the cat you love," Tree went on after a moment's silence. "What does it mean to you, ThunderClan?"

Bristlefrost closed her eyes, letting out a long sigh. "It's where I was born," she replied. "It's Bramblestar and Squirrel-flight, and the Clan Firestar built—a noble and true Clan."

"Yes." Tree gave his shoulder a couple of licks. "Every Clan seems to think it's the noble and true Clan. Funny, that, don't you think?"

Well aware of the challenge in his words, Bristlefrost glared at him. "I would never speak for other Clans," she retorted, "but I know that in ThunderClan's case, it's true. All I've ever wanted is to be a good ThunderClan warrior."

The words were tumbling out of her now. "ThunderClan is the home of my mother and father, and all my kin. Thunder-Clan means playing with Fernsong and my littermates in the nursery. It means helping Flipclaw when Ashfur made him act as a medicine cat. It means sharing prey with Thriftear beside the fresh-kill pile."

"So it's not just your Clan," Tree meowed. "It's your family."

"Yes," Bristlefrost agreed.

"But what if you had your own family?" Tree suggested. "Most cats grow up, choose a mate, and have kits. When you have your own family, those become the most important cats in the world, and you make your decisions with them in mind. What if you had your family somewhere else?"

Bristlefrost thought about that for a moment. "Tree, you're talking about yourself," she replied at last. "Rootspring told me that you've considered leaving the lake, leaving the Clans. He says he's not sure you would ever have stayed in SkyClan if it weren't for Violetshine. Are you feeling that way again?"

Tree did not reply for a moment. He just gazed thought-fully across the Moonpool, before agreeing with a slow nod of his head.

"I've never been a true Clan cat," he admitted. "I really love Violetshine, and I want to be with her and our kits. But I believe that the rights of individual cats, and their happiness, are more important than a Clan's rules."

Bristlefrost narrowed her eyes. "Is it strange having the Sisters so close by?" she asked. "You couldn't have stayed with them if you'd wanted to, could you?"

Tree winced, and Bristlefrost momentarily regretted her casual tone. *It must have been hard for Tree to be turned away as a young cat. But as I understand it, toms can't live among the Sisters.*

"I wouldn't have wanted to stay," he replied, meeting her eye with an expression that told her not to push any further. "But yes, it is strange having them here. When they made camp on SkyClan's current territory and the others drove them off, I thought that was the last I'd see of them. But then you and Rootspring went to fetch them. And I have to admit . . . they seem better prepared to deal with this sort of thing than the Clans are, even though these are your ancestors."

Bristlefrost opened her mouth to say something in defense of the Clans, but then stopped herself. *He's not wrong.* "How do you think they can help us?" she asked.

Tree sighed. "I haven't figured that out yet. Anyway, back to you, young warrior. Why is it so easy for you to ignore real love to follow an arbitrary rule? You know SkyClan wasn't exactly eager to accept a rogue like me, but I wore them down with my abundant charm."

"But—" Bristlefrost began.

Tree ignored her attempt to interrupt. "Maybe you and Rootspring could find a home away from the lake," he continued. "Away from the Clans. It isn't so bad out there."

"Never!" Bristlefrost couldn't believe any cat could suggest that. "I'm a Clan cat, through and through. I always will be."

Tree blinked at her in surprise. "I wouldn't stick around if I knew I could be happier somewhere else," he told her.

"It would be too much of a change," Bristlefrost objected.

"Only as big a change as I made, when I became a—well, a sort of Clan cat, so many moons ago."

"Don't be a fool." A new voice joined the conversation. "Clan cats carry their Clan in their blood. It isn't so easy to let that go."

Bristlefrost started with surprise, and turned to see that Mothwing had woken up.

"Even though I wasn't born in RiverClan," the medicine cat continued, "it hasn't been easy to switch Clans. I still miss my old Clan, and I would never have left it if I hadn't been forced to. ShadowClan couldn't have given me a warmer welcome, but I still long for RiverClan's camp. For its scent, for the river itself . . ." Her voice cracked, and she couldn't go on, turning her head away and licking vigorously at one forepaw.

"Why don't you go back, then?" Bristlefrost asked.

"I don't see RiverClan in the same way anymore," Mothwing meowed, still not looking at Bristlefrost. "Not since Mistystar forced me out and refused to take back the cats who fought against the false Bramblestar. Even if things have changed since then . . . nothing can wipe out those moments."

She's being too proud, Bristlefrost decided, though she didn't speak her thoughts aloud. *I can't imagine ever being so angry at ThunderClan that I wouldn't want to go back.* But then she thought again of Rootspring: of the way she loved him, and of Tree's words. *Only as big a change as I made . . .* Tree seemed happy. Well, most of the time.

Could I ever leave ThunderClan?

And then a thought came that she didn't want to have:

What's left of ThunderClan now?

Both Mothwing and Tree were staring at her, and she couldn't imagine what they thought they saw in her face. A shiver went through her, and she knew that she had to get away.

"We ought to eat something," she blurted out. "I'll go hunting. No need to come with me."

Racing out of the Moonpool hollow and onto the moor, Bristlefrost drew in great gulps of air, relishing the cool, fresh taste. She could just make out the line of the hills, dark against a sky where dawn was beginning to break.

The springy moorland grass beneath Bristlefrost's paws felt good, too, as she paced away from the Moonpool, all her senses alert for the first trace of prey. Her thoughts winged like homing birds to the time when she and Rootspring had hunted on their quest to find the Sisters. *We worked so well together.* Each had seemed to know exactly what the other was thinking. Fear rose inside Bristlefrost as she realized they might never have that again. *Oh, StarClan, let him be all right.*

While she searched for prey, Bristlefrost tried to shake off her feelings of dread, but they surged over her as if she had plunged into icy water. *What will become of ThunderClan if we can't get Squirrelflight back?* She respected Graystripe—he was truly a noble cat—but he was an elder. How long would he be able to lead the Clan without nine lives? Would they just . . . go on without StarClan?

And if we do, what will my place in the Clan be then?

Bristlefrost had always wanted to be a ThunderClan

warrior. But what would happen to her if ThunderClan wasn't ThunderClan anymore?

Pushing these dark thoughts away, Bristlefrost tried to concentrate on her hunt. Soon she came to a rocky hollow with a puddle of water at the bottom and several dark holes gaping among the stones. Rabbits were out feeding or drinking at the pool.

Bristlefrost pinpointed one that had moved a little farther away from the burrows, and darted in to grab it by the neck. It let out a squeal of terror, while the rest of the rabbits stamped a warning with their huge hind legs, then vanished in a flash down the holes.

"Thank you, StarClan, for this prey," Bristlefrost murmured, though she was unsure if any of the starry spirits would be listening.

Her thoughts pulled again to Rootspring, trapped in the Place of No Stars. She remembered him running toward Willowshine's body, explaining that her spirit had tried and failed to reunite with her remains.

Because if you die in the Dark Forest, you die in real life.

She dropped the rabbit, suddenly nauseated. Rootspring was a strong fighter, but still—what if he was overpowered in the Dark Forest? She would never see him again.

There's so much I want to say to him. She knew that they'd decided they couldn't be together—that neither of them was ready to leave their own Clan. But suddenly it didn't seem like such a clear decision.

I need to speak to him. I need to hear his voice.

She realized she would need to have a conversation with Mothwing when she got back.

The dawn light was strengthening as Bristlefrost returned to the Moonpool, and a spot on the horizon glowed golden where the sun would rise. She laid her prey down beside Tree and Mothwing, shrugging off their thanks, and the three cats ate in near silence.

"You ought to sleep," Mothwing meowed, when nothing was left of the rabbit except for fur and bones. "We'll wake you if you're needed."

"Okay." Bristlefrost curled up on a patch of grass away from the water's edge, but she felt very far from sleep. Instead, her gaze drifted over to the Moonpool.

"I hope he's okay," she murmured, hardly aware that she was speaking her thoughts aloud. "I wish I could go after him."

"You really, really don't want that," Mothwing responded, her eyes understanding while her words and her tone were dismissive. "The Dark Forest is called the Place of No Stars for a reason. Even having cats from there walk in your dreams is terrifying. And as for dreaming yourself there . . . Shadow-sight may have accomplished it, but it's still difficult and very dangerous. Remember what happened to Willowshine."

Bristlefrost sat up again, suddenly alert. "I know that what happened to Willowshine was terrible," she mewed. "But like Shadowsight, other cats have entered the Dark Forest through their dreams and come back safely. My mother did, over and over again. So that should mean that there might be a way for *me* to get there. I could at least find out if Rootspring is okay."

And be sure I get to speak with him again, she added silently.

Mothwing let her pelt ruffle up, clearly disturbed, then smoothed it down again. "It's better if you don't think like that," she told Bristlefrost firmly. "Nothing is like it was back then. I watched Willowshine die. I saw Shadowsight struggle to hold on. We both saw Rootspring snatched by some dark spirit through the Moonpool, and who even knew that the Moonpool could be a portal to the Dark Forest?"

"But I—" Bristlefrost tried to break in.

Mothwing shook her head decisively. "*Stop it.* You're barely older than a kit, so you can't understand. But I was alive when cats first battled in the Dark Forest, and I'm alive now. *It's different.* Ashfur has changed the rules, and only he knows what they are."

Bristlefrost was silent for a moment, absorbing this wisdom. But still, hope fluttered like bird wings in her chest. *I know the rules are different. But isn't it worth the risk if I can make contact with Rootspring?*

"Please, Mothwing, tell me how to do it. I heard what you said, and I'll be careful. But this is so important to me."

"You *didn't* hear what I said, then. Not really," Mothwing replied, her voice cold. "Anyway, you already know how to do it. You heard what we said to Willowshine. But there's no way I'm sending another cat into that awful place."

"You wouldn't be *sending* me," Bristlefrost pointed out. "I'm a warrior. I can make up my own mind."

"You might as well let her," Tree advised the medicine cat. "Now that Bristlefrost has it in her mind to go, she won't rest until she tries it, whether any cat approves or not."

Mothwing let out an exasperated hiss and gave her pelt a shake. "The pair of you are ganging up on me," she complained. "Okay, Bristlefrost, but don't blame me if it all goes horribly wrong."

"I won't, I promise," Bristlefrost meowed. *If it all goes wrong, I won't be able to blame any cat.* A tiny worm of apprehension woke in her belly, but she resolutely ignored it. "Remind me what I have to do."

Mothwing still hesitated for a heartbeat, before she began to speak. "You can make a connection to the Dark Forest if you open yourself up to your negative emotions. Let all your anguish and fear, all your anger, everything you've ever grieved over, flow through you as you try to sleep. If you do that, then the Dark Forest will find *you*, in your dreams." She paused for a moment, then added, "But there's one thing I want to warn you about. Before Willowshine went to sleep, I suggested that she should focus on some of her dead Clanmates, because they might help to pull her through."

"Oh, I can do that!" Bristlefrost exclaimed.

"No, I'm not telling you to do that." Mothwing gave her whiskers an irritated flick. "I'm telling you *not* to. Something went wrong for Willowshine, and it might have been . . ." For a moment her amber eyes were haunted. "It might have been the advice I gave her that killed her."

Bristlefrost nodded, not really understanding, but deeply compassionate for Mothwing's pain, that somehow she might have sent her beloved apprentice to her death. "Okay, I won't," she meowed.

Mothwing sighed. "You need to be sure of what you're getting into. The Dark Forest is more frightening, more desolate, than any place you can imagine."

Bristlefrost gazed back at the medicine cat, straightening up resolutely with her head and her tail held high. *I can face the danger,* she thought. *I can take any risk, if I can get Rootspring back.*

❧

CHAPTER 15

Shadowsight crouched beside Snowtuft in the shelter of a low-growing yew tree. Through the dark branches, his gaze was fixed on Ashfur and Squirrelflight, who still stood glaring at each other with their backs arched. Though he was relieved to have found the ThunderClan cat, he felt entangled in bonds of fear like the twining stems of ivy.

What am I going to do now?

As he watched, Shadowsight began to realize that somehow Squirrelflight looked more *real* than Ashfur. He decided that must be because she had come through in her own body, whereas Ashfur had shed Bramblestar's, and stood there in his spirit form. Peering closer, Shadowsight spotted Bramblestar's body, an inert lump of tabby fur, lying close by among the wilting grasses.

I'm here as a spirit; my body is still beside the Moonpool, Shadowsight thought. *But I can't work out what's happening to Bramblestar. Where is his spirit?*

One thing Shadowsight did know: He couldn't fight Ashfur by himself. "Will you help me, Snowtuft?" he asked. "I want to distract Ashfur so that Squirrelflight can get away."

Snowtuft turned toward him, eyes wide with shock and fear. "Absolutely not!" he growled. "I've seen the island where Ashfur keeps spirit cats. He controls them with his mind. I don't know how he manages it, but I'm not risking ending up like that, thank you very much."

"Island? What island?" Shadowsight asked. Could that be where Ashfur was keeping Bramblestar?

Snowtuft only shook his head. "You really don't want to know."

Frustrated, Shadowsight decided that all he could do was wait, and listen to Squirrelflight and Ashfur in the hope that would give him an idea. He crept forward to the very edge of the shadow cast by the yew branches, so that he could hear what the two cats were saying to each other.

When he had first seen them, Squirrelflight had been standing protectively over Bramblestar's body, as if defying Ashfur to attack either of them, but now he guessed that she had given up on taking her mate with her. She was trying to walk away from Ashfur, but the evil cat kept dodging around her to stand in her way. Squirrelflight flexed her claws over and over, as if she was longing to take a swipe at him but kept thinking better of it.

Eventually she stood facing him, her shoulder fur bushing up angrily. "I'm not going along with any of this," she hissed.

"Don't be mouse-brained," Ashfur growled, looking down at her arrogantly. "It will all be worth it when I control the forest and StarClan. We can be together, and I'll forgive you for betraying me to the Clans."

"Never!" Squirrelflight spat.

"But you must see that I'm the better choice," Ashfur meowed, with a disdainful glance at Bramblestar's limp body. "Right now, with all the power I have over the Dark Forest and StarClan, I may be the most powerful cat who ever lived!"

And he calls her mouse-brained! Shadowsight thought. *He has a whole swarm of bees in his brain.*

"Powerful?" Squirrelflight glared at the spirit cat. "The sort of power you had in ThunderClan, where you turned cats against you and provoked a battle where so many of them died? That's not a power I want any part of. Power is inspiring cats to *want* to follow you—like Bramblestar did."

"Bramblestar is lost and defeated," Ashfur growled. "He couldn't even find his way back to his body to reclaim his next life."

"Oh, shut up!" Squirrelflight exclaimed, clearly at the end of her patience. "I'm not listening to your rambling anymore. I'm going to find a way back through the Moonpool—alone, if I have to."

Fury flashed in Ashfur's blue eyes, and he drew his lips back, baring his teeth at Squirrelflight. "After all this," he snarled, "why would you *still* choose Bramblestar over me?"

Squirrelflight let out a *mrrow* of genuine laughter. "Don't you understand, fur-for-brains?" she asked. "This isn't about Bramblestar—although I *do* choose my own mate, thank you. You could be the only cat left in the world, and I still wouldn't choose you, not after everything you've done."

She tried to barge past him, but once more Ashfur

intercepted her, thrusting at her with his chest.

"Are you ready to fight me?" Squirrelflight demanded. "Because that's what you'll have to do, if you want to stop me."

"No, I don't want to harm you," Ashfur meowed. "I still love you."

Squirrelflight's only response was to turn away from him with a disgusted hiss.

Ashfur blinked and looked away briefly with a dip of his head. To Shadowsight's surprise, he seemed genuinely hurt, as if he couldn't believe that the dark ginger she-cat had rejected him.

How could Ashfur possibly think Squirrelflight would go along with him, now or ever? Shadowsight wondered. Then he realized that Ashfur wasn't thinking straight at all. His obsession with Squirrelflight was making him ignore what was right in front of him.

"Why are you forcing me to do this?" he asked plaintively. "If you would just admit that you love me, I could stop."

"I'm not forcing you to do anything, you stupid mange-pelt," Squirrelflight retorted. "I'm not taking the blame for all the evil things you've done."

Ashfur seemed torn between fury and real bewilderment about why Squirrelflight was being so hostile. The two cats began to circle each other, neck fur bristling and tails lashing. Shadowsight held his breath, expecting that they were about fight at last. He crouched, muscles tensing as he prepared himself to leap in and fight alongside Squirrelflight—whatever good that would do—but instead of attacking, Ashfur stepped back, seeming to relax. There was a malignant light in his blue eyes that told Shadowsight the danger wasn't over.

"I have something to show you," Ashfur announced to Squirrelflight. "Something you'll want to see before you make any rash decisions about attacking me."

Shadowsight didn't know what he should hope for. Part of him wanted Squirrelflight to fight Ashfur and get it over with, but he wasn't sure that she could defeat him, here in the Dark Forest where his power was greatest. And in this fearsome territory, a living cat had much more to lose.

Besides, he thought, *if she goes with Ashfur, we might find out something he has been hiding from us—something we can use to defeat him.*

Squirrelflight was hesitating, as if she too was struggling to decide what she ought to do next. But finally, she stepped back. "Fine, you can show me whatever it is," she meowed. "Even though I suspect it's all some stupid trick."

Shadowsight cast a final glance at Bramblestar's inert body. Then he turned to leave, glancing at Snowtuft. Would the Dark Forest cat follow? But the white tom merely nodded and fell into step behind Ashfur and Squirrelflight, as though his help were assured. Shadowsight was impressed by the Dark Forest cat's loyalty. Together, they followed at a safe distance as Ashfur and Squirrelflight set out through the Dark Forest. Every paw step was an effort for Shadowsight, for with each one the forest seemed more terrifying still. Out of the corner of his eye he thought he could see the trees moving, though they were quite still when he faced them head-on. The ground seemed to shift beneath his paws: A downward slope became a ridge that he had to climb; stretches of marsh opened up without warning, so that he shuddered at the thought of being swallowed up. Worst of all, if he tried to look into the distance, he spotted patches of the same roiling gray fog that Snowtuft had shown him earlier. It seemed to be closing in, as if it were a predator and he was the prey it was stalking.

Thoroughly confused, Shadowsight wondered how Ashfur knew, in the midst of the shifting landscape, that the place he was heading for would still be where he'd left it.

Eventually, Ashfur led the way through a grove of young hazel saplings, their trunks blackened as if they had been struck by lightning. When they emerged on the far side, Shadowsight found that he was gazing down at a dark lake with an island in the middle—little more than a stretch of mud with a few decaying trees sagging at odd angles.

"Is that the island you told me about?" he asked Snowtuft.

The Dark Forest cat gave a tense nod. "That's it."

Peering more closely through the dim light, Shadowsight became aware of a crowd of spirits on the island; they were pacing slowly back and forth, and as he crept nearer, he could make out that their eyes were eerily blank. They seemed not to be in control of their own paws.

Maybe Ashfur could find his way to this place because he was drawn to the spirits.

Staring in horror, Shadowsight realized that some of the spirit cats were known to him. He recognized Spiresight, and Conefoot, Rosepetal, Berrynose, and Stemleaf, and several others.

What's happened to them? he asked himself. *What has Ashfur done?*

Ashfur and Squirrelflight were standing at the edge of the black lake. Shadowsight managed to creep into earshot under cover of the clumps of dead bracken that dotted the downward slope. Snowtuft followed him, though he could tell that the Dark Forest cat grew more reluctant with every paw step.

"Take a good look," Ashfur directed Squirrelflight. "This is how powerful I am. All these cats were once strong warriors, and now they do *my* bidding. They are my paws, and I'll use them to crush the Clans, in your name, Squirrelflight." He turned to her with a gleam of triumph in his eyes. "See, here's a familiar face. . . ."

On the island, a cat stepped forward to the edge of the crowd of spirits. Shadowsight let out a gasp. *Bramblestar!*

Squirrelflight stiffened as she gazed at her mate; Shadowsight could see relief and pain on her face. "I wasn't sure he was still here," she murmured to Ashfur. "You made it sound like he was really dead."

Shadowsight knew exactly how the ginger she-cat was feeling. His own heart hurt to see the real ThunderClan leader, reduced to a spirit and with weird blank eyes that were surely a sign he was under Ashfur's control. But if his spirit still survived, that meant it had to be possible for him to find his way back to his body. He could still claim his next life—he could still come back to ThunderClan.

Hope sparked within Shadowsight, every hair on his pelt

tingling with it. *I have to find a way to help Bramblestar get back to the real world.*

Ashfur half closed his eyes, his expression fixed in concentration. Instantly Bramblestar's head jerked and his ears pricked up as if he had heard a call that Shadowsight could not. He padded all the way to the edge of the island, to where a narrow muddy path stretched across the dark water to the mainland. A dark gray tabby tom sat on guard at the far end, and rose to his paws as Ashfur called out to him.

"Let him pass, Darkstripe."

The dark gray tabby tom dipped his head and stepped back to let Bramblestar pass along the path and join Ashfur and Squirrelflight.

At first Shadowsight hoped that might be a good thing, but as he halted in front of Squirrelflight, Bramblestar showed no sign of recognition, and his eyes were still blank.

"See how weak your former mate is now," Ashfur gloated, wafting his tail toward the ThunderClan leader.

Squirrelflight gave a contemptuous snort. "If you think showing me that I still have a mate to fight for will make me join you," she growled, "you're even stupider than I thought."

At the sound of her voice, Bramblestar's eyes blinked and cleared, restored to their familiar warm amber. He seemed to see his mate for the first time, and cried out, "Squirrel—"

Her name was broken off as Ashfur let out a snarl and the terrible blank film covered Bramblestar's eyes again.

Let him go, you mange-pelt! I'll show you! Shadowsight extended his claws toward Ashfur, feeling the hideous evil of the Dark Forest like bubbling blood coursing through his whole body. It felt like heavy paws pressing down on his back. He paused, forcing himself to take a breath. *It's getting to me. I have to keep control.* He crouched low to the ground, feeling doubtful that he would ever be able to move again.

Ashfur stepped away, leaving Squirrelflight and the spirit of Bramblestar facing each other. A ghastly chill surged through Shadowsight as the power-crazed cat spoke:

"I'll show you . . ." His voice was soft and menacing. "I'll show you just how *foolish* it is to stand against me."

Without warning, Bramblestar reached up a paw and swiped at Squirrelflight. She was taken by surprise; her mate's spirit claws scratched her face, leaving tracks of blood along her muzzle.

Squirrelflight reared back in shock, letting out a cry of alarm. Still controlled by Ashfur, Bramblestar began to circle her, his claws extended and his teeth bared.

Shadowsight glanced at Snowtuft in dismay. "That vile cat is making Squirrelflight's own mate attack her! We have to do something."

Snowtuft shook his head. "There's nothing we can do."

Meanwhile, though Squirrelflight's ears were flattened and her whiskers were quivering in fear, she still whirled to face Ashfur boldly. "What do you think you're doing?" she demanded.

Ashfur's reply was too muffled for Shadowsight to make it out, though it sounded as if he was addressing Bramblestar.

He fixed a furious glare on the ThunderClan leader; Shadowsight wondered, with a surge of hope, if he was finding it hard to control him, and was angry that Bramblestar would try to fight back.

After a moment of apparent struggle, Bramblestar turned away and launched himself at Squirrelflight again. But now Squirrelflight was ready for him, and dodged aside just in time. Shadowsight held his breath as Bramblestar repeated the same move over and over, while Squirrelflight managed to step out of his way or push him off without causing him harm.

"Bramblestar!" she yowled as he snapped at her throat. "Remember who you are! Fight against Ashfur . . . *please!*"

For a heartbeat, her appeal seemed to work. Bramblestar stumbled and pulled away from her, his eyes focusing once more. "I'm sorry," he choked out. "Squirrel—"

"No!" Ashfur screeched.

Back under his control, Bramblestar attacked again. This time, he flung Squirrelflight to the ground, his claws poised over her throat. Desperate to escape, she lunged to bite his leg, but Bramblestar seemed hardly aware of it.

He doesn't feel pain! Shadowsight thought, horrified. *How can Squirrelflight possibly win this fight?*

Somehow, Squirrelflight managed to wriggle free, and pinned her mate to the ground before he could recover his paws. For a moment she held him there, but seemed not to know what to do next.

Ashfur was tearing at the ground in rage. "How can you love a cat who is prepared to fight you to the death?" he yowled.

"I am ready to destroy everything for you!"

I can't let this go on, Shadowsight resolved. *Ashfur is so obsessed, he might turn on Squirrelflight at any moment. If he takes this too far, he might even kill her. Though I'm a medicine cat, and not a trained warrior . . . could I even make a difference?* He paused, feeling weighed down by hopelessness, but then he shook his pelt in an attempt to cast off the feeling. *That's the Dark Forest, getting to me . . . or at least I'll choose to believe it is. Together, Snowtuft and I can at least distract Ashfur long enough to save Squirrelflight!*

Turning to Snowtuft, he murmured, "Maybe if we attack Ashfur, we'll break his concentration—and then Bramblestar might be able to snap out of his control. I know it's a scary idea, but it's all I can think of. . . ."

Snowtuft stared at him, backing away. "Have you got bees in your brain? This isn't my fight, and I'm certainly not going to die for it." He took a step away into the bracken, then halted, looking over his shoulder. "Good luck to you," he meowed gruffly, before he vanished into the darkness.

It's up to me, then. Shadowsight felt even more afraid now that he was left alone, but he knew he had no choice. *I must do something.*

By now, Bramblestar had thrown Squirrelflight off and the battle was on again, the two cats circling each other, with Squirrelflight darting aside every time her mate leaped at her.

How long can she keep avoiding his attacks? How long before she gets tired?

His paws shaking, Shadowsight crept through the under-growth, working himself into a position behind Ashfur. Paw step by paw step, he sneaked up on him. . . . *Any moment now, and I can pounce. . . .*

Ashfur whipped around and swiped a paw through the air. Catching Shadowsight off guard, he easily batted him to the ground.

"Stupid kit," he growled. "Did you think you could sneak up on me? This is my territory. No cat can get the better of me in this place." His blue eyes flared with mingled pride and fury as he stood over Shadowsight. "I know everything that happens in the Dark Forest," he boasted.

Shadowsight braced himself for the killing blow he knew was coming, when Ashfur suddenly spun around and stared at a point in the forest. Shadowsight followed his gaze, but there was nothing there.

"Yes, I see you too," Ashfur meowed, apparently to no cat. "My faithful young warrior!"

Just for a moment, Shadowsight spotted a dark shadow in the shape of a cat, at the edge of the trees that surrounded the dark lake. *That shape's familiar . . . ,* he thought. *Who—*

But the shape blinked out and was gone.

Meanwhile, with Ashfur distracted, Bramblestar had come back to himself. Shadowsight saw his eyes glowing amber, and he leaped backward in the act of slashing at Squirrelflight with claws extended. "Squirrelflight! Run!" he yowled. "I'll follow you!"

The ThunderClan she-cat darted away, racing toward the dark trees. Bramblestar began to run after her, but Ashfur let out a furious yowl, turning away from Shadowsight.

Bramblestar stumbled to a halt. "Keep going!" he called to Squirrelflight, in the last heartbeat before Ashfur had him fully under control again.

The dark ginger she-cat glanced back once at the edge of the trees, as if even then she wanted to return.

"Squirrelflight!" Ashfur screeched. As if his voice had made her decide to run, she fled into the shadows and disappeared.

A warm glow enveloped Shadowsight as he watched her escape. *Maybe now there's a way I can save Bramblestar,* he thought, his heart soaring with hope.

Ashfur padded up to Bramblestar and thrust his muzzle a mouse-length from the ThunderClan leader's face. "You've stolen Squirrelflight from me," he snarled. "Again! I'm going to destroy your pitiful Clan and all the others when I lead my followers back into the living world."

StarClan, give me strength! Shadowsight prayed, even though he knew that the ancestral spirits probably could not hear him in this dark place.

Then he leaped at Ashfur, landing squarely on his back. With Ashfur's attention on Bramblestar, he managed to sink his teeth into the evil cat's shoulder.

Ashfur let out a screech, rearing up to shake Shadowsight off. Shadowsight dug his claws into Ashfur's pelt, clinging on with all his strength. Gazing down at Bramblestar, he saw the leader's eyes glowing amber once more. "Go! Now!" he yowled.

Bramblestar hesitated. Ashfur reared up again; this time, Shadowsight lost his grip and thumped to the ground, the impact driving his breath out of him.

"Back to the island, mange-pelt!" Ashfur ordered, gaining control of Bramblestar again.

But Shadowsight would not give up. His chest heaved as he fought for breath and launched himself at Ashfur once again.

"Bramblestar, I know what I'm doing!" he gasped out as Ashfur raked his claws across his shoulder. "If I distract him, he can't control you. You have to go! Follow Squirrelflight! Get back to your body! Get back to the real world!"

Ashfur let out a howl of rage, putting all his strength into attacking Shadowsight. Pain from his blows flooded over the medicine cat. *I know I'm no match for him, but it doesn't matter. I just have to stay alive and keep him busy, just for long enough . . .*

Shadowsight was pinned down, half suffocated under Ashfur's body, but he managed to turn his head and see Bramblestar once again restored, his amber eyes full of horror at what he was witnessing. For a moment, Shadowsight was afraid that the ThunderClan leader was going to leap into the battle to try to save him.

"No!" he choked out. "Go!"

To his relief, Bramblestar obeyed; he dipped his head in gratitude, then raced away from the lake, following in the paw steps of his vanished mate.

Ashfur had not seemed to notice that his prisoner had escaped. Scrambling to his paws, he grabbed Shadowsight by the scruff with no more effort than if he had been a kit. Taking a couple of paw steps forward, he hurled Shadowsight into the black water, where he bobbed for a heartbeat like a pine-cone in a stream.

"Good riddance!" Ashfur snarled.

As the lake engulfed him, Shadowsight realized that the black water was not water at all. It felt more like soft pelts, enfolding him, tightening around him and gently stopping his breath. He was shocked by the icy cold, and could feel his strength draining away. Despair seeped into his mind; he felt as if the whole world were decaying and soon everything would be just as dark and hopeless as this forest. *There's no way out. . . .*

Shoving back these dark thoughts, Shadowsight struggled to the surface before he could lose any more energy. He was hurt and exhausted by the fight against Ashfur, but he knew he could not stop trying. With a massive effort, he flailed his paws and propelled himself forward until he could haul himself back up onto solid ground.

Ashfur was standing with his tail to him, glancing around as if looking for any sign of Bramblestar. Shadowsight leaped for him again, trying to pierce Ashfur's thick pelt with his claws. But Ashfur spun around and sank his teeth hard into Shadowsight's leg, and raked his claws down the top of his head, shredding his ear.

The pain was so intense that Shadowsight collapsed, darkness swirling around him. He struggled to rise to his paws, but the injured leg could not bear his weight.

"Bramblestar!" Ashfur shrieked; clearly, he had realized that the ThunderClan leader was gone. "Come back! Come back now! You *will* obey me!"

Shadowsight could just make out the line of trees where

the ThunderClan leader had disappeared; there was no sign of him returning.

But now Shadowsight's vision began to narrow, and the Dark Forest seemed to fade around him. The last thing he saw was Ashfur, still screeching impotently into the darkness.

I did it. I saved Squirrelflight and Bramblestar!

Then blackness claimed him, and he knew nothing more.

CHAPTER 16

Bristlefrost lay stretched out on a sun-warmed rock at the edge of the ThunderClan camp, her eyes slitted against the dazzle of the sun's rays. She could sense the busy life of the Clan going on around her: the squeals of happy, playful kits, the purposeful padding of the warriors' paw steps, the rich scent of the well-stocked fresh-kill pile.

It's so peaceful here. And yet . . . something feels wrong.

The lap of a rough tongue on her shoulder fur distracted her. Rolling over onto her back, Bristlefrost opened her eyes to see her mate, Rootspring, lying beside her, his blue eyes full of love as he gazed at her.

It feels so good to see that he's safe, and everything's all right. But in the midst of her contentment, Bristlefrost seemed to sense a cold breeze ruffling her fur. *Then why do I feel . . . disturbed?*

"Are you in the right place?" she asked Rootspring. "Shouldn't you be somewhere else?"

"I'm exactly where I want to be," Rootspring purred reassuringly. "I chose ThunderClan, remember? I knew that I needed to be with you, so I left SkyClan."

Bristlefrost's sense of uneasiness grew stronger, yet it was so tempting to push it aside and bask in the sunlight and happiness of her life in ThunderClan with Rootspring.

I know that our life together is wonderful. He's happy. I'm happy. So what's the problem?

Rootspring's father, Tree, came padding across the camp, his yellow pelt gleaming in the sunshine. "Greetings, Bristlefrost," he meowed, sitting down at the edge of the rock where she lay beside his son.

"Greetings," Bristlefrost murmured in response, wondering what the SkyClan tom was doing in ThunderClan's stone hollow.

"Didn't I tell you that you and Rootspring belong together?" Tree asked her, affection in his amber gaze. "What are you worried about? My son has chosen you. Isn't that what you wanted?"

"I'm still not sure," Bristlefrost confessed, coming to the heart of her uneasiness. "I can't remember what happened, and I never thought Rootspring would make that choice. I thought . . . I thought we both loved our Clans too much to change?" She shook her head, her brain feeling as if it were stuffed with thistle-fluff. "Why can't I remember?"

She knew that Rootspring was close, so close that their pelts were brushing, and yet she felt equally certain that he was very far away. She could see him, but her chest ached with anxiety, as if she were searching but could not find him.

What's going on? she asked herself, her panic rising. *Why do I feel so worried, so scared that I could almost throw up? Why does this moment of happiness feel like something I can never have?*

Instead of relaxing into her closeness to the tom she loved above all others, Bristlefrost felt as though her happiness were taunting her, teasing her as if it were an enemy, letting her escape for a brief heartbeat before reaching for her with outstretched claws.

As her anxiety and fear swelled inside her, the sunlight vanished; Bristlefrost couldn't sense the presence of other cats around her anymore. Suddenly, she realized she wasn't in the camp, but in a cold, dark forest where the trees massed threateningly around her. When she looked around for Rootspring and Tree, they had vanished, too.

With a shudder that shook her right down to the tips of her claws, Bristlefrost realized that this was a dream. That happy life with Rootspring as her mate was never going to happen. Instead, her fears for him, and her anguish at their impossible future, were the terrible emotions that had formed her pathway into the Dark Forest.

Mothwing was right, Bristlefrost thought, shivering with fear. *I've drawn the Dark Forest to me.*

"Rootspring! Rootspring!" she called out, but there was no answer. Bristlefrost hadn't been sure what the Dark Forest would look like, but she had imagined a sort of dark reflection of the forest she knew. Here she didn't recognize anything.

As she paused, uncertain what to do next, she heard a frightened, angry yowling close by. The sound turned her blood to ice, but she hurried toward it, ducking under a bush and circling a massive oak tree with gnarled roots that seemed to reach out and entangle her paws.

Bristlefrost emerged from the shadow of the oak to find herself at the edge of a clear space that stretched down to the shore of a dark lake. Beside the water, two cats were circling each other, their fur bushed up and their tails lashing. Shock struck Bristlefrost like a bolt of lightning as she recognized Squirrelflight and Bramblestar—her Clan's true leader, and his mate and deputy—about to attack each other.

"Oh, no!" she whispered aloud. "That can't be!"

Beyond the two cats, a low, muddy island lay in the center of the lake. Along its shore stood a line of spirits, all staring at the combat with blank, eerie gazes. Bristlefrost's horror deepened as she realized that she knew some of them.

Her appalled gaze fixed on an orange-and-white tom. *Is that . . . Stemleaf?* Her heart gave a horrible jolt to see the dead spirit of the cat she had once loved, the cat who had been her good friend and loyal Clanmate, now trapped in this terrible place. Rosepetal was there, too, and Bristlefrost ached to see her former mentor unable to join StarClan. She also spotted the impostor's former deputy, Berrynose, and other cats who in life had been brave warriors loyal to their Clans. But they had fallen in their fight against the impostor. Ashfur had devastated the Clans, and now he was holding the spirits of the dead prisoner in the Dark Forest. *It's a crueler punishment than I ever could have imagined. . . .*

Bristlefrost tore her gaze away from the island, back to her Clan leader and deputy. Another cat was standing close to them, a gray tom she had never seen before, watching. impassively as Bramblestar sprang at Squirrelflight, aiming for her throat with bared fangs.

Who is that third cat? Bristlefrost wondered. *It's like he's making them fight each other!*

She looked around at the other cats. None of them seemed to notice her, or react to her presence. *Does that mean they can't see me?* she wondered. When she'd talked to her mother about walking in the Dark Forest, Ivypool had made it sound like she was simply there—she could do all the things she could do in the real world, like hunt, fight, and speak. Now Bristlefrost had the eerie sense that she was invisible to the others. *But maybe that's a good thing,* she reminded herself. *Maybe I don't want them to know I'm here.*

Squirrelflight had slipped aside, avoiding Bramblestar's attempt to tear out her throat. Then the third cat let out a startled yelp and spun around. A smaller cat was creeping up on him, his belly fur brushing the ground as if he were stalking prey.

Shadowsight! What is he doing?

The young medicine cat was bunching his muscles to spring, but before he could attack, the gray tom swiped a paw through the air, catching him a hard blow on the side of his head.

At the same moment, as the strange cat was distracted, Bramblestar stumbled, his fighting move halted in mid-leap. He pulled away in horror from trying to attack Squirrelflight, as if he was in control of himself once more.

That other cat has to be Ashfur. . . . Bristlefrost blinked in surprise to see what the impostor had looked like all along. Back in the living world, she had only ever seen him in the muscular dark tabby body of Bramblestar.

So Shadowsight is attacking Ashfur to save Squirrelflight and Bramblestar. . . . I've come just in time! I have to help Shadowsight somehow!

She drew a breath to call out to him, but then Ashfur turned and fixed a malignant blue gaze right on her. Bristlefrost jumped, startled. *Oh, no. Can he see me after all?*

Ashfur spoke, as if answering her question. "Yes, I see you, too, my faithful young warrior!"

Bristlefrost shuddered at the memory of the time she had spent serving him, and later plotting against him, when she thought that he was Bramblestar. Then Shadowsight turned to look at her, too, and as their gazes locked, everything went dark.

Opening her eyes, Bristlefrost found herself back in the living world, near the Moonpool where she had fallen asleep. The sun had risen on a bright, blustery day where clouds raced one another across the sky.

"Rootspring! Shadowsight!" she called hoarsely as she scrambled to her paws; for a moment she couldn't believe that she had lost her connection to that desolate forest.

Then she spotted Tree and Mothwing standing at the edge of the Moonpool, talking together softly as they exchanged worried glances. While she was happy that she'd helped Shadowsight, disappointment crashed over her as she realized that she had messed up her chance of helping Rootspring. *I went there to talk to him, and I didn't even see him!*

Bristlefrost drew herself to her paws and approached the

other cats. *Shadowsight—is he all right?* As she drew closer, she saw that the young medicine cat lay beside them, his legs jerking horribly in his sleep.

"I was there in the Dark Forest!" she gasped. "I saw him fighting Ashfur." Turning to Mothwing, she added, "He's not a trained warrior. He took such a massive risk, attacking that mange-pelt. Will he be okay?"

Suddenly Shadowsight's whole body convulsed, as if he was being mauled by an invisible cat. At Mothwing's side, she watched in renewed horror as long tears appeared in Shadowsight's ear, and a gash opened up in his leg, spilling blood onto the stones.

Dismay leaped into Mothwing's amber eyes, but she stayed calm, reaching out a paw to pin down Shadowsight's shoulder, to stop him rolling into the water. At the same moment, Shadowsight's amber eyes slammed open, and his jaws stretched wide in a screech of pain, echoing among the rocks around the Moonpool.

CHAPTER 17

Rootspring sat beside Willowshine in the shelter of a holly bush. They had moved away from the island so that they could decide on their next move without fear of discovery. Now they crouched with their heads close together, keeping their voices low.

"We have to save those cat spirits from Ashfur's prison," Rootspring meowed.

Willowshine nodded, though her expression was doubtful. "Be careful, Rootspring," she warned him. "Don't do anything rash. That's what got me killed, after all."

A mixture of grief and anger flooded over Rootspring at the thought of the RiverClan cat's unnecessary death. "I'll keep you safe from Ashfur," he promised, even though he wasn't sure how he was going to do that.

"When I came through to the Dark Forest," Willowshine told him, "I was attacked by a cat I'd never seen before—a gray tom with brilliant blue eyes. Was that Ashfur?"

"Yes, that's him," Rootspring mewed.

"He killed me," Willowshine continued. "I never had a chance. And when my spirit left my body, he appeared there and dragged me into the Moonpool," Willowshine continued.

"It was only when we arrived here, in the Dark Forest, that I was able to get away from him."

Rootspring was still thinking about the terrible fate of the cat spirits trapped in the middle of the dark lake. "I wonder if there's something weird about the water around the island," he mused. "I haven't seen any other water in the Dark Forest. If it were normal water, the RiverClan spirits would be able to escape, but they all look afraid of it. Perhaps we can make some kind of a bridge for them? But what if they're all still under Ashfur's control . . . ? Or . . . maybe they're not under his control at all? That's why he needs Darkstripe to guard them?"

He let his voice die away. He had not forgotten that Darkstripe was guarding the only way on or off the island, and any plan they made had to take account of him. He tried to remember the stories he had heard as an apprentice about the previous time the Clans had fought against cats of the Dark Forest, but that had taken place many moons before SkyClan had come to live beside the lake. And the cats from the other Clans, who had lived through that terrible time, were all reluctant to speak about it.

I wish they had talked about it more, he thought regretfully. *I wish that I'd asked more questions.*

While he struggled with the problem of what he would do next, a sudden rustling in the dark undergrowth distracted him from the problem. He sprang to his paws, claws unsheathed, ready to fight or run if the newcomer was Ashfur or one of the cats under his control.

But the cat who came bursting into the open was Squirrel-flight. She skidded to a halt, panting and staring at him and the RiverClan medicine cat.

"Rootspring? Willowshine?" she meowed. Grief welled up in her green eyes. "Is it really you? Are you dead?"

Willowshine dipped her head to the ThunderClan deputy. "I am," she responded, sadness in her narrowed eyes. "I tried to reach the Dark Forest in a dream, after Rootspring saw Ashfur drag you into the Moonpool—but I couldn't get back to my body. Ashfur brought me here, too. Now I'm stuck with all the others who can't find the way to StarClan."

"I'm so sorry." Squirrelflight's voice quivered as she touched her nose to the young medicine cat's ear. "I never meant for any of this to happen. I just wanted to save Bramblestar." Turning to Rootspring, she asked, "How did you die?"

"I'm not dead!" Rootspring assured her. "I'm . . . well, what happened to you happened to me too. I followed Shadowsight to the Moonpool, and then Willowshine pulled me in. Now that we've found you, we're going to figure out a way to get you out of here."

Squirrelflight stepped up to him and touched her forehead to his. "I feel honored," she mewed, "that three cats from three different Clans—not even my own Clan—would risk themselves like this to save me."

"Three cats?" Rootspring pricked his ears alertly. "Then you've seen Shadowsight?"

Squirrelflight nodded. "Just now," she replied. "He attacked Ashfur so that Bramblestar and I could escape."

Willowshine tilted her head in surprise. "Bramblestar *escaped*?" she asked.

"That's amazing," Rootspring meowed. He suddenly felt hope expanding inside him like a flower unfolding its petals. Glancing around, he added, "So where is he? And what happened to Shadowsight?" Fear for his friend surged up inside him so that he almost wanted to vomit. "Was he hurt?"

"I don't know," Squirrelflight replied. "He was okay when we got away. As for Bramblestar," she continued, "everything was so confused that I lost track of him. I can only hope he's safe somewhere. I have to find him, so that I can lead him back to his body."

"We'll help you," Rootspring promised. "But we have to help the other cat spirits who are trapped here, too."

"I'm glad Leafpool died before StarClan was closed off," Squirrelflight murmured, memory clouding her green gaze for a moment. "At least I don't have to worry about *her* spirit."

"He's keeping them all trapped on an island in the middle of—" Rootspring began.

"Yes, I've seen the island," Squirrelflight interrupted, brisk and alert again. "But the only way to help the spirits is to free them from Ashfur's control."

"But how would we do that?" Willowshine asked. "And what do we do with them afterward? There's still no StarClan for them to go to."

"Suppose we take this one step at a time," Squirrelflight responded. "We don't know what will happen to cats when they die from now on, or whether StarClan will ever be able to come back."

I really don't want to worry about that just now, Rootspring thought. *As if we don't have enough to cope with!*

"When he was away from the island, Bramblestar was able to fight Ashfur's control, provided that Ashfur was distracted," Squirrelflight continued. "But that might be because he was a leader, with more lives waiting for him. Maybe his spirit is stronger than the spirits of the cats who have lost their only life."

"Bramblestar is free now . . ." Rootspring was thinking aloud. "And he knows what it's like to be controlled by Ashfur. If we can find him, he might know how to help the other spirits."

Squirrelflight nodded. "Yes, and I'm sure if we can find him, he'll be able to return to his body. Ashfur wore it when we entered the Dark Forest, then just left it where we came in. If we can reunite his spirit with it, perhaps he can help the others, and then return to the living world just as he was before any of this happened."

Rootspring couldn't help letting out a sigh. In spite of the hope that Bramblestar would soon be himself again, the task in front of them seemed as massive as trying to push a boulder up the spiral path from the Moonpool. And even if they succeeded, they still could not be sure what would happen to the Dark Forest, or to StarClan. "I wish we had StarClan to help us," he murmured.

"There's no point in wishing like that," Squirrelflight meowed firmly. "StarClan has given us plenty of help since the Clans were first created. Now it's time for the living Clans to help StarClan. Ashfur is responsible for all this. We need to focus on getting back to the living world with Bramblestar, so we can rally our Clans and stop him once and for all. And since I can't find Bramblestar, the next best thing is to find his body and stash it somewhere Ashfur can't find it."

"And you saw it? You know where it is?" Rootspring asked, beginning to feel more positive.

Squirrelflight nodded. "This place is so confusing, but I think I can find the way. Follow me."

Rootspring padded along at the ginger she-cat's shoulder as she headed through the trees; Willowshine brought up the rear.

With every paw step Rootspring felt more and more uneasy. He thought he was being watched, though as he flicked his gaze from side to side he could see nothing. From time to time he thought that he could sense movement: the earth swirling beneath his paws, or a tree lowering its branches with twiggy paws reaching out to grab him. He wanted to know if his companions could feel it too, but as Squirrelflight strode confidently on, and Willowshine kept silent watch from behind, Rootspring clenched his jaws on his misgivings and trudged on grimly.

Though Squirrelflight had to pause once or twice, tasting the air and gazing around to check her direction, it was not long before she halted at the edge of a forest clearing and announced, "This is the place."

In front of him Rootspring saw a stretch of bare earth where feeble clumps of grass poked up into the pale, sickly light. Dying trees surrounded it, interspersed here and there with clumps of dry bracken. There was no sign of the powerful tabby-furred body of Bramblestar.

"Are you sure?" he asked.

"I'm absolutely certain." Squirrelflight's voice cracked. "He was right here. He has to still be here somewhere!"

She began to search among the tree roots and bracken clumps, working her way around the edge of the open ground. Rootspring helped, circling in the opposite direction, while Willowshine kept watch. But when the two cats met at the far side of the clearing, they had found nothing.

"He's not here," Squirrelflight sighed despairingly. "We're too late."

"Ashfur must have taken it," Rootspring meowed.

"And what is he going to do with it?" Squirrelflight asked. Rootspring could tell that she was on the edge of panic, her green eyes wild and her voice shaking. "Maybe he'll destroy it—maybe throw it into that awful dark water! And then there's no getting Bramblestar back."

"I don't think he'll do that," Willowshine put in, padding up to join them. "I think he'll keep it safe in case he wants to use it again."

Squirrelflight shuddered. "That's almost worse!" She took a deep breath, obviously fighting for control. "I began to hope when I found that Bramblestar's spirit was still alive, but how can we ever escape from this horrible place if he can't be reunited with his body?"

"Don't give up." Rootspring rested his tail on Squirrelflight's shoulder; it felt odd to be comforting a senior, more experienced cat, and one who had been Clan deputy. "I promise you, we're not going to leave until we find Bramblestar *and* his body."

Squirrelflight cast him a grateful glance, then drew a gasping breath at the sound of rustling from a nearby clump of bracken. She whipped around, hope lighting up her face. "Bramblestar, is that you?"

There was no reply. Squirrelflight took a couple of paces toward the bracken, then halted, frozen. Rootspring padded up next to her and peered through the dry fronds, which made a kind of tunnel through the undergrowth. At the end of the tunnel, he could see a shape walking toward them: a sleek-furred tom with blank eyes.

"Stemleaf!" he gasped hoarsely.

At the same moment, Squirrelflight yowled, "Run! Stemleaf probably isn't himself. More likely, Ashfur has sent one of his spirits after me," she added. "We have to lose him."

Before she had finished speaking, the three cats spun around and hurtled into the trees, dodging around bushes and bramble thickets in a frantic dash to shake off Stemleaf's pursuit.

Glancing over his shoulder, Rootspring couldn't see the spirit cat. "I think he's—" he began, only to break off with a squeal of alarm. He had thought they must have outpaced

Stemleaf, but as they skirted another clump of brown, dead bracken, the orange-and-white tom was standing there waiting for them. Rootspring skidded to a halt just in time to stop himself from crashing into him, and doubled back to race away beside Squirrelflight and Willowshine.

How did he do that? Rootspring asked himself as he ran. *He was behind us.*

As they ran, the eerie landscape of the Dark Forest seemed to shift and change around them. Scrambling up a rocky slope, Rootspring was unprepared for the ground to fall away under his feet; he rolled downward, striking stones as he went, and landed bruised and panting in a narrow gully. As he struggled to his paws, he spotted a flash of orange-and-white fur, as Stemleaf wove his way among the boulders in his inexorable pursuit.

"This way!" Squirrelflight gasped.

Rootspring followed her along the gully, with Willowshine treading in his paw steps. Within heartbeats the sides of the gully fell away and the landscape opened up into a stretch of swamp where dead reeds rattled their tops in uneven gusts of wind.

Before Rootspring was aware of what was happening, white mist curled around him like a massive cat's paw, and he lost all sight of his surroundings and his companions. "Willowshine! Squirrelflight!" he called out, but his voice sounded muffled, as if it couldn't carry farther than the ends of his whiskers. He staggered to and fro, his head spinning, and the mist soaking into his fur. He had lost all sense of direction.

He was stumbling to a halt, ready to give up and sink down onto the marshy ground, when he felt claws dig into his shoulder. "This way, mouse-brain!"

It was Squirrelflight's voice; Rootspring had never felt so relieved to hear another cat. The ThunderClan deputy dragged him backward, and suddenly he broke out into clear air, to see her and Willowshine standing on a shallow hillock that rose up out of the swamp. The clinging mist was dissipating rapidly. As the last shreds of it vanished, Rootspring found that he was facing Stemleaf, who was staring straight at him across the marsh.

Steadily, with unhurried paws, the spirit cat headed toward them. "Run!" Squirrelflight urged again.

As he turned to follow her, Rootspring felt as if his paws had turned to stone. His legs ached and his breath was coming in tortured gasps. *I'm sure we're lost,* he thought. *But at least that should mean we can shake off Ashfur and his spirits.*

Yet no matter how far they ran, how swiftly they dodged from one patch of cover to the next, Stemleaf's spirit seemed able to follow them. Whenever they caught a glimpse of him, he was moving with determination, not scrambling after them, or even seeming to need to scent or look for them.

It's as if he always knows where we're going to be, Rootspring thought.

Once, as they circled around and headed toward a dead tree they had already passed in their desperate flight, Stemleaf was standing beside it, calmly waiting for them.

As he darted away, Rootspring's belly churned with horror.

He couldn't explain how the spirit cat could anticipate their every move. And somehow it was worse because Stemleaf was a cat they had known and liked when he was alive. He had been one of the rebel cats who had lost his life fighting bravely against the usurper. *How terrible would he feel now, to know that he was doing the usurper's bidding?*

Rootspring was beginning to think that he couldn't go on putting one paw in front of another when he heard a cat calling from somewhere ahead of them. "Squirrelflight! Squirrelflight!"

"That's Bramblestar's voice!" Squirrelflight gasped, hope kindling in her eyes as she halted and gazed around.

The undergrowth rustled around them. But it wasn't the ThunderClan leader who stepped into the open. Instead, four spirit cats, their eyes blank and staring, broke out of the bushes and surrounded them. All four spoke at once, still mocking their prisoners with the voice of Bramblestar.

"There you are!"

CHAPTER 18

Shadowsight woke with a yowl, blinking painfully in the bright light of day. His leg and his ear were burning as though Ashfur's claws were still fastened in his flesh, but he knew at once that he wasn't in the Dark Forest any longer. A huge surge of relief swept over him, to be back among the Clans and still alive.

As his eyes grew used to the light, Shadowsight realized that his body hadn't moved: he was lying beside the Moonpool. He felt the cold touch of a nose along his leg, and turned his head to see Mothwing examining him carefully.

"Lie still," the medicine cat ordered. "You're going to be okay, but you have to rest."

Shadowsight found it hard to obey. Twisting his neck, he managed to get a clear view of his leg, and saw that it was really bleeding. He suppressed a shiver at the sight of the wounds he had received in the spirit world appearing on his physical body. *So it is true: You can die in real life if you die in the Dark Forest,* he thought. Even Icewing's warning hadn't prepared him for seeing the wounds on his own body. He felt chilled at the thought of how close he had come to death.

"I'll get you some poppy seed for the pain," Mothwing

meowed, padding over to where she and the other medicine cats had stowed the herbs they had brought earlier.

Shadowsight tried to sit up, but he couldn't put any weight on his injured leg, and he could feel blood congealing across his ear. As he looked around, he spotted Tree and Bristlefrost sitting together a couple of tail-lengths away; his heart thumped harder as he focused his gaze on Bristlefrost.

"Was that you?" he asked her. "Were you in the Dark Forest?"

"Yes, I was," Bristlefrost replied.

"Did you see Bramblestar escape?"

The ThunderClan warrior's ears flicked up in surprise. "No—did he really escape?"

"I think so," Shadowsight told her. "Ashfur was calling out to him, and he sounded furious."

"That's good news!" Bristlefrost exchanged a glowing glance with Tree. "Then maybe there's hope of getting him back. I was trying to find Rootspring," she added, "but I found you instead, and I couldn't manage to stay there for very long. Ashfur saw me, but I couldn't *do* anything." She gave a frustrated twitch of her whiskers.

Then she seemed to notice that Shadowsight was staring at her in alarm.

"*Rootspring* is there now?" he asked. "Why? How?"

Bristlefrost sighed. "Of course . . . you don't know. He . . . well, he was *pulled* in. Through the Moonpool, like Squirrelflight was. We couldn't see who did it, though Rootspring seemed to see—it must have been a spirit."

Shadowsight shook his head. "Great StarClan! Is he okay?"

"I don't know." Bristlefrost's voice cracked as she spoke. "I had hoped to see him when I went in . . . but I couldn't stay. I hoped *you* might have seen him."

Shadowsight met her eyes and shook his head sadly. "I wish I had," he mewed. "But the Dark Forest is a big, confusing place. My not seeing him doesn't mean that he isn't all right."

Bristlefrost took a deep, shuddering breath, as though she was trying to hold on to her courage.

"How did you get in?" Shadowsight asked.

"I dreamed my way there," Bristlefrost replied.

Shadowsight nodded, impressed. "It isn't easy. It took me a few tries before I could focus on the darkness enough to stay . . . but even so, it isn't for everyone."

Bristlefrost was opening her mouth as if to ask what he meant, when Mothwing returned and set down a leaf in front of Shadowsight with two or three poppy seeds on it.

"Walking in the Dark Forest is very dangerous," Mothwing said, leaving Shadowsight wondering how much of their conversation she'd overheard. "I hope that your injuries show you how serious this is. Dreaming your way into the Dark Forest isn't like just nipping over to the Gathering Island or visiting another Clan." Giving him a gentle prod, she added, "You'll be all right. Lick those up, then lie down and rest."

Shadowsight obeyed, feeling the skillful rasp of Mothwing's tongue as she cleaned his wounds. Soon the pain in his leg and ear started to fade slightly, but the voices of the others sounded a little strange, especially when they were speaking behind him. With an unpleasant jolt, he realized that he could not move his wounded ear anymore.

"I fought Ashfur," he began, knowing how important it was for the others to learn what had happened. "I think Squirrelflight and Bramblestar both got away while I distracted him, but I couldn't bring them back here with me. And then Ashfur bit my leg, and I woke up." He paused for a moment, and then went on, "I have to go back."

"Over my dead body!" Mothwing exclaimed. "I'm your medicine cat, and I absolutely forbid it. Besides, what do you think you could do, with those injuries you have?"

"She's right," Tree meowed, cutting off Shadowsight's instinctive protest. "Surely you've done enough? No cat could ask more of you."

"But Rootspring and Squirrelflight are still in the Dark Forest," Bristlefrost pointed out. "And Bramblestar, if he really did escape from Ashfur. We can't just leave them there and hope for the best!"

"Some cat should go back and help the trapped spirits, too," Shadowsight agreed. "So many cats are trapped there, under Ashfur's control."

Bristlefrost nodded sadly. "I saw Stemleaf, and many others."

Mothwing's eyes widened. "Willowshine?" she asked anxiously.

"No, I didn't see Willowshine," Bristlefrost replied.

"I didn't see her, either," Shadowsight added, noticing how

deeply Mothwing still grieved for the cat who had been her apprentice. "Maybe she's also escaped Ashfur. Maybe she and Rootspring have found each other."

Mothwing let out a long sigh. "I hope you're right."

"Ashfur is planning to take over StarClan and the living Clans," Shadowsight continued. "As well as the spirits he's controlling, he seems to have many of the Dark Forest cats working for him."

"How many are there?" Bristlefrost asked.

Shadowsight shook his head uncertainly. "I can't be sure."

"Ashfur is worse than a fox in a fit," Tree grunted.

"It's all come out of his obsession with winning back Squirrelflight," Shadowsight meowed. "Of course Squirrelflight wants nothing to do with him, but however many times she says no, Ashfur is clearly going to attack the Clans, and he's going to do it soon. I *need* to go back."

"With a leg you can't use and a wounded ear?" Mothwing mewed. "I don't think so."

Shadowsight could only think that he had to go, with or without his medicine cat's permission. "I'll cope somehow," he insisted. "I have to."

The sun was rising higher in the sky, its rays glittering on the surface of the Moonpool. Shadowsight drew a long breath, thankful for the warm touch on his fur after the dreary chill of the Dark Forest.

A moment later, he stiffened at the sound of rustling in the bushes at the top of the spiral path. Tree and Bristlefrost sprang up, and Bristlefrost unsheathed her claws, only to relax as the newcomer emerged into the open: It was Tigerstar.

"Shadowsight!" he called, bounding down the path. "Thank StarClan you're alive!"

His eyes were full of relief as he halted beside the group of cats. Warmth crept through Shadowsight's pelt at the sight of his father, but at the same time he realized that there was no way Tigerstar would allow him to go back into the Dark Forest. He tried to get up to greet his father, wobbling on three legs, and Tigerstar's expression changed to deep shock at the sight of his son's injuries. He sank down at Shadowsight's side as if his own limbs wouldn't support him anymore.

"You got those injuries in the Dark Forest?" he meowed. A shudder passed through him; Shadowsight found it hard to meet his wide, stricken gaze. "Haven't you listened to a word I've told you about how dangerous it is in there?"

Shadowsight sat down again beside his father, and he and Bristlefrost told the story of what had happened in the Dark Forest. Tigerstar listened without interrupting, only the horror in his eyes showing what he felt.

"I'm bringing you back to ShadowClan now," he announced briskly when the tale was at an end. "You've done the best you can; you've tried to make up for the way Ashfur tricked you. No cat can blame you, or expect more of you now."

Shadowsight felt a sinking in his belly at his father's words; clearly, Tigerstar did not expect to be disobeyed. He took a deep breath, bracing himself to defy his father.

"No," he mewed. "I have to go back in."

Tigerstar glared at him. "Have you got bees in your brain?"

he demanded. "No way are you going anywhere near that place again."

"But I *have* to," Shadowsight argued. "I'm needed there."

His father let out an irritable snort. "You almost didn't make it back," he pointed out. "Just look at you! What if you're not so lucky next time?"

"I think Shadowsight is right," Bristlefrost meowed, facing up to the angry ShadowClan leader. "Rootspring is still in the Dark Forest. Bramblestar and Squirrelflight, too. We can't leave them behind. I tried to dream myself in," she added, "but I couldn't make myself stay. Somehow, Shadowsight can focus well enough to stay in the Dark Forest, and that's why we need him."

Tigerstar didn't reply, though Shadowsight saw the fur rise along his spine, revealing the fear he wouldn't express out loud. "I can't allow it," he snapped at Shadowsight.

"Tigerstar, you're not thinking this through," Mothwing said. Shadowsight stared at her—after her reaction earlier, he had been sure that she would take his father's side. "At first I thought he shouldn't go, but now I'm not so sure. Shadowsight knows the way in," the medicine cat continued, "and if we don't support him, we may all end up regretting it. If we can avoid a battle like the first one we fought against the Dark Forest, then we must, right? We have to get our cats back and stop Ashfur before it's too late."

An expression of dull fury gathered on Tigerstar's face as he listened to golden she-cat. "I do not appreciate all of you arguing with me," he grumbled. "In any case, Shadowsight needs to rest before we make a decision. And Mothwing—remember that *I'm* your Clan leader now."

"And Shadowsight and I are your medicine cats," Mothwing retorted. "We have to act for the good of the Clan—for the good of *all* the Clans."

"Fine," Tigerstar snarled. Reaching out a paw, he gently pushed Shadowsight down onto his belly. "Now get up."

Shadowsight did his best to balance, but his injured leg gave way under him and he flopped down onto the stones again. His fur burned with embarrassment, even though he knew that his father was only trying to protect him.

"All right, maybe I'm not fit to fight Ashfur again just yet," he muttered.

Mothwing sighed. "Right now, you would lose a fight with a mouse."

"But my leg will get better," Shadowsight went on, reluctantly accepting the judgment of the older medicine cat. "I'm going back—and soon. Rootspring, Bramblestar, and Squirrelflight are still in there, and who knows what danger they're facing?"

CHAPTER 19

❧

Rootspring was surrounded. Stemleaf and the other blank-eyed spirit cats had closed in on him where he stood with Willowshine and Squirrelflight on either side. After their first words, the spirits had remained eerily silent, but Rootspring couldn't doubt the menace in their stance and their bristling fur.

He looked frantically around, trying to see a gap between the spirits where they might make a dash for freedom. But though there was enough space between the spirit cats that a single cat might slip through, he wasn't sure that all three of them could escape that way.

And I don't want to think about what will happen if they get their claws into us.

The dead Clan cats, led by Stemleaf, were closing in, creeping closer and closer, the gaps between them narrowing with every heartbeat. Rootspring could see in their eyes that they meant to hurt him and the others, whether they tried to flee or not. He remembered that even if he could slip past them and shake off their pursuit, he was still in the Dark Forest, and he might be stuck there forever.

Trying to escape can't make this any worse. And if they chase me,

Willowshine and Squirrelflight might be able to make a break for it.

Rootspring lowered his head and charged toward the nearest pair of dead-eyed cats, feeling the brush of their fur against his as he barreled between them. For a single heart-beat, he struggled with panic at the thought that he had failed: that they would bundle him to the ground and pin him down, where he would be helpless, at their mercy.

Then he felt nothing at all, except for the slap of his paws on the ground as he ran and ran.

Yes! I've escaped!

But Rootspring knew scarcely a moment of triumph before a paw clamped down hard on his tail. He yowled in shock at the pain in his hindquarters as his momentum carried him on a few paw steps further, only for his whole body to fly backward and hit the ground with a thump. A groan rose from deep in his chest as he realized that he had been caught.

Rough paws clawed at his shoulders. Rootspring twisted his neck to see the spirit of his own Clanmate, Sandynose, dragging him back to the others.

"Sandynose!" he exclaimed desperately. "It's me, Rootspring. Don't you recognize me?"

But the former SkyClan cat did not respond; there was no emotion in his blank eyes, as if he had never seen Rootspring before.

"Okay, you can sheathe your claws," Rootspring went on, gasping as Sandynose dug harder into his shoulder. "I get the point. I'm not going to try to escape again. . . ."

But the spirit cat didn't let up, dragging and pushing

Rootspring through the undergrowth, seeming not to care about the branches that raked his side, nor the sharp stones that he stumbled over.

As they returned, Rootspring struggled to dig up at least a scrap of optimism and courage from within his heart. Even if he never made it out of the Dark Forest, he told himself, but ended up stuck there as another mindless follower of Ashfur, the Clans would surely unite against their enemy now. Bramblestar had escaped, which meant he might make it back to the Clans to tell his story. And if the Clans united against Ashfur and his followers, surely they would be able to defeat him.

I have to believe that!

But when Sandynose dragged him back to his companions, and Rootspring saw a battered and dazed Squirrelflight being beaten and pinned down by Stemleaf, while Berrynose stood guard over Willowshine, he felt as if his last traces of hope were vanishing like rain sinking into dry ground.

I don't think we will ever escape this place.

Rootspring crouched near the shore of the island, feeling the mud soak into his belly fur and between his paw pads. Darkstripe was standing nearby, his claws flexing in and out; Rootspring knew the Dark Forest warrior was ready to leap on him if he so much as twitched a whisker.

More than anything, he wanted to talk to Squirrelflight, but Stemleaf and the other spirit cats had dragged her and Willowshine away to a different part of the island. Now and again, he caught a glimpse of the ThunderClan deputy and the dead medicine cat, but there were too many cats around them for him to make any kind of rescue or escape attempt. And Ashfur had all of them in his control.

Even the sight of Darkstripe, the large, lean tom's yellow eyes so cold and pitiless, sent a chill through Rootspring. It seemed that Ashfur couldn't control the Dark Forest cats—so how ruthless would Darkstripe have to be to be helping Ashfur *willingly*? That alone told Rootspring how stupid he would be to launch an attack against him.

It just won't work.

The thought of the danger he was in, of how securely he was trapped, made Rootspring's heart sink so fast he was surprised it didn't break out of his chest and drop down into the mud at his paws. There was no way out. He and Squirrelflight would be imprisoned in the Dark Forest forever. What terrified Rootspring most of all was the knowledge that, sooner or later, Ashfur would come for them, too, would turn them into blank-eyed slaves, mindless and condemned to do his bidding in this terrible place between life and death.

Even if I were willing to leave my Clan, I would never get to be mates with Bristlefrost, he realized wretchedly. *I'd never even get to see her again.*

The thought stirred something within Rootspring. Determination hardened inside him, to do everything he could to escape. He hated the idea of leaving Squirrelflight and Willowshine behind, but he knew that he was going to have a better chance of freeing them if he himself was free. *Maybe I could find Bramblestar and help him. . . .*

Rootspring rested his chin on his paws, slitting his eyes as if he were falling into a doze. Instead, he slyly looked all around, trying to work out which would be the best way for him to run, which direction offered the best chance of escape. He noticed that Stemleaf and the other trapped spirits were mostly gathered around Squirrelflight and Willowshine.

Of course they are. If Ashfur had to choose, there's only one cat he'd try to make sure could not get out of here.

Realizing this was his chance, Rootspring let himself sink onto one side, close his eyes, and pretend to slip into deeper sleep, though he didn't know if cats in the Dark Forest even needed to sleep. In spite of his frantic flight away from Stemleaf, and being dragged across the forest as a prisoner, he did not feel the least bit tired. But none of the cats around him paid him any attention, so he assumed they were not aware of anything unusual.

Rootspring extended all his senses to make sure that he couldn't hear or scent any of Ashfur's spirits padding in his direction. Once he was fairly certain that no cat was heading toward him, he rolled over onto his belly, his limbs tensed and ready. He cracked open his eyes and saw that a gap in the crowd had opened up between him and the shore of the island, with all his captors' attention on Squirrelflight.

This is it!

Taking a deep breath, and swallowing his fear as if it were a tough piece of prey, Rootspring crept forward as silently as he could. He gradually drew closer to the gap, hoping to give himself the best chance of a head start. He risked one glance over his shoulder, and spotted Squirrelflight gazing at him, a sudden light in her green eyes. She sprang to her paws so quickly that Rootspring was afraid she was about to sound the alarm, to alert Darkstripe and Ashfur's other followers so that *she* could escape.

Instead, Squirrelflight let out an ear-splitting screech and leaped on the nearest cat—Berrynose—thrusting him aside and dodging between two others as if she were making her own bid for freedom. All the spirit cats converged on her, leaving Rootspring clear.

Rootspring wanted to call out to her, to tell her not to give up, and reassure her that he would do all he could to find Bramblestar and help get her out of there. But he knew he couldn't risk alerting his captors.

Unseen, Rootspring slipped away, clenching his jaws and his muscles to keep from bolting for the edge of the island, in case the sucking sound of his paw steps in the mud gave him away. It was hard to control his movements, especially with his ears swiveled backward, straining to pick up any sound from the center of the island.

He was drawing closer to the shore when he heard a furious yowling break out behind him. They had noticed he was gone; Squirrelflight's distraction had only lasted so long. Stemleaf's voice was raised in a chilling wail as he gave chase.

Rootspring dodged back and forth, looking for a safe space to take cover, even while knowing there was no such thing as a safe space in the Dark Forest. But mist had begun to gather, ragged strips of it floating through the trees like ghostly paws stretching out to capture him. Through the pale fog, Rootspring saw the massive trunk of a tree looming up in front of him. He tried to skid to a halt, but he was too late; he ran full-pelt into it, his head thumping against the rough bark.

The whole forest spun around Rootspring as he tried to skip past the tree and keep heading for the shore, but the mist was thickening with every heartbeat. Somehow, there seemed to be more trees than he remembered, appearing out of nowhere to cut off his escape.

Hindered by both the trees and the mist, Rootspring could not pick up speed. Above the sound of his paws on the ground and his panicked breathing, he could hear his pursuers drawing closer.

At last, he emerged through a gap in the trees. The air was clearer here, and the shore was closer, but at once Rootspring spotted Stemleaf and Sandynose pressing in on him from one side, while from the other side, Dark Forest cats he did not recognize were charging toward him.

It's no use, he thought despairingly. *They've caught me!*

Hot rage swelled up inside Rootspring, driving away his despair and kindling new resolve within him.

"I'll show you!" he yowled. "I won't let you take me alive!" *If I am even still alive, here in the Dark Forest.*

Baring his teeth, he charged at Stemleaf with his claws unsheathed, trying to ignore the voices in his head that were telling him it wasn't these cats' fault. He didn't like the way he was forced to attack, but compassion and understanding for the trapped spirits would not help him survive now.

The former ThunderClan warrior was taken by surprise, darting aside to avoid Rootspring's onrush. Rootspring went flying past him, barely feeling the scratch of claws along his flank. At once the ground gave way under his paws. Losing his balance, he went rolling and tumbling down a steep slope, until . . .

Splash!

As the water surged over his head, Rootspring realized he had fallen into the dark lake that surrounded the island, struggling just as he had on that day, many moons ago, when he was an apprentice goaded by Kitepaw and Turtlepaw. Then, he had almost lost his life. Now, as the cold and stagnant water swirled around him, he forced his eyes open only to see that it was completely opaque. He couldn't swim; he couldn't even tell which way was up, or how deeply he had plunged.

This isn't ordinary water . . . it's like it's seeping through my body.

He could feel his strength draining away as his memories overwhelmed him: memories of the day he had fallen into the lake because of his arrogance, his rage against the cats who were taunting him.

And there was no Bristlefrost to save him now.

But the thought of Bristlefrost gave Rootspring the will to survive. His determination to live swelled within him, fueled by his wish to see her again. Bristlefrost was the cat he cared about the most, and he was *not* going to leave her to wonder what had happened to him, to live out her life never knowing where he had gone, or why he had not come back to her.

I don't want to die like this, alone, without Bristlefrost. I want to go on fighting Ashfur by her side. And if I must die today, then I want my death to mean something.

Even though the dark water was sapping his strength, Rootspring flailed his legs to turn himself what he thought was the right way up. Then he kicked hard, forcing himself upward until his head broke the surface. He gulped in mouthfuls of air, still paddling frantically until he felt solid ground beneath his working paws. Clambering out onto a muddy bank, he scrambled for cover in the hollow of a dead tree, listening for sounds of the spirit cats who had pursued him.

After a moment, he heard voices drifting across the water from the island.

"He's dead. He must be dead."

"Yeah, there's no way any cat could escape from the water."

Relief tingled through Rootspring's body as the voices gradually grew more distant. The Dark Forest cats had given up and were heading back. He was about to emerge from his hiding place and flee in the opposite direction, but then he remembered that he was still trapped in the Dark Forest, with no way out. And something inside him refused to let him leave without doing all that he could for Squirrelflight.

In spite of his desperation to put as much distance as possible between himself and Ashfur's prison, he followed the lakeshore until he reached a rotting tree that leaned out over the water. He scrambled up into the branches until he had a good view of the island, flinching as the stinking bark flaked off the trunk under his claws.

Rootspring could see that the spirit cats had wrestled Squirrelflight to the ground; Berrynose and Rosepetal were holding her pinned down with their paws on her shoulders and hindquarters.

Willowshine, the other prisoner, was approaching them. Watching her, Rootspring was glad to see some cat trying to help Squirrelflight, but at the same time he was apprehensive. He didn't expect a medicine cat to be able to hold her own against all these fierce warriors.

Ashfur's followers will hurt both of them, or worse. . . .

Willowshine was drawing closer, seeming to wait for the right moment to attack, to rescue Squirrelflight. Rootspring's breath came short as he watched her, and he flexed his claws, wishing that he could give the medicine cat his strength and his fighting skills.

Now, Willowshine! Now!

But as the moments passed, a sick realization crept into Rootspring's belly. Willowshine wasn't going to attack. *She's not waiting for the right time—she's being controlled by Ashfur!* Rootspring's gut clenched in horror as he saw her pad up to the ThunderClan cat and stand there watching, her eyes no longer narrowed.

Squirrelflight tensed, tossing her head. "What in StarClan's name is happening?" she demanded.

Willowshine said nothing, just went on staring at Squirrelflight out of wide, *blank* eyes.

Squirrelflight's whole body seemed to shrink inward in despair. Rootspring felt devastated, too.

Does that mean Ashfur's here? Rootspring looked around, but could see no sign of the evil tom. *But I've hardly taken my eyes off Willowshine since we were captured,* he told himself. *So when could Ashfur have taken control of her?*

A cold feeling spread from Rootspring's ears to the tips of his claws, as if he were turning into a cat made of ice. He realized with horror that Willowshine must have been Ashfur's creature from the very first, when she pulled him into the Moonpool. She had only been *pretending* to help him. Maybe she had even set him up to follow Mapleshade into the collapsing cave, so that the falling rocks or the fog would kill him.

No wonder she looked surprised when I turned up by the lake!

He realized too that somehow she must have been connected to the other spirit cats—that would explain how Stemleaf had been able to follow them when they were trying to escape, always turning up wherever they ran.

And that's why she kept her eyes slitted, Rootspring thought. *It wasn't the light hurting them at all. It was so I wouldn't see that her eyes are blank!* He let out a groan, disgusted with himself. *I should have realized that from the very beginning!*

But as his fury ebbed, a pang of pity for Willowshine stabbed through Rootspring. He remembered her when she was alive, how loyal she had been to her Clan and her calling as a medicine cat. It hurt him deeply to see her like this, reduced to obeying Ashfur's evil commands.

But Rootspring's situation was so perilous that he had to push Willowshine's problems to the back of his mind, telling himself that all was not lost. If he and the other Clan cats could defeat Ashfur, she would be free of him, able to travel on to StarClan with the rest of the spirits.

What can I do? he asked himself desperately. *Maybe I should try to find Shadowsight. I guess he must be around here somewhere.*

But just as he thought that things could not get any worse, Rootspring's gaze was drawn to more movement on the island. Ashfur himself appeared, dragging something from behind the roots of a fallen tree that coiled up into the air like snakes poised to strike. Rootspring drew in a harsh breath as he recognized what it was: a limp body covered in dark tabby fur.

Bramblestar!

Rootspring wondered what Ashfur would want with the ThunderClan leader's body now. Surely it had already served its purpose. Then he realized that it wasn't that Ashfur wanted it for himself anymore: He just didn't want Bramblestar to have it, or be able to reunite with it. Rootspring imagined the ThunderClan leader desperately searching the Dark Forest for it, and for Squirrelflight, his hope of finding them gradually draining away, because even though his spirit was free, he couldn't return to the living world and the leadership of ThunderClan without his body.

Has Ashfur really already won?

As Rootspring sat gazing out at the island, he heard the scrabble of claws at the bottom of the tree. Tensing, he spun around, sliding out his claws as he braced himself to fight to the death.

The newcomer was a skinny white tom with a nasty scar running across his belly. At first, Rootspring thought that one of Ashfur's spirits had caught up with him, until he noticed that this cat's eyes weren't blank. *So he's a Dark Forest cat . . . but is he in league with Ashfur or not?*

"Don't come any closer," he warned with a threatening growl.

"Keep your fur on," the white tom grunted as he clambered up the tree, though he stopped on a lower branch, well out of the range of Rootspring's claws. "I'm a friend."

"I don't have any friends in the Dark Forest," Rootspring snarled.

"You don't? Then you're not the cat I think you are. I can see you're a living cat. Don't you have something to do with that scrawny little gray tabby I met a while ago?"

"Shadowsight?" In his amazement, Rootspring forgot to be wary. "You've seen Shadowsight?"

The white tom nodded. "Yeah. He was fighting Ashfur, and then he just . . . disappeared. I guess he went back to the living world."

Did he? Rootspring hoped the young medicine cat had made it home. Still, he wished some cat had seen it happen. In any case, these words made Rootspring slightly less distrustful of the Dark Forest tom. His story agreed with what Squirrelflight had said earlier. He only prayed Shadowsight had managed to escape.

"So who are you, and what do you want with me?" he asked.

"My name is Snowtuft," the tom replied. "I helped Shadowsight, and I'll help you, if you like."

Rootspring narrowed his gaze, still not sure if the tom

could be trusted. *I've already been deceived by one cat,* he thought, with another pang of sorrow for Willowshine. *But StarClan knows, I could do with some help. Maybe if I stay on my guard . . .*

"Why do you want to help me?" he asked.

"I don't like the way the forest is shrinking," Snowtuft replied.

"Shrinking?" asked Rootspring. He remembered the bizarre feelings he'd had when he was following Mapleshade at Willowshine's orders—like he was moving in circles, the forest seeming to fold back on itself. "Is that what's happening?"

"Oh, yes." Snowtuft nodded. "There are plenty of places I remember that just . . . don't exist anymore. A few cats, too." He paused, looking troubled. "Anyway—most of all, I especially don't like the creeping mist. I reckon it's something to do with Ashfur, so if I can do anything to help you living cats get rid of him, I will."

That makes sense, Rootspring thought. The little he'd seen of the changing forest and the terrifying mist was enough for him to imagine how a cat must feel if he had no chance of escaping this place. "Okay," he meowed. "I'm called Rootspring. I'll be glad of your help if you really mean it. But put a paw wrong, and I will rip your pelt off."

Snowtuft let out a grunt, sounding half amused, then scrambled farther up the tree until he could crouch on the branch at Rootspring's side. "I saw what happened on the island," he told Rootspring. "What are you going to do now?"

Rootspring was growing calmer, reassured that Snowtuft

didn't seem hostile. It was encouraging to be facing a cat whose eyes appeared normal, not blank and unfocused, as he'd seen in Ashfur's followers. Even so, his muscles remained braced, ready to fight if the Dark Forest cat should suddenly turn on him.

Rootspring's heart ached to think of Willowshine, Stem-leaf, and the countless other spirit cats who were trapped on the island. *I can never fully trust a Dark Forest cat . . . but the Dark Forest is filled with cats I could trust, if only I could free them from Ashfur's control!*

"I have to work out a way of breaking Ashfur's hold over the spirit cats," he murmured to Snowtuft at last. "Then maybe we'd have a chance of defeating Ashfur once and for all."

I just wish I had the faintest idea how to pull that off!

CHAPTER 20

✿

Bristlefrost paced restlessly along the edge of the Moonpool, every hair on her pelt urging her to plunge into its depths and force her way back into the Dark Forest. Only her knowledge of how stupid that would be was holding her back. *I'd just end up cold and wet . . . and no closer to Rootspring.*

"We *can't* give up on him!" she insisted to Mothwing. The medicine cat looked infuriatingly calm, sitting beside the pool with her tail wrapped around her paws. "I know he's in real trouble just now," Bristlefrost continued. "He's strong and brave, but can he really get himself out of it without any cat's help?"

She didn't know what was going on in the Dark Forest, but she could imagine Rootspring's determination, as well as his fear, and she felt her heart shaking with pride and terror. "I can't believe Ashfur has caught him," she told Mothwing. "And I don't believe he's dead. And as long as that's true, I'm going to do whatever I can to go back into the Dark Forest and find him."

Stepping away from the side of the Moonpool, Bristlefrost cast a glance up at the cliff overlooking the hollow. Tree stood there, with Tigerstar at his side, both cats gazing down at her with a mixture of curiosity and disbelief.

Even after everything that's happened, they still don't believe I'm the right warrior to go back there. They don't think I can help. Despair threatened to overwhelm her. *And maybe they're right. . . .*

At least Tree was looking optimistic, though Bristlefrost wondered if that might just be a desperate hope. He would surely snatch at any possibility if he thought that it might save his son's life.

Bristlefrost began her restless pacing again, but she had hardly taken more than a couple of paw steps when she heard movement from the bushes at the top of the hollow. She glanced over her shoulder, half expecting to see the Sisters returning. Instead it was Graystripe who appeared, thrusting the branches aside with his powerful shoulders, and following him, her slender figure slipping through more easily, came Bristlefrost's mother, Ivypool.

Relief flowed over Bristlefrost like a cool breeze on a hot day. It was heartening to see ThunderClan cats: Graystripe, who had returned so unexpectedly to lead the Clan, and Ivypool, who as well as being her mother was one of their strongest and bravest Clanmates, and had visited the Dark Forest countless times in the buildup to the Great Battle.

Maybe she can help me!

Bristlefrost bounded to the bottom of the spiral path to meet Graystripe and Ivypool as they padded down. "It's so good to see you!" she exclaimed.

Graystripe gave her a friendly nod. "I thought it was time to find out what's going on," he meowed. "And Ivypool seemed to think I needed an escort. Maybe she thought I would get lost."

"Clan leaders don't go wandering around on their own," Ivypool retorted, with a glimmer of amusement in her eyes as she looked at Graystripe. Stepping forward, she touched noses with Bristlefrost. "I wanted to see you," she murmured. "Your father and I are worried about you."

"You don't need to be," Bristlefrost responded, though she wondered if that was true. "I'm fine."

"So what has been happening?" Graystripe asked. "I suppose Rootspring and Shadowsight are still over there, in the Dark Forest?"

"There's no sign of Rootspring," Bristlefrost told him, a heavy feeling in her belly as she spoke the words. "Shadowsight came back, after he fought with Ashfur. He wants to go there again, but he's too badly wounded."

Graystripe gazed along the shore of the Moonpool to where Mothwing sat beside Shadowsight's inert body. "Poor little scrap," he muttered. "I'd better have a word with Mothwing."

He headed toward the medicine cat, leaving Bristlefrost and Ivypool behind. Bristlefrost turned to her mother, but before she could speak, Tigerstar came hurrying down the path, brushed past them with a brief nod, and went to join Mothwing and the others. Tree, however, stayed where he was at the top of the hollow; Bristlefrost realized that nothing mattered to him right now except for the return of his son.

"Ivypool, there's something that I have to tell you," she

mewed, turning to her mother. "And I don't think you're going to like it."

Ivypool's ears twitched up. "Why am I not surprised?" she murmured. "What have you done this time?"

"I . . . I've been into the Dark Forest," Bristlefrost replied.

Ivypool's blue eyes widened. Bristlefrost realized that whatever her mother had been expecting, it wasn't that. "How did you get there?" she asked.

"I dreamed myself in. I listened to what Harestar said, and what Mothwing told Willowshine, and it worked." She gave her whiskers an impatient twitch. "But it was no use. When I got to the Dark Forest, I only managed to stay there for a few heartbeats. Ivypool," she continued, leaning closer to her mother, "you've got to help me. You trained in the Dark Forest, spying for ThunderClan. Please tell me how you did it."

For a few moments, Ivypool hesitated, her blue eyes dark with thought. Bristlefrost dug her claws hard into the ground; she was convinced her mother was going to refuse.

"No," Ivypool murmured. "I know the place better than you. I should be the one to go."

Bristlefrost's chest clenched. "No—"

"Don't argue," her mother said, firmly. "If you knew the Dark Forest as well as I do, you'd know it's no place for such a young warrior."

Bristlefrost stood as tall as she could make herself. "Maybe not," she replied. "But this is my fight. This is my problem to solve."

Ivypool stared at her for a long moment, her dark blue

eyes two pools of shimmering sadness. Then she let out a long sigh. "I don't like this, but I suppose I can't convince you not to go?"

"No—I have to. I have to find Rootspring and help him!"

Ivypool gave her a hard look, and when she spoke, her voice had an edge as sharp as fangs. "I went through all that with my sister," she meowed. "And now you're telling me you want to mate with a cat from another Clan?"

"I wish I could!" Bristlefrost couldn't stop her voice from shaking. "But you don't need to worry," she went on more calmly. "Rootspring and I have talked about it, and we decided it's not possible. We've realized we're both too loyal to our Clans to think of leaving them." *Though I'm beginning to have doubts. . . .* Bristlefrost knew enough not to share that last part.

"Thank StarClan for that," Ivypool murmured. "I know it's hard—but, believe me, it's for the best."

"But all the same, I can't leave him alone in the Dark Forest," Bristlefrost declared.

A light seemed to flicker in Ivypool's eyes, her sadness chased away by relief and pride. "You're so very brave," she said, stroking her tail along Bristlefrost's side. "*So* brave."

"Please tell me what to do."

"I can only tell you what worked for me," Ivypool responded. "You know about thinking dark thoughts as you go to sleep?" Bristlefrost nodded. "Well, my thoughts were very dark," Ivypool continued. "There was a time when I was furiously jealous of Dovewing, because she was so special, and I . . . I wasn't. I think that was what carried me over into the

Dark Forest—at first, anyway. And afterward it got easier . . . maybe because I was scared out of my fur every time I set paw there. Or maybe because I knew that ThunderClan needed me to be there."

"*You* were so brave—" Bristlefrost began, only to break off as Ivypool slapped her tail over her mouth. Following her mother's gaze, Bristlefrost saw that Graystripe had left the group of cats beside the Moonpool and was heading toward them.

"Don't say anything about this to Graystripe," Ivypool warned her in an undertone. "He's Clan leader now, and if he forbids you to go, you will have to do as he tells you."

Bristlefrost had time for a brief nod before Graystripe padded up to them.

"Well, the medicine cats seem to know what they're doing." The old gray warrior's voice was a deep rumble in his chest. "Though I'm not sure Tigerstar agrees with them." He gave his pelt a shake. "Time we were off, Ivypool."

Bristlefrost began to relax as Graystripe took the first paw steps up the spiral path. Then she grew tense again as he turned and looked down at her, fixing her with a compelling look from his yellow eyes.

"I suspect there are things you could tell me, if I asked you to," he meowed, "but I won't ask. I trust you, Bristlefrost. You're a brave and intelligent warrior, and I know you'll make the best decisions for your Clan. And for a certain young Sky-Clan tom. Do what you must—and may StarClan light your path."

"Thank you," Bristlefrost whispered, dipping her head in deepest respect.

Graystripe continued up the path. Before Ivypool followed him, she pressed her muzzle into Bristlefrost's shoulder. "Graystripe is right," she mewed. "You're brave and capable, and if any cat can do this, you can. But . . ." Her voice shook, and she took a deep breath to steady it. "Take care, my dear daughter," she added, then raced up the path without waiting for a reply or looking back. Bristlefrost watched until she and Graystripe had disappeared through the bushes.

With new determination, Bristlefrost padded back toward the Moonpool to join Tigerstar and the two medicine cats. Before she reached them, Shadowsight came limping up to meet her, still balancing on only three legs after the injuries he'd picked up in the Dark Forest. At least the bleeding had stopped from the wounds on his leg and his ear; Mothwing had poulticed them with herbs, wrapped around with cobweb. Now Shadowsight seemed calmer, no longer in such pain.

"Shadowsight, you know how to stay in the Dark Forest," Bristlefrost began eagerly. "Please, will you tell me how I can stay there, too?" *And maybe with Ivypool's advice, I can find Rootspring this time.*

For a few heartbeats, Shadowsight was silent, blinking uncertainly. "I'm not sure," he replied at last. "I'd like to help you, Bristlefrost, you know that, but I think maybe being able to stay in the Dark Forest isn't a *good* thing."

Bristlefrost lashed her tail in frustration. "What does that mean?"

Shadowsight looked down. "Sometimes when I'm in the Dark Forest, I can feel it seeping into my thoughts. I feel darker, angrier, more hopeless. I think that's what the older cats mean when they say the Dark Forest can 'turn a good cat bad.'"

Bristlefrost stared at him. "There's nothing wrong with you, Shadowsight," she said evenly. "Every cat feels that way in the Dark Forest."

"But most of you wake up," Shadowsight insisted. "Don't you see that that's a good thing, Bristlefrost? You wake up because you can't feel that bad for that long. It isn't in you."

"Oh, Shadowsight." Bristlefrost sighed. "You think it *is* in you, somehow?"

"I don't know." The young tom's eyes were sad. "I'm just not sure this is a talent you would want."

"But I *do* want it, Shadowsight," Bristlefrost insisted. "I want to save Rootspring. I'm not worried about myself. We could at least try, couldn't we?" Her voice was taut with desperation. "Please, Shadowsight."

Once again, Shadowsight hesitated for a moment. "We can't be sure what will happen," he reminded her gently. "I might be able to help you cross over to the other side, but that doesn't mean that you will be able to return *as yourself.* Do you understand?"

Bristlefrost clenched her jaws on a wail of fear. In her brief visit to the Dark Forest, while she was dreaming, she had seen enough to know how terrifying it would be to go back there. She couldn't imagine what she would feel if the Dark Forest somehow got *inside* her—if it changed her from within.

But I know that I have to. I have to take the chance—for Rootspring.

"Shadowsight, will you come with me?" she asked impulsively. "I could do with a friend—especially a friend who has been to the Dark Forest before."

"What?" Tigerstar had padded up to his son's side without Bristlefrost's noticing. Now his yowl cut across any response that Shadowsight might have made. "Absolutely not! No way will I agree to that. Over and over again, I've come too close to losing my son for good." He turned to Shadowsight. "Your luck is going to run out if you go on tempting fate like this."

Shadowsight looked torn between his father's anxiety and Bristlefrost's desperate appeal. "I want to go with you, Bristlefrost," he meowed. "I know you won't be able to save Rootspring by yourself. But Tigerstar isn't exaggerating when he talks about the risks. And to be honest, I'm not sure I could do it again and come back . . . myself."

"If you're seriously considering this," Tigerstar growled, "I'll have you dragged back to the ShadowClan camp and put under guard in Ashfur's old prison."

Shadowsight met his father's furious gaze steadily. "I was freed from that prison," he responded. "I'm back to my medicine-cat duties now, and I won't go back."

"We'll see about that!" Tigerstar snorted. "I'm not just your father . . . I'm your Clan leader. And it's my job to protect you."

Shadowsight gazed at his father for a moment, then suddenly straightened. Bristlefrost thought that in spite of his wounds and his weakness, he had somehow taken on extra authority. "I respect you, Tigerstar," he began, "as my father and my Clan leader. And I appreciate your support. But I'm old enough to make my own decisions. I'm a medicine cat, and I'll use my abilities to help the Clans in any way I can."

"Whether I approve or not?" Tigerstar snarled.

"Whether you approve or not," Shadowsight repeated steadily.

Mothwing had padded up to join Bristlefrost and the others, dipping her head to the furious Tigerstar. "There's no point in pretending any longer that Shadowsight isn't a full medicine cat," she told him. "And that means that in a real emergency, not even a Clan leader can tell him what to do."

A light seemed to glimmer in Shadowsight's eyes at Mothwing's taking his side, after all the problems he'd had with her in the past. *She's finally accepting him as a real medicine cat again,* Bristlefrost thought.

Tigerstar stared at Mothwing, eyes blazing, looking as if he had so much to say that he couldn't get a single word out. Eventually, he took a deep breath and let it out again as if he was doing all he could to control himself.

"I'm wondering whether a medicine cat with more experience than Shadowsight might be a better choice to escort Bristlefrost," he meowed, clearly making a massive effort to speak calmly. "How about you, Mothwing, since you're ShadowClan's senior medicine cat now?"

Mothwing's eyes narrowed, as if she suspected that the ShadowClan leader was flattering her, while Shadowsight seemed to be suppressing a growl. Bristlefrost guessed he was annoyed that Tigerstar didn't seem to have listened to anything that he had just said.

"I'm not sure you're right," Mothwing responded calmly. "Since Willowshine died, I've been feeling the pull of my old Clan, and wondering whether they need me, now that they don't have a medicine cat anymore. If they do, I should probably stay on this side of the Moonpool. Besides," she added, "as a cat I cared for very much once pointed out, I don't exactly have an easy relationship with StarClan." She looked down at her paws, and Bristlefrost felt the weight of her grief for Willowshine. "Anyway," she said after a moment, looking up, "I believe that Shadowsight is by far the best cat to take this on."

"Fine." Tigerstar kept his voice calm, but his eyes still flashed with anger. "I suppose my opinion is worthless. Let's get on with it, then." He spun around and paced off around the edge of the Moonpool.

Bristlefrost watched him go, then turned back to Shadowsight. There was no time to lose. "Okay, what do I do?" she asked.

Shadowsight rested his tail on her shoulder, a comforting gesture. "I think, before we go any further, we should ask for advice. Maybe there's another way to travel into the Dark Forest—a way to go there but keep the dark thoughts at bay."

"What do you mean?" asked Bristlefrost, frustrated. "Advice from whom? I want to get to Rootspring as quickly as I can." *And tell him that I love him,* she added silently.

"The Sisters have been very patient with us," Shadowsight went on, "but I think it's time to check in with them and see what they've come up with."

Bristlefrost took in a breath. *The Sisters—of course!* They had made clear they were willing to help the Clans, and Bristlefrost could think of no group better suited to guide them through the tricky corridors of the spirit world.

Shadowsight turned to Tree, who had watched everything in silence from the top of the hollow. The two cats just stared at each other; Bristlefrost thought it was as if some silent discussion was passing between them.

Eventually, Tree nodded. "I'll go and speak to them," he meowed.

"They said they were willing to help in any way they could," Shadowsight told him. "They seem to know a lot about the spirit world . . . the darkness and the light."

"And they were willing to help. Yes, it's time to ask them," Tree agreed. There was none of the usual reluctance in Tree's eyes that Bristlefrost had seen before when his kin were mentioned. She guessed that nothing was more important to him than helping his stranded son.

The yellow tom padded around the top of the hollow and vanished through the bushes. After all that had gone wrong, Bristlefrost felt the first tingle of hope in her pads. *Maybe we really can pull this off.*

After Tree left, Bristlefrost hunted again, bringing back fresh-kill for Mothwing, Shadowsight, and Tigerstar. By the time they had eaten, it was past sunhigh. Bristlefrost stood with Shadowsight beside the Moonpool, as they waited for

Tree to return with the Sisters from their temporary camp. The young medicine cat was standing on all four paws now, though he looked a little unsteady, and he still could not move the ear that had been injured in the Dark Forest.

While they waited, Bristlefrost felt confidence growing inside her, that somehow the Sisters would be able to help her stay in the Dark Forest without changing herself, so that she could rescue Rootspring. However, she was aware that Tigerstar didn't share her certainty; the ShadowClan leader was shifting his paws impatiently and muttering under his breath, the words too low for Bristlefrost to catch.

"Whatever these Sisters decide to do," he mewed aloud after a while, "Shadowsight must be kept safe. That's the most important thing, and I won't allow anything else."

Before either Shadowsight or Bristlefrost could respond, movement among the bushes at the top of the path announced the return of Tree. He slid out into the open, followed by several of the Sisters. With their thick pelts and wide shoulders, the she-cats were finding it harder to wriggle their way through the branches.

Tree led the way down the path, with Snow, the white cat who was the Sisters' leader, hard on his paws. Several of her campmates followed; Bristlefrost recognized Sunrise, the plump, pale yellow she-cat, and Flurry.

Snow stood beside Tree, confronting the Clan cats, curiosity and annoyance mingling in her expression. "You sent for us?" she asked.

Tigerstar opened his jaws to respond, but Tree forestalled

him, casting a warning glance at the ShadowClan leader. Tigerstar turned half away with an angry shrug.

"The Clans have come up with a way they could use your help," Tree replied to Snow.

"Yes, so you said." Snow's tone was resentful, and her gaze unfriendly. "And we've always been willing. It's you Clan cats who aren't happy to accept us."

Terrified that the white she-cat was going to refuse, Bristlefrost couldn't stop herself, as if she had leaped down a crevasse with all four paws. "A good cat is trapped in the Dark Forest," she meowed. "I need to cross over so that I can bring him back . . . but I need to find a way to stay there, while keeping the darkness from getting inside *me*. We thought maybe you Sisters could help me do that."

Tree took a step forward, bringing him to Bristlefrost's side. "Remember that it's my son, Rootspring, who is trapped," he told Snow. "He nursed alongside Moonlight's kits. He is kin to many of the Sisters, including Sunrise."

Snow kept her blue gaze fixed on Tree. "I've never known a tom like you, Tree," she huffed. "Not one who's had such a *presence* in our lives after leaving us."

Tree glanced at Bristlefrost and rested the tip of his tail on her shoulder. "We're here to do anything we can for a cat we both love," he stated calmly.

For the first time, Bristlefrost did not feel her usual flush of embarrassment, nor her instinct to protest about her feelings for Rootspring. All she cared about was convincing the

Sisters to help the Clans. Once again she imagined him, alone and fearful in the Place of No Stars, and her heart yearned to join him there.

". . . very well," Snow was meowing when Bristlefrost began paying attention again. "We Sisters and the Clans have formed some kind of bond recently. We owe each other a lot. But after we help you today, that has to be the last time the Clans call on us for a favor. At some point, our destinies need to diverge."

Tree inclined his head respectfully to Snow. "If you help us now, the Clans will consider all debts paid."

"But that shouldn't stop you Sisters from asking help from the Clans," Shadowsight put in. "If you ever need us in the future, we will be here."

At that, Tigerstar seemed about to speak once more, then clamped his jaws shut as if stopping himself from arguing.

Snow rolled her eyes. "Once Sunshine and her kits are fit to travel," she meowed, "we will be seeking out some new territory, away from the lake." Then a spark of amusement kindled in her blue eyes. "I've half forgotten what peace and quiet is like—there's always *something* going on around here!" she lamented.

Bristlefrost and the rest of the Clan cats stepped back respectfully as Snow gathered the rest of the Sisters around her. Their heads close together, they began to discuss in low voices what they were going to do.

"I'm so relieved we've found a way for the Sisters to help,"

Bristlefrost murmured to Tree. But glancing at Rootspring's father, she didn't see the same optimism reflected in his face. "What's wrong?" she asked.

"Don't raise your hopes too high," Tree sighed. "That only gives them too far to fall. There's no guarantee that this is going to work. Even if the Sisters can help you strengthen your connection to the Dark Forest, that does not mean that . . ." He let his voice trail off, as if the words were like rose thorns in his mouth. Then, after a moment, he braced himself and went on. "It doesn't mean that you will be able to find Rootspring. And it doesn't mean that you'll ever find your way back here, to the land of the living. Are you sure that you want to take such a risk?"

Bristlefrost felt a sudden warmth toward the yellow tom. Even though he was desperately afraid for his son, he was still giving her the chance to back out.

"I've never been more sure of anything in my life," she responded unhesitatingly, touching Tree's shoulder with the tip of her tail. "This is what I'm meant to do."

CHAPTER 21

❧

Shadowsight stood at the edge of the Moonpool, beside Bristlefrost and the other Clan cats, his claws working impatiently as he watched the Sisters. Their discussion had come to an end, and now they had fallen silent, standing shoulder to shoulder and seeming to stare off into the distance, at nothing.

After a few moments, Snow gave her pelt a shake and transferred her blue gaze to Shadowsight and the others. "The spirit of our sister Moonlight is here with us," she explained. "She is proud to see us all working together."

Shadowsight tried to draw hope from the white she-cat's words, to make himself believe that what they planned to do would be a success.

But he could see that his father did not share his optimism. Tigerstar had never been convinced that the Sisters could help, and his expression was doubtful as he faced Snow. But his only response was a shrug, as he meowed, "Go ahead, then."

The Sisters exchanged bemused glances. "We can't perform the ceremony now," Snow stated. "It is much too early in the day. It must be performed as the sun begins to set."

Shadowsight saw his father open his jaws and spoke loudly before Tigerstar could make some kind of derisive comment. "You have our thanks, for any help you can give."

Snow dipped her head toward him, gratitude in her eyes, and cast a glance toward Flurry. "My campmate tore her pads on some thorns, on our way to this . . . this Moonpond. Would you perhaps be able to find something for it?"

"Well, I don't know—" Tigerstar began.

"Of course we can," Shadowsight interrupted. "I'll do that right away. Tigerstar, would you like to help me?"

He wasn't sure if that was the right thing to say, when his father had been so reluctant to call on the Sisters, and so angry that Shadowsight had insisted on traveling to the Dark Forest. He was unprepared for the look of pleased surprise that spread over Tigerstar's face.

It must mean something to him, Shadowsight thought, *that I want him to be part of this.*

Then Tigerstar gave a sudden start, as if he had just remembered that he was a Clan leader and not a medicine cat. Shadowsight could tell from the rumble in his throat that his father was about to protest that he shouldn't be involved in medicine-cat business. But before he could speak, Shadowsight caught his eye, and with a twitch of his whiskers indicated that he would like a word with him in private.

"Uh . . . sure," the ShadowClan leader muttered. "I'd be glad to help."

"Mothwing, do we have any chervil leaves, or marigold?" Shadowsight asked his fellow medicine cat.

Mothwing shook her head. "No, I used all we had on your leg and ear."

"Then we'll have to go and find some. Come on, Tigerstar."

Tigerstar's ears twitched in surprise at being ordered around by his son, but he followed without any protest.

Before they left the hollow, Shadowsight stopped to examine Flurry's paw. There was a nasty gash right across her pads, and he could imagine how much it had to be hurting her. But at least there hadn't been time for infection to set in.

"Give it a few good licks," he instructed the orange-and-white she-cat. "Make sure that it's completely clean. I'll be back soon to make you a poultice for it."

Flurry dipped her head. "Thank you," she mewed.

As Shadowsight headed up the spiral path with Tigerstar following him, he spotted Bristlefrost down below; the ThunderClan warrior was approaching Snow.

"Do we really have to wait until sunset?" she asked. "Is there really nothing we can do now?"

Snow looked genuinely regretful as she shook her head. "I'm afraid not," she replied. "We have to wait."

Heading across the moor, his senses alert for the sight or scent of the healing herbs, Shadowsight could tell that his father was growing tense. "Is something the matter?" he asked.

Tigerstar halted and let out a gusty sigh. "It's a terrible thing, for a father to come so close to losing his son," he explained. "And so often, too. I wish that you weren't being pulled into all this . . . this mystical thistle-fluff all the time. Dovewing and I feel that danger is creeping up on you, just as if a fox were stalking you."

Shadowsight drew his tail down his father's side. It felt odd to be the cat doing the comforting, when Tigerstar and Dovewing had always been the ones taking such care of him when he was younger. But this was why he had wanted to speak to Tigerstar privately, to reassure him about what was unfamiliar territory for a warrior, and to explain why he felt such a compulsion to return to the Dark Forest.

"As a medicine cat, I'll never understand a parent's feelings for their kits," he began, "but I have many cats that I care for, and worry about, and I'd do anything for them. Rootspring saved my life once, and I feel such a strong sense of duty and loyalty to him because of that. But what I feel even more," he continued, "is a sense that all of this—everything that's happened—is vital for the Clans' survival. All five of them. I could not turn my back, even if I wanted to."

Tigerstar grunted thoughtfully, and gave Shadowsight a long, considering look. The appraisal made Shadowsight uneasy, and he wondered whether his father had really understood what he was trying to tell him.

At last Tigerstar let out a long sigh. "When you and your littermates were kits, your mother and I worked so hard to protect you from anything that might cause you harm. Especially you. You were such a fragile little scrap, and you used to have those seizures. . . . Well, I see now that Dovewing and I have to take a step back. Pouncestep and Lightleap are warriors now, and we have to accept that they might be badly injured in battle—or even killed," he added with another heavy sigh. "So I guess that goes for medicine cats, too. Your battles aren't the same, but you still have to take risks for your Clan." He leaned forward and pressed his muzzle into Shadowsight's shoulder. "I'm sorry I lost my temper. I'm proud of you."

Shadowsight felt as though a whole litter of kits were chasing their tails in his chest and belly. He knew indescribable joy that at last his father was seeing him for what he was, but at the same time he was acutely embarrassed. "Thank you," he choked out.

Tigerstar let out a warm purr, while Shadowsight glanced around, desperate for a distraction.

"Look, here's chervil!" he exclaimed, spotting the fresh green color and white flowers of a clump growing beside an outcrop of rock. He darted across to it and began biting off the stems close to the ground. Tigerstar watched him, with a deeply thoughtful look, and said nothing more as they headed back toward the Moonpool, with Shadowsight carrying a bunch of the healing herbs.

As they approached the top of the hollow, they heard the sound of paws on the earth. Tigerstar dropped into a crouch and slid out his claws, the fur on his shoulders rising as he prepared to defend them both. But the newcomer was only Mothwing, appearing from behind a nearby gorse bush.

"What are you doing, creeping around up here?" Tigerstar asked, relaxing with an irritated twitch of his whiskers.

"I've been making dirt, not that it's any of your business,"

Mothwing retorted. "Oh, well done, Shadowsight, you've found chervil. I've checked Flurry's paw, and it's thoroughly clean now."

She turned toward the bushes at the top of the spiral path, but before she had taken more than a couple of paw steps, Tigerstar halted her with a raised paw.

"There's something I have to insist on, Mothwing," he meowed. "I've accepted that going back into the Dark Forest is something Shadowsight must do. But he can't do it alone."

Mothwing gave him a look from narrowed amber eyes, as if she were wondering how such a mouse-brained cat could ever become Clan leader. "No cat is suggesting he should," she responded.

"Of course not," Shadowsight agreed, setting down his bundle of herbs. "You know that I'll just be a guide for Bristlefrost. She's a warrior, and she'll be doing any fighting that needs doing. I promise you, that's how it's going to be."

Tigerstar stared at Shadowsight for a long moment. Shadowsight wondered if he was going to change his mind, even after everything that he had just said. Then he saw resignation creep into his father's eyes.

"I don't like it," he growled brusquely. "No father could. But I suppose I have to accept that you are special. Tawnypelt was right about that, when you were just a kit, having fits that were actually visions of the Tribe of Rushing Water. You were far too young then to have ever heard of the Tribe, so it has to be significant that you could see them."

Shadowsight tried to remember that, and for a moment

he seemed to call up the memory of sparkling, falling water, and a vast cave where light flickered unevenly on the walls and roof. But he wasn't sure how much of what he thought he could remember was real; the time when he was a kit felt so very long ago.

"Maybe you really do have a duty," Tigerstar went on. "A destiny—one that might extend over more than just Shadow-Clan. After all, there must be a *reason* that you've been continually pulled into all the crises we've suffered around the lake, even when you were a kit." A gleam kindled in his eyes as he added, "It's been a long time since I was a cat with a destiny, so it's hard for me to accept. And you have always been a cat that I do not truly understand."

"I'm not really . . . ," Shadowsight began, feeling hot embarrassment surge over him again.

Tigerstar ignored the interruption. "Even so, I am your father, and destiny or not, that means I only want to keep you safe. You said all of this is vital for the future of the Clans, and maybe you're right, but that doesn't stop me being afraid for you. Choosing between my son and the Clans is a harder choice than you might think." He heaved a sigh from the depths of his chest. "I love you all the same, Shadowsight, and I trust you. If you're determined to see this through, I will support you. Even if that means you have to go with Bristle-frost into the Dark Forest."

For a moment, Shadowsight wasn't sure whether he had heard his father's words right. *He really means it. He really does believe in me!*

"Thank you," he meowed, vastly relieved. "I'm proud that you trust me."

Tigerstar blinked at him affectionately, his face suddenly serious. "Shadowsight, I want you to make me one more promise—that you *will* return. Your mother and I have already grieved for you once, and I doubt we could go through it again."

Shadowsight had to force himself to hold his father's gaze. He didn't want to lie, and he didn't think that Tigerstar would actually stop him, even if he told the truth—that he couldn't guarantee he would return safely. At the same time, something within him was compelling him to tell Tigerstar what he wanted to hear.

"Yes, I promise," he mewed solemnly.

I only hope I can keep that promise.

The sun was dipping down behind the hills, casting dark shadows across the Moonpool. Snow rose to her paws, gathering her Sisters to her with a flick of her tail. At the movement, Shadowsight and the other Clan cats, who had been talking quietly together at the water's edge, fell silent, each one turning to fix their attention on the Sisters.

A shiver passed through Shadowsight, as if a chill wind had blown over him. *But whatever awaits us in the Dark Forest . . . this time we have the Sisters' protection, and we have each other.*

CHAPTER 22

Rootspring and Snowtuft crouched underneath a bush near the edge of the trees, hidden from Ashfur and his cats on the island. Rootspring's belly was churning with anxiety about Squirrelflight, and how Ashfur now had Bramblestar's body back in his power.

"We have to do something to free her," he meowed to Snowtuft. "There has to be a way."

Snowtuft shook his head disbelievingly. "There are too many cats on the island," he responded.

Even though Rootspring knew that the skinny white tom was right, he still refused to give up. "Suppose we attacked Ashfur," he wondered aloud. "Would that break his hold over the island cats? Then we could catch them up on what's happening. They're all good, loyal Clan cats . . . I know they would help us if we could just *reach* them."

Snowtuft let out a grunt; clearly he wasn't optimistic. "I suppose it might be worth a try. . . ."

With Rootspring in the lead, the two cats crept forward, weaving their way through the shelter of bramble thickets and clumps of bracken until they came within sight of the island again. Peering from behind a rotting tree stump, Rootspring saw that Ashfur's followers were standing idle, making a ring around Squirrelflight but not trying to attack her. The ThunderClan deputy's head and tail were drooping, as if she felt completely defeated, and utterly without hope.

"Where's Ashfur?" Rootspring muttered. "I can't see him—and I can't see Bramblestar's body, either. What has he done with it?"

While he was still speaking, Ashfur reappeared from behind the fallen tree's roots. But this time he did not have Bramblestar's body with him.

What has he done with it? Rootspring repeated to himself, sinking his claws into the ground. An image invaded his mind, of the ThunderClan leader's body reduced to a few scraps of blood-soaked fur, destroyed so completely that his spirit would have no hope of returning to it. *No, that's too awful. I can't bear to think about that. . . .*

As he watched the evil gray tom addressing his followers, Rootspring thought that he looked agitated. "I know he's lost his hold on Bramblestar's spirit," he murmured to Snowtuft. "Squirrelflight thought that might be because Bramblestar's a leader with nine lives, but what if there's a chance that his hold on the others can be broken, too? We might not be able to help their spirits reach StarClan, but at least we could free them from the influence of that vile, crow-food-eating excuse for a cat."

"To do that, we'll have to get Ashfur away from them,"

Snowtuft responded. "But how are we going to lure him off the island?"

Before Rootspring could reply, let alone start to make a plan, he heard a rustling in the undergrowth behind him. He spun around, claws extended and teeth bared, braced for an attack. Part of him hoped that some of Ashfur's followers had tracked them down.

I'm just in the mood to tear their stinking pelts off!

But as the newcomer shouldered his way into the open, Rootspring relaxed with a gasp of relief. The muscular body, dark tabby pelt, and amber eyes were the most welcome sight in the world, even though there was an insubstantial look about him, reminding Rootspring that he was a spirit.

"Bramblestar!" he exclaimed.

The spirit of the ThunderClan leader gazed at Rootspring for a long time, a deep sadness in his eyes. *He probably thinks I'm dead,* Rootspring thought.

He returned Bramblestar's gaze, until he was completely certain that this really was the ThunderClan leader's spirit, and not some trick of Ashfur's. His eyes were their usual warm amber, not the dreadful blank stare of the spirits doing the evil cat's bidding.

As his certainty grew, the hope that Rootspring had scarcely dared to feel swelled so strongly inside him that he half expected his chest to burst.

"Bramblestar, it's really you!" he meowed thankfully.

The ThunderClan leader dipped his head. "Rootspring.

I'm sorry to see you in this place."

"But I'm not dead," Rootspring assured him. "Willowshine brought me here, and now I'm trying to free Squirrelflight from the island."

Bramblestar's ears flicked up. "Squirrelflight is on the island?"

Rootspring pointed in that direction with his tail. Bramblestar peered out from behind the tree stump; a low growl rumbled in his chest as he spotted his mate surrounded by Ashfur and his followers.

"I think Ashfur has your body there, too," Rootspring told him. "I can't see it now, but it was there earlier. We thought—"

"'We'?" Bramblestar interrupted. He swung around again, seeming to notice Snowtuft for the first time. His eyes narrowed. "I've seen *you* before," he snarled. "In the battle against the Dark Forest."

"But now Snowtuft is *helping*," Rootspring protested, while the skinny white tom shrank away from the ThunderClan leader. "We were going to lure Ashfur off the island, so that we could try breaking his hold over the other spirits. I know it's not much of a plan. . . ."

Bramblestar seemed to dismiss Snowtuft with a grunt, though he still had a glint of suspicion in his eyes, as if he couldn't quite believe the Dark Forest cat was not part of one of Ashfur's plots. "It's enough to know that some cat hasn't given up."

In spite of their danger, and the apparently hopeless task in front of them, the ThunderClan leader's praise sent warmth spreading through Rootspring from ears to tail-tip. "You'll have to be careful," he warned Bramblestar. "Ashfur has your body, and he can still control your spirit with his mind unless he's distracted enough for you to throw him off."

Bramblestar nodded gravely. "But this may be my only chance to reunite with my physical form." His expression darkened as he added, "That's exactly why I *must* be involved. Ashfur stole my body, and my place within my Clan. He used them to do terrible things to so many honorable warriors, he sowed division and conflict, he turned friends and allies against one another, and he weakened the cats' belief in StarClan. All while posing as me. His jealousy of me twisted him so much that he set his sights on destroying all the Clans for good—and he has very nearly succeeded in doing it."

"But he *won't* succeed," Rootspring insisted. "We'll stop him. We *have* to. Even if we're not sure how we're going to do it," he added.

Bramblestar purred agreement. "StarClan appointed me the leader of ThunderClan," he meowed. "And that means I'm willing to risk anything, even if that means I die, or get trapped here forever. I *must* save my mate, and ThunderClan, and *all* the Clans. I *have* to put this right."

"But you're in more danger than—"

The ThunderClan leader interrupted his protest. "From what you tell me, you and Snowtuft don't exactly have any ideas, do you? That's where I come in. . . ."

* * *

Bramblestar didn't take long to explain what they needed to do, speaking in short, decisive bursts. *The sign of a true leader,* Rootspring realized.

"Well?" the dark tabby tom asked when he had finished. "Do you think it will work?"

"It has as good a chance as any," Rootspring replied.

Snowtuft glanced from Bramblestar to Rootspring and back again, his mouth twisting wryly. "It's a good plan," he commented, "but I have to admit I'm having second thoughts about going along with it."

Bramblestar gave an irritated flick of his tail, but Rootspring felt more sympathetic toward the Dark Forest cat, who seemed to be trying to make himself into something nobler. "Why are you really helping us?" he asked curiously, not sure he was satisfied by the explanation Snowtuft had given him beside the lake.

Snowtuft blinked, clearly deep in thought. "When the Dark Forest started shrinking," he began, "I just felt resigned. I thought that maybe everything was going to disappear forever, and that I and the other cats who ended up here would just disappear along with it."

The bleak prospect sent a shiver through Rootspring. "Weren't you afraid?"

"You'd think so," Snowtuft responded, "but no, I wasn't . . . not really. I've always believed I deserved to be here, because . . . Well, why else would I be here? I must have done some bad things when I was alive. Things that earned me my place here.

I've always felt that my story was going to end badly."

Rootspring touched his shoulder with the tip of his tail. "It doesn't have to," he meowed.

Snowtuft shrugged. "Maybe. Anyway, right when the forest starts to shrink, here come some good cats: Shadowsight, and you, Rootspring, and now Bramblestar. Good cats in need of help. Maybe that's a sign that my last actions before I fade away ought to be good ones."

Rootspring glanced at Bramblestar and saw that the ThunderClan leader looked just as moved by Snowtuft's story as he felt himself. His amber eyes glowed with deep sympathy, and he dipped his head toward Snowtuft, a gesture of respect.

Snowtuft cleared his throat, obviously embarrassed, then straightened up, giving his pelt a shake. "Okay," he mewed. "Are you sure this idea of yours will work? I'm not exactly thrilled that I'll be the bait in your trap, but I'm willing to give it a try."

"It's going to work," Bramblestar assured him, rising to his paws, every hair on his pelt bristling with resolution. "It's all or nothing now."

Snowtuft took a deep breath and then broke out of cover, bounding down the slope directly toward the island. At the same time, Rootspring and Bramblestar slid through the undergrowth in the opposite direction, ending up—still in hiding—close to the narrow strip of land that joined the island to the main part of the forest. Darkstripe stood on guard there, his gaze roving along the edge of the trees.

"Hey, Ashfur!" Snowtuft's loud yowl echoed through the

dank air of the Dark Forest. "Ashfur, are you there?"

After a moment, Ashfur emerged from the crowd of cats and padded toward the shore opposite where Snowtuft was standing.

"What do you want?" he demanded.

"There's something you should know," Snowtuft replied.

For a moment, Ashfur seemed uninterested; Rootspring dug his claws hard into the ground, praying that the gray tom wouldn't just turn away and rejoin his followers. Then he saw Ashfur tilt his head curiously; his gaze sharpened as he stared at Snowtuft, and Rootspring thought he could see a flicker of eagerness in his eyes.

"Maybe he wants to take Snowtuft under his control," he whispered to Bramblestar. "Or promise him enough to get him on his side."

"All right, what are you meowing about?" Ashfur asked at last. "Spit it out!"

"I'm not sure," the white tom replied, "but I think I've found the place where Bramblestar's spirit is hiding. He's underneath a fallen tree, and he looks like he's injured. The tree might be trapping him."

Ashfur's eyes narrowed in suspicion. "Why are you telling me this?"

Snowtuft repeated the reason he had discussed with Bramblestar and Rootspring. "You're in charge here—any cat can see that," he replied. "And I reckon if I help you get Bramblestar, then you'll help me by making sure my corner of the Dark Forest stays strong, for as long as it might last."

As the white tom was speaking, Rootspring couldn't help looking at Bramblestar, wondering what it felt like to hear cats plotting your death, even though Snowtuft was lying, his words only part of a ruse. But Bramblestar's gaze was fixed evenly on the two cats below, his expression giving nothing away.

"Okay," Ashfur growled. "I'll deal with this myself. Wait there."

Turning, he padded along to the strip of land where Darkstripe was on guard, paused briefly for a word with the dark gray tabby tom, then crossed and followed the shoreline to where Snowtuft was standing.

"Lead on," he snapped.

Snowtuft obeyed, heading for the trees well away from where Bramblestar and Rootspring were crouching.

"I hope Snowtuft can escape once Ashfur realizes he's been tricked," Rootspring murmured. "Ashfur will kill him, or worse, if he catches him."

Bramblestar nodded. "That's the risk he agreed to. He's a brave cat."

Once Snowtuft and Ashfur had disappeared into the trees, Rootspring felt Bramblestar's muscles tense. "Are you ready?" the ThunderClan leader asked.

Rootspring nodded. "We think Ashfur was keeping your body among the roots of that fallen tree," he mewed. "You have to make for that first."

"I remember," Bramblestar replied. "Let's go!"

Bramblestar sprang to his paws and hurled himself down

the slope toward the island. Rootspring pounded along at his shoulder, letting out a furious screech of challenge. At the sound, Darkstripe whirled around, his eyes bulging in horror at the sight of the two ferocious cats charging down at him. With a squeal of terror, he fled onto the island, vanishing into the crowd of cat spirits.

"He always was a coward," Bramblestar muttered through gritted teeth.

The two cats' flying paws carried them across the strip of land within heartbeats. Rootspring let the more experienced Bramblestar take the lead, admiring the way he sent Ashfur's followers flying with fierce swipes of his forepaws.

But as soon as the cat spirits hit the ground, they sprang up again as if they weren't hurt in the slightest. Their fur was bristling and their claws extended, all of them looking ready to leap back into the battle and fight to the death—or whatever unknown fate awaited them now.

Rootspring stared at them in dismay, feeling his courage drain away like water into parched ground.

How can we possibly defeat cats like these?

Bramblestar was heading straight for the fallen tree. Rootspring braced himself and followed hard on his paws, trying to imitate his swiping motions. But he wasn't as strong or experienced as Bramblestar. As he struck out at Stemleaf, the spirit warrior closed in on him, bringing him to a halt. They tussled together in a flailing knot of legs and tails, Rootspring desperately trying not to look into Stemleaf's blank eyes.

I still remember him from when he was alive. I can't bear seeing him like this.

Rootspring had lost sight of Bramblestar, but he caught a glimpse of Squirrelflight, struggling in the midst of a heaving mob of Ashfur's followers. The spirit cats were too closely massed around her for her to make an escape. Behind her, Darkstripe was lurking, as if he was waiting for just the right moment to enter the fray.

Or finding an excuse not to enter it at all . . ., Rootspring thought.

He threw Stemleaf off him with a massive heave, and hurled himself toward Squirrelflight. A moment later he saw Bramblestar launch himself into the crowd of cats from the other direction, thrusting them aside as he fought to reach his mate.

Rootspring tensed, staring at him, then let out a growl of frustration as he realized that this was still the spirit Bramblestar; the ThunderClan leader hadn't found his body yet. Obviously, he had been distracted by seeing Squirrelflight so embattled.

Then, as Bramblestar was still struggling toward his mate's side, throwing off the spirit cats who tried to sink their claws into his fur and drag him down, Rootspring spotted Darkstripe again. He was sneaking around the edge of the fight, slowly and deliberately making his way toward the Thunder-Clan leader.

"Bramblestar, look out!" Rootspring yowled.

He barreled across the island, feeling the scrape of claws

along his flanks as the spirits that Ashfur controlled tried to stop him, bundling into Darkstripe and knocking the Dark Forest tom off his paws just before he reached Bramblestar.

Holding Darkstripe pinned under all four paws, Rootspring took in a gasping breath and looked around him. He was not far now from the fallen tree; relief shook him like a gale blustering through him from ears to tail-tip as he spotted Bramblestar's body lying limply across one of the roots.

"Bramblestar!" he screeched, gesturing with his tail. "Over there!"

The ThunderClan leader's head whipped around, and instantly he changed course, his paws flashing as he headed toward his body. At the same moment, Rootspring felt Darkstripe's claws sink into his neck fur as the larger tom tried to throw him off. Losing his balance, he fell to the ground, and he and Darkstripe went rolling over together.

The whole Dark Forest seemed to lurch. The ground gave way under him, and with Darkstripe still clinging to his fur, Rootspring felt himself go tumbling down a muddy slope.

Instinctively, he stabbed all his foreclaws into the mud, halting his descent. Behind him, he heard a screech of terror, and a moment later, Darkstripe skidded helplessly past him, plunging into the dark water that surrounded the island.

Taking a couple of heartbeats to catch his breath, Rootspring started to climb back up the slope. He had not taken two steps when a blinding pain stabbed through his tail. *Something's holding me back,* he realized.

Turning his head again, he saw Darkstripe rearing up out

of the water. His claws were fastened in Rootspring's tail as he tried to drag him down.

He was glaring up at Rootspring with a mixture of evil intent and fear in his yellow eyes. Rootspring guessed that he couldn't swim, and he hated to imagine what the dark water was doing to him. *Does he want to drown me, or save himself?*

Kicking out with all his strength, Rootspring jerked on his tail, feeling the fur painfully rip out as he freed himself. Scrambling back up the slope, he heard Darkstripe behind him, choking and thrashing, but this time he did not turn around to see what was happening to the villainous cat.

Good riddance to him. . . .

Staggering back toward the center of the island, Rootspring was just in time to see Bramblestar reach the fallen tree roots where his lifeless physical form lay. The ThunderClan leader leaped onto his body and seemed to sink into it like a raindrop disappearing into the lake. Rootspring stared, his breath coming short, as he willed Bramblestar to get up.

But the body didn't move.

Is it too late? Rootspring wondered in anguish. *Oh, StarClan . . . Bramblestar has been out of his body for too long. He can't get back!*

A moment later, Rootspring saw one of Bramblestar's paws jerk—such a tiny movement that he wasn't even sure at first that he had actually seen it. But then the body began to wriggle and writhe more strongly; Bramblestar's eyes opened, and he took a huge gasp of air as he scrambled to his paws.

Rootspring saw panic in the ThunderClan leader's eyes, but it was only a brief flash. Almost at once he looked stronger, sturdier, as he turned his head first one way, then the other. He stretched out his forelegs as if he were waking up from a long, ordinary sleep.

Squirrelflight struggled free at last from the cats surrounding her, and bounded up to her mate, her eyes glimmering with the same happiness and hope that Rootspring could feel surging within his own heart. Had Bramblestar really returned, after everything they'd gone through to find him?

Then the ThunderClan leader drew himself up, standing tall and proud and strong, and let out a wordless yowl that seemed to reverberate through the whole of the Dark Forest.

Yes! He's alive!

All around Bramblestar, the spirit cats were standing in confusion, staring at him and at one another. Although their eyes remained blank, they seemed to recognize him. The ThunderClan cats in particular seemed not to know what to do next; they certainly did not look as if they wanted to carry on fighting. Rootspring spotted Rosepetal drawing away from the others, shuddering as if some great conflict was taking place inside her.

Even the Dark Forest cats seemed taken aback, as if they were thinking twice about attacking the magnificent warrior who had suddenly appeared in their midst. In the few moments of indecision, it was Squirrelflight who took the lead.

"This way!" she called, gesturing with her tail at a gap between Ashfur's followers that gave the living cats a clear run to the strip of land leading off the island.

Bramblestar followed her as she streaked along the narrow path across the rippling dark water, Rootspring bringing up the rear, panting loudly as he tried to find every scrap of speed and strength in his entire being.

But almost as soon as the three cats reached the shore, a pale gray shape appeared at the edge of the trees.

"Great StarClan, no!" Rootspring groaned. "Ashfur!"

Immediately Bramblestar halted, dropping into a fighting stance with his tail lashing; a growl of sheer fury erupted from his chest. Briefly, Rootspring halted beside him, glancing over his shoulder at the island where Ashfur's followers were already massing to give chase.

"No!" he gasped to Bramblestar. "You're not used to being back in your body yet. Let me keep Ashfur busy. You and Squirrelflight need to get out of here."

And then I'll have to make sure that I survive, too.

Without waiting for Bramblestar's response, Rootspring plunged ahead, racing up the slope to meet Ashfur as he hurtled down. Once he was in striking distance, Rootspring leaped into the air, straight at Ashfur, aiming his foreclaws at the vile tom's eyes.

For a heartbeat, the speed of his attack seemed to stun Ashfur; in a panic, the gray tom took a few desperate steps backward. Rootspring's claws swished harmlessly through the air.

In the moment's respite, Rootspring half turned. "Get out of here!" he yelled at Bramblestar and Squirrelflight. "Go!"

The pause in Rootspring's attack gave Ashfur an opening;

roughly, he yanked Rootspring's legs out from under him. Rootspring hit the ground with a painful thump that drove all the air out of his body.

Before he could recover, Ashfur pinned him to the ground with his powerful hind paws while he aimed swipe after swipe at Rootspring's head. His blue eyes blazed, like he was furious that he had been so nearly defeated by a younger and less experienced cat.

This is it, Rootspring thought as he writhed helplessly under the weight of Ashfur's paws. *I'm going to die here, in the Dark Forest. Bristlefrost, I'm sorry. I'll never see you again.*

But just as he felt his strength draining away, his vision darkening, Ashfur's weight suddenly vanished. Rootspring sat up, gasping for breath, and saw Snowtuft wrestling on the ground with the evil tom.

Where did he come from?

The skinny white cat raised his head, while his claws dug deep into Ashfur's shoulders. "What are you waiting for?" he yowled at Rootspring. "Run, mouse-brain!"

But it was too late. Ashfur's followers were already pouring off the island; they were so determined to come to their leader's rescue that they paid no attention at all to Bramblestar and Squirrelflight.

Bramblestar looked ready to hurl himself into the fight, but Squirrelflight pushed him back, clearly arguing with him. In the end, both ThunderClan cats bounded off into the trees.

Good, Rootspring thought. *Bramblestar has to escape, so that he can lead the Clans against Ashfur.*

Snowtuft leaped away from Ashfur and gave Rootspring a massive shove. "I said, run!"

Side by side, the two cats pelted toward the trees, passing within a mouse-length of the Dark Forest cats, who instantly swerved to give chase. Rootspring could hear Ashfur's voice raised in a furious screech.

"Get them! Don't let them get away!"

Rootspring thought he could feel the panting breath of the spirit cats on his hindquarters as he plunged into the darkness under the trees. He and Snowtuft dodged this way and that, weaving a path through the undergrowth in the hope of throwing off their pursuers. The forest seemed denser than before, thick white tendrils of mist curling through the trees as if they were forming a trap for the fleeing cats. But at least the yowls of their pursuers were fading. Rootspring hoped they had fallen behind, or lost their trail.

Snowtuft was gasping out directions, and not long after they entered the trees, Rootspring caught sight of Bramblestar and Squirrelflight just ahead. "Bramblestar!" he yowled.

The ThunderClan leader and his deputy halted and waited for Rootspring and Snowtuft to catch up. "Rootspring! Are you okay?" Bramblestar asked. "I think you must be the bravest cat I've ever set eyes on."

Rootspring shrugged, embarrassed. "I'm fine," he responded; although he could feel blood trickling from the wounds Ashfur had given him, he did not think any of his injuries were serious.

"We're fine, too," Squirrelflight meowed. "We—"

"Do we have to stand here gossiping?" Snowtuft cut in irritably. "We still have half the Dark Forest on our paws, or have you forgotten about that little problem?"

Rootspring knew that the white tom was right. He could still hear the sounds of pursuit in the distance, and they were gradually getting louder again. "Okay," he responded tersely. "Which way?"

"Follow me," Snowtuft replied. "I can show you how to get out of here."

"Thank StarClan!" Bramblestar exclaimed.

Snowtuft took the lead, racing ahead with Bramblestar and Squirrelflight hard on his paws. Rootspring tried to follow, only to see a shadow flicker at the edge of his vision.

A heartbeat later a wet body slammed into him, pushing him down to the ground. Rootspring tried to cry out, but the weight of his attacker held him down, pushing his muzzle deep into the debris of the Dark Forest floor, cutting off his air so that he could not make a sound.

Don't leave me here . . . , he begged silently, as his senses began to spiral away into oblivion.

CHAPTER 23

❧

The sun was going down, casting long, dark shadows across the Moonpool. Bristlefrost fluffed out her fur against the chill, remembering what the pool had been like when it was frozen over, at the very beginning of the Clans' troubles.

She exchanged a glance with Shadowsight as the Sisters finally rose to their paws and stepped toward the edge of the water. Bristlefrost could tell that the young medicine cat was as nervous as she was about going back into the Dark Forest.

She spotted a resigned look on Tigerstar's face as she and Shadowsight padded toward the Sisters. Snow dipped her head and pressed it against Bristlefrost's, then Shadowsight's. "I wish both of you well as you—" she began.

The sound of splashing from the pool interrupted the white she-cat's words, followed by desperate gasps for air. Along with every cat, Bristlefrost spun around to see Squirrelflight paddling furiously, pushing a weaker Bramblestar toward the bank.

Caterwauls of joy and amazement rose up from the cats on the bank, echoing around the hollow. "Bramblestar! Squirrelflight!" Tigerstar yowled. Even the Sisters joined in.

Bristlefrost's heart surged with hope. *It's the trapped cats—Squirrelflight and Bramblestar! They've escaped!*

Within a heartbeat, all her misgivings vanished, and she looked eagerly toward the pool to see if Rootspring was following. But so far there was no sign of him. *Surely he'll come through soon?* she asked herself. *He has to!*

Tigerstar and Snow bounded forward to lean out with their forepaws, dragging the ThunderClan leader and deputy safely out of the pool. Both cats stood panting, then gave their pelts a shake, scattering droplets over the cats who surrounded them.

"Bramblestar, it's great to see you back!" Tigerstar exclaimed. Then misgivings seemed to strike him. "Can we be sure this is the real Bramblestar?" he added anxiously.

"It is," Squirrelflight assured him. "I saw his spirit return to his body. And after everything that's happened, I'll never mistake another cat for my mate ever again!" Purring, she twined her tail with Bramblestar's, and he leaned in to give her an affectionate lick around her ears, before closing his eyes and resting his head on the back of her neck, as if he needed her to keep himself upright. *Which he might*, Bristlefrost thought.

More cries of amazement and delight greeted the ThunderClan deputy's words.

"Bramblestar is alive and back among us!" Tree exclaimed eagerly. "And Squirrelflight has returned to the living world. Incredible."

"I can hardly believe this!" Mothwing agreed. "How did you manage it?"

"I met up with Rootspring and a Dark Forest cat called

Snowtuft," Bramblestar explained. "Together, we stormed the island where Ashfur was keeping my body, and I managed to force my way back into it."

"Then we fought our way out," Squirrelflight added.

But the two cats were too weary to talk for long. While their shining eyes showed how glad they were to have made it back home, their legs were shaking with exhaustion, and within a couple of heartbeats they collapsed to the ground, resting their heads on their paws.

Bristlefrost turned back to the Moonpool and saw that the water had grown still again, except for the perpetual ripple from the waterfall. A cold, heavy weight settled in her belly. "Where *is* Rootspring?" she asked. "What's happened to him?"

Squirrelflight raised her head, her eyes stretching wide with a stricken look. "He was just behind us," she replied between gasps of air. "He should have followed us out. . . ."

Now the gaze of every cat was fixed on the surface of the pool. They stared at it for a long time, but no other cat emerged. Bristlefrost struggled to contain her anguish, but when she looked toward Tree and saw her own dread reflected in his amber eyes, she could not help her gasp. "What happened?" she repeated. "Why isn't he here?"

"I don't know," Bramblestar responded, looking just as troubled as his deputy. "He was right on our paws. . . . Something must have gone wrong. It's so dangerous there, in the Dark Forest."

"Ashfur is controlling the spirits of Clan cats who have died since all this began," Squirrelflight added. "And several

Dark Forest cats are following him, too."

Tree's head drooped, his teeth clenched as though he was fighting the urge to wail aloud in grief.

Meanwhile, Tigerstar stepped forward, his gaze flicking from Shadowsight to Bristlefrost and back again. "We have to rethink our plan," he meowed. "Bramblestar and Squirrelflight have returned to us, and they need help. Only Rootspring is in the Dark Forest now, and he has . . . what we might call unusual gifts. Perhaps he can take care of himself."

Tree overheard the ShadowClan leader's words, and a look of utter horror settled on his face. He opened his jaws, then instantly clamped them shut again, as if he knew that no argument would persuade Tigerstar to send his son back into the forest now. Bristlefrost guessed that Tree was now also weighing the danger of risking the lives of two more healthy cats to save one from the Dark Forest.

Shadowsight scarcely seemed to be listening to his father. "Bramblestar and Squirrelflight need medicine-cat help," he pointed out. "They can hardly breathe."

He hurried to their side, joining Mothwing, who had also stepped forward and was examining the two cats.

"It's amazing," she mewed, disbelief in her voice. "This is the first time I've ever seen a cat *physically* cross between the Dark Forest and the living world , but I can't see any damage— even for Bramblestar, who was there for so long, and out of his body. They should be okay, but they're going to need treatment." Turning to Tree, she continued, "Will you go out and look for some herbs? Juniper berries would be best, but it's the wrong season. Coltsfoot leaves will do nearly as well."

Tree dipped his head in agreement. Bristlefrost could tell that Mothwing had given the worried father a task to keep him occupied, to distract him from his grief and fear.

"I'll go too," Tigerstar meowed. "I suppose you know what this stuff looks like?" he added to Tree.

Bristlefrost was relieved to hear that. At least there would be some cat to watch over Tree while she was gone. *Because I'm still going into the Dark Forest. I have to. . . . Some cat has to save Rootspring.*

As Tree headed for the bottom of the spiral path, with Tigerstar at his side, he cast a glance back at Bristlefrost. Her emotions were surging through her so fiercely that it took a massive effort for her to nod at him. *I will do everything I can,* she assured him silently.

With all the other cats distracted, watching Mothwing, Bristlefrost inclined her head to Snow and returned to her position at the edge of the Moonpool.

"You still want my help?" Snow asked. "I thought the leader said . . ."

Bristlefrost glanced around to where Shadowsight was helping Mothwing tend to Bramblestar and Squirrelflight. For all her worries about Rootspring, it gave her hope to see her leader and deputy alive, and close together once more. *No matter what happens to me, ThunderClan is going to be okay.*

Almost the last traces of sunlight had faded from the sky. Bristlefrost knew that within a few moments it would be too late, and she would have missed her chance.

"I need to go," she whispered to Snow. "I need to find him. Do you understand?"

At that moment, Shadowsight looked up and spotted her. His jaws dropped open, but Bristlefrost vigorously shook her head. *Don't say anything!* She didn't want the older cats to realize and stop her.

Shadowsight gave a slight nod and slowly, quietly, made his way to her side. "I'm coming with you," he mewed softly.

"You are?" Bristlefrost was surprised. "But what about Tigerstar? What about the risks?"

Shadowsight shrugged. "Tigerstar isn't here, is he? So I can't ask permission. Besides, he's accepted my path as a medicine cat, so I don't *need* his permission. Bristlefrost, we can't leave Rootspring behind. He would never leave us. And we've been through so much together, haven't we, the three of us?"

Bristlefrost felt her throat tighten. She nodded, unable to reply.

Snow dipped her head to both of them, then faced the water once more. She lowered her head, her whiskers brushing the surface as she seemed to whisper to the pool.

"This is the end of your adventure," she mewed. "Our love guides you home, and brings direction to your dark wander. *You* are the guardian of the land, not spirits. Through us, the land will call to you, if you listen." Turning to Bristlefrost and Shadowsight, she continued, "Lie down beside the Moonpool and close your eyes."

Bristlefrost obeyed, shivering as the chill of the stones struck through her fur. She felt a twinge of uneasiness at being so close to the water. *What if my body rolls in while my spirit is in the Dark Forest? Will I drown?*

Then, as she felt Shadowsight's tail brush against her side, she began to feel lighter. A cold wind ruffled her fur. Snow's whisper rose into a chant, and it now seemed to come from many voices; Bristlefrost guessed that the other Sisters were adding theirs. Even so, the sound was fading so that Bristlefrost couldn't make out the words.

After a few moments, she dared to open her eyes. The decaying landscape of the Dark Forest stretched all around her, sending a chill through her whole being that had nothing to do with the cold. She could not see Shadowsight, or any other cat, but she could still hear Snow and the Sisters, their chanting now no more than a faint echo that never quite went away.

Summoning all her courage, Bristlefrost rose to her paws and turned in a slow circle. *If I'm alone here . . . I don't know if I can bear it.*

There was still no sign of Shadowsight, until Bristlefrost had almost rotated back to her starting point. Then the ShadowClan cat popped into view out of nowhere, his eyes still closed.

"Shadowsight!" Bristlefrost gasped in relief.

The young medicine cat opened his eyes, blinking as he gazed around. A look of dismay spread over his face, and he shivered. "This place is just as terrible as I remember," he muttered.

"We should get moving," Bristlefrost meowed, bracing herself to face whatever danger the Dark Forest would spring on them. "We have to look for Rootspring."

Side by side, the two cats began to move cautiously through the forest. With every heartbeat, they stayed alert for the sound of approaching paw steps. Bristlefrost knew that any cats they met here would be enemies, poised to attack. Ready to kill.

By now, the Sisters' chanting had faded into silence, their song at an end. Bristlefrost had known that would happen, but the realization that she and Shadowsight were quite alone made her heart thump and the fur on her shoulders begin to rise.

What if we never make it back?

"Shut up!" Bristlefrost muttered through her teeth to the voice in her head. "I'm not listening to you!"

Beside her, Shadowsight drew to a halt; Bristlefrost could feel his muscles tense. "What's wrong?" she asked, drawing to a halt beside him.

"I think I heard movement over there," Shadowsight responded in a whisper, gesturing with his tail.

Both cats dropped into the hunter's crouch and slithered forward, ignoring the scratch of thorns that stabbed through their pelts and the slimy sensation of the ground against their belly fur.

At last, they reached the top of a rise and looked down into a small, gloomy clearing that was shrouded in mist. As Bristlefrost gazed down, the white tendrils parted briefly, showing her the figure of a familiar yellow tom. For a moment, her heart soared with relief.

We've found Rootspring!

But as the mist cleared still further, her heart plummeted again, and she felt as though all her courage and optimism were leaking out through her paws. Rootspring stood surrounded by a ring of Dark Forest cats.

On the edge of the circle, Ashfur was staring at Rootspring with a mixture of arrogance and satisfaction, as if Rootspring were no more to him than a moss ball made to amuse kits.

In the midst of the spirit cats, Rootspring was facing a skinny white tom Bristlefrost had never seen before. The two cats were maneuvering around each other, their teeth bared and their claws extended. Clearly, they were about to leap into battle.

A battle to the death.

"Snowtuft!" Shadowsight gasped. He looked utterly grief-stricken as he stared down into the clearing.

"What?" Bristlefrost asked.

"That's Snowtuft—the white tom," Shadowsight explained. "He's a Dark Forest cat; he fought against the Clans in the Great Battle, but I thought he had changed. He was *helping* us!"

"Well, he's not helping us now," Bristlefrost mewed grimly, though she had to admit that the white tom looked oddly reluctant to spring into the attack.

Ashfur obviously agreed with her. "Get on with it, you mangy white coward!" he yowled.

Looking utterly terrified, Snowtuft hurled himself at Rootspring, who dodged neatly aside and whirled to kick at his adversary with his powerful back legs. Snowtuft staggered and collapsed on the ground. Rootspring sprang on top of him and the two cats wrestled across the ground, scraps of yellow and white fur flying around them like rain in a storm.

As soon as the fight began, the watching spirit cats let out yowls of encouragement to Snowtuft, and loud jeers aimed at Rootspring. Bristlefrost stared at their writhing bodies; they looked as if they were fighting an imaginary battle of their own.

"That's . . . grotesque," she whispered. "Oh, Rootspring . . ."

Then among the spirit cats, Bristlefrost spotted a tom she knew well, a tom she had thought she might never see again.

Stemleaf!

There in the Dark Forest, Bristlefrost stared in horror as the Clanmate she used to love cheered on the killing of the tom she couldn't live without.

CHAPTER ONE

Leaf rolled over and stretched her paws out in front of her, raking the thin soil with her claws, then rolled again onto her back and slowly opened her eyes. The sky above was a soft gleaming gray, pale and unmarked by clouds. All she could see was the very top of one tall tree at the edge of her vision. Leaf felt almost as if she could tumble into the sky.

Her stomach rumbled.

There'll be time for sky-gazing after the First Feast, she thought, letting out a huge yawn and flopping back onto her stomach again. She got to her paws and loped over to the big tree and scratched the back of her ears against its gnarled trunk.

Through the sparse trees that grew on the northern slopes, she could see Aunt Plum and all the other Slenderwoods rising from comfy piles of leaves and clambering down from flat rocks, heading over to the thin bamboo stalks that pushed up between the trees. Leaf shook herself and padded toward the place where she had seen some growing the night before. Sure enough, every few paw-lengths she was able to break off a bunch of tender shoots with thin green leaves sprouting. But she stopped before she had gathered them all.

Greedy cub now, hungry cub later, Aunt Plum always said, and she was right.

Leaf held the bunch of shoots tightly in one paw and hurried across the forest floor to the big clearing. The other Slenderwood pandas had all gathered there already, each sitting with their back to a tree, a respectful distance away from one another.

"Come along, Leaf," said Plum, with a yawn. "The Great Dragon won't wait for you."

She said that a lot too. Leaf grinned and sat down at the base of the same tree as little Cane and his mother, Hyacinth. Cane wriggled on his stomach toward the small pile of shoots in front of Hyacinth, but she gently reached out a paw and rolled him away.

"Not quite yet, little one," she said. Cane squeaked in disappointment, and Leaf knew how he felt. The bamboo in her paws smelled delicious, but no panda could begin to eat before the blessing.

Aunt Plum scratched her back against the tree trunk and cleared her throat. "Great Dragon," she said, holding her own shoots out in one paw. "At the Feast of Gray Light your humble pandas bow before you. Thank you for the gift of the bamboo, and the wisdom you bestow upon us."

Leaf bowed her head, and so did all the other pandas in the clearing, including Cane, who dropped his muzzle until his nose rested on the forest floor. There was a short pause before they all looked up again, and the sound of happy crunching filled the clearing. Leaf brought her bamboo to her nose, smelling the fresh, cool scent, and then started to pick off the leaves. She formed them into a small bundle before chomping down on the tasty green ends. Hyacinth stripped the tougher bark from the outside of her bamboo, and passed the softer green shreds from the inside down to Cane, who gobbled them up with gusto.

"The Dragon could be a bit more generous with his gifts," one of the older pandas grumbled, his mouth full of bamboo splinters.

"And you could be more grateful for what you have, Juniper Slenderwood," said Plum, eyeing him sternly through the pawful of green leaves.

"Juniper *Shallowpool*," Juniper muttered.

"There is no shallow pool now, Juniper," said Hyacinth gently. "We're all Slenderwoods now."

"Yeah, if you won't be a Slenderwood, you ought to be *Deepriver*, or *Floodwater*," said Grass, with a snide look over her shoulder toward the edge of the river. Juniper got to his paws with a huff and turned his back on the other pandas, settling on the other side of his tree and chewing on the woody stems of his First Feast.

Leaf watched him with a pinched feeling growing in her heart. That was mean of Grass. Juniper was a crotchety old panda, but she couldn't exactly blame him—she couldn't imagine what it would be like to have her home there one day and vanished the next, swallowed up by the rising river. She had never known any home but the Slenderwood, with its tall, wavering trees and sparse bamboo.

"All of you are stuck in the past," Grass snorted, rolling over onto her back and licking her muzzle. "Nine times a day we thank the Great Dragon for feeding us, but why? Who has seen so much as a dragon-shaped cloud since the flood? Juniper's right—the Dragon has abandoned us."

"Not what I said," grumbled Juniper, without turning around.

Leaf turned to look at Plum, and so did several of the others. Leaf half expected her to snap at Grass, but she just shook her head.

"That isn't how it works, Grass," she said calmly. "The Dragon cannot abandon us. The Great Dragon *is* the Bamboo Kingdom. As long as there are pandas, and there is bamboo to feed us, the Dragon is watching over us." She held up the next long stem of her feast, as if that settled the matter. For a while there was silence, only broken by crunching.

"Do you remember that summer," Crabapple put in, using a long black claw to pick a bamboo shoot out of his teeth, "before the flood, when Juniper's pool dried up? The Dragon Speaker warned us all. You found a deeper pool in plenty of time—remember that, Juniper?"

Juniper just grunted again, but Hyacinth smiled to herself as she nudged a pawful of leaves toward Cane. "Oh, remember the time with the sand foxes?" she said. "Old Oak Cragsight had to take the message to them by foot, right up to the White Spine peaks. Only just made it in time to warn them about the avalanche."

"I thought it was a blizzard?" said Grass, her cynical expression melting a little.

"No, it was an avalanche," grumbled Vinca, wriggling his back against the tree to scratch between his shoulder blades. "*Beware the white wave*—that was the Speaker's message. I remember it distinctly."

Leaf wriggled onto her back again, trying to take her time over the last mouthfuls of her feast. Once they started on this topic, the older pandas could go for hours—they would still be here reminiscing when it was time for the Feast of Golden Light, and the Feast of Sun Climb after that.

Leaf knew that Plum was right, that the Great Dragon was still out there, watching over them. She believed it, truly, she did. But when Plum and the others told their stories of the time before the flood, when the river had been calm and narrow enough to cross, the bamboo plentiful, and every panda had had enough food and space to have their own territory, Leaf couldn't help wondering why things weren't like that anymore.

Oak Cragsight would have gone to the sacred spot on his territory and received the Dragon Speaker's message about the danger to the foxes, as all the pandas would have. That was how Plum said it had worked—the Great Dragon would send its prophecies to the Speaker, and the Speaker would pass them on to the other pandas, who would spread the word of the Dragon to all the other creatures of the Bamboo Kingdom. The pandas were special, the Dragon's chosen messengers.

But still, not one of them had known about the flood until it was upon them. Why had the old ways failed? Had the Great Dragon not warned the Dragon Speaker, or had the Speaker known and just not warned the other pandas?

"What do you think happened to the Dragon Speaker?" Leaf said. She knew it was a question without a real answer—no panda knew where Sunset Deepwood had gone.

"I think it's obvious," said Vinca with a heavy sigh. "It's been a year, and we must face the truth: Speaker Sunset must have died in the flood."

Leaf expected at least some of the other pandas to disagree with him, but to her dismay none of them did. Even Aunt Plum hung her head in quiet grief.

"I met him once," said Hyacinth. "I was only a cub, but I'll always remember how he talked to me as if I were a full-grown panda. He told me that one day I would see the signs too, and maybe I'd be the one to stop an illness from spreading or save a nest or . . . He made it sound as if I could be a hero."

"He was one of the wisest Dragon Speakers," said Plum softly.

"But if Sunset is dead," asked Grass, "why hasn't a new Speaker been chosen? Unless we truly have angered the Dragon so much that it's left us all alone."

Plum shook her head. "We must not lose faith. The Dragon

will send us a new Speaker when the time is right."

The silence that followed this was gloomy. Leaf suspected that all the Slenderwood pandas were asking themselves the same question: *How much longer?*

Leaf got up and shook herself from head to tail. The feast was over, and she didn't really want to stay here and chew over the past any longer.

"I'm going to find Dasher," she announced.

"If you're away for the Feast of Golden Light, don't forget—" Aunt Plum began.

"I'll do the blessing," Leaf reassured her. She trotted across the clearing and bumped her nose against the older panda's cheek as she passed. "Don't worry."